Reign By Wrath

The Rogues

Ruby Vincent

Published by Ruby Vincent, 2023.

Prologue

Bitterness seeped through my lips, leaving an acrid kiss on my tongue.

I coughed—rough and hacking and dragging my senses back to the surface. Blinking, I came to, straining as my vision cleared.

What happened? Where am I?

I squeezed my eyes shut, forcing tears to fall. My eyes were watering, it was so blurry. And what was that noise?

I opened my eyes again, fighting to adjust in the dim. *Why can't I see? What's wrong with...?*

Twisting my neck, I saw past the couch to the staircase—where the smoke freely billowed down. *Smoke?*

"It's about time you woke up. You're the one who wanted this little chat. You're wasting your own time."

I turned with difficulty, achy bones creaking. It was hard. Tight pressure around my wrists and ankles proved I was bound.

A vision in white stood on the very spot Wesley spat out his bloody tooth. She lowered her face mask and smiled at me. "Hello, Luna."

"Everleigh?" I croaked, then immediately started hacking. My lungs shredded trying to force out smoke that kept flooding in. "W-what's... going on? Where are the guys?"

"Your boyfriends are safe. I sent them away so we could have some privacy. You wanted to meet me. Here I am. What do you think?" Everleigh twirled, spinning the lace edges of her ivory summer dress. "Am I what you expected of the Phantom?"

The words barely penetrated. My head hurt so much, the idea of putting two thoughts together drove a spike through it. Smoke was filling the room, making it even more impossible for my blurry eyes to focus, or my tortured lungs to breathe.

"Hello." Everleigh snapped her fingers in my face. "Focus, Sinclair. We don't have much time. This place is about to burn down with you in it."

The fog blew out of my mind. Sense came back to me, latching on to that statement as the ladder to bring me back. "What did you just say?"

"You going to make me waste time repeating myself, or are you going to ask me what you really want to ask me?" She flicked my nose. "Quickly, bitch. It's getting a little too smoky in here for my taste."

I gaped at her. Everleigh Starling? Saylor's best friend with the model looks, and the dreamy eyes that spent too much time looking at my fiancé—

"You're the Phantom?"

She winked. "That's right. Love the nickname, by the way. Much better than the Book Lady. Now that we're here, did you enjoy my performance?" She laughed. "All that weeping and wailing on the café floor. I keep telling Maman I was meant to be an actress."

She frowned into my wide eyes. "What? You don't get it? Damn, you're stupid," Everleigh muttered. "I'm Jezebel12. I gave you the link to my site for your boring little revenge against me, Saylor, and the others. You weren't going to dig dirt up on me on your own, and I couldn't have you sending the T.O.D.ers after me. I don't need stalkers."

Everleigh shrugged. "I also don't particularly care if people know about the Book Lady. I started doing it to get information from stupid, horny idiots that you can't get when those horny idiots are dressed. That information led to your mother, which led to your sister, which led to you. So yeah, I'm glad everyone knows. The Book Lady is my greatest accomplishment."

"But..." I searched for the words and found only one. "Why?"

"Why did I send those guys after your sister?" She pushed out her lips in mocked sadness. "Ah yes, poor little Winter."

"No," I said. "Why... are you a psychotic bitch?"

Everleigh laughed out loud. "For the same reason you are. Revenge. There's something I needed and your sister got in the way. Thankfully— Well, thankfully for me, you were much more obedient and did what you were told. You hung the flag."

"A flag? That's why you did all this? You had Winter tortured all for a fucking flag!" I tried to shout but wheezed it instead. I went into another coughing fit, jerking and banging my back against the coffee table legs. "Why d-didn't you just hang it yourself!"

"It had to be a Sinclair. When your sister died, I gave up. Those bastards were supposed to drive her to follow my orders, not kill herself. I almost killed them myself... then you showed up." Everleigh looked around. "Time to go. See you in hell, Sinclair."

Everleigh turned and walked off.

"Wait! That's it? You destroyed my family for a flag and that's all you have to say? Why?" I screamed. "Tell me why!"

"I'm actually not into the evil-villain-monologuing. Especially in a burning building." Everleigh snapped her fingers. "Come."

"I can't come." I thrashed against the table legs. "You tied me up."

"Not you."

A tall, silent figure dipped in black stepped out of the hallway. His face so like Rafael's beheld me coldly.

"Shoot her."

Ice dumped down my spine.

"I want to see her die for myself," Everleigh continued, tone light and cool as could be. "Do this and your freak boys are safe. No one touches them. No one even gives them dirty looks. The Dumont brothers won't die of anything except old age."

Leon Dumont drew his gun and leveled it on my chest. The expression on his face was no different from the one he had when we drank tea.

"No, wait!"

Dumont flicked off the safety.

"Tell me why," I screamed. "Just tell me why!"

"Why?" The first crack in her amused, happy mask appeared. "It's simple. I've been waiting almost ten years to make that bastard pay for what he did to my father. For years I've searched for him. For years I couldn't get close. Then, Daddy's little girls enrolled in Regalia University."

Daddy's little girls? Jack?

"I've waited so long," she hissed. "Finally, he's going to come. He can't hide from me anymore." The smile she flashed me turned my stomach. "Don't let it get to you that you'll die without ever meeting your father. I promise, I'm sending him to hell right after you."

She jerked a chin at Rafael's father. "Do it."

"Forgive me, Miss Sinclair-Bowden. I truly wish there was another way."

"Mr. Dumont, don't—"

Bang!

Pain ripped through my chest.
Darkness came for me again, and didn't let go.

Chapter One

"...hadn't come to this..."

"...no other way..."

"Winter."

Voices mingled in my head. Teasing me. Taunting me. Disturbing my rest.

Wasn't I promised eternal peace? Or did my rage and vengeance earn me the other kind of eternity?

Was that why I kept hearing *him*?

"...must act..."

No, go away. I just want to sleep. Let me sleep.

"There's no time!"

My eyes snapped open. Shooting up, ferocious pain ripped through my chest, tearing a cry from my lips. I hunched over, gasping and clutching my stomach.

Blue-and-black-paisley teardrops swam before my eyes. *What is this? What's going on?*

I looked around, trying to breathe as my vision came into focus. I was in a small room. Bland forest wallpaper lined the space, its black and white a complement to the white cabinets, black wall lamps, and black-and-white carpet. Barring the bed I lay on, that was the end of the décor. The room didn't even have windows—providing a clue to where I was.

One thing I knew for certain was that I wasn't on campus or in the hospital. None of the dorms or frat houses at my rich school were this small or sparsely decorated. I also knew another thing—

I gently rubbed my chest, feeling the definite lack of a bullet wound.

—I'm not dead.

What happened? I was in the Gallery, there was smoke everywhere, and Leon Dumont...

I felt the punch through my gut like it just happened.

"...have me do..."

My head snapped up. That was one of the voices I heard in my dream. Wherever I was, I wasn't alone.

Sliding off the bed, I took slow, measured steps to the door—wincing the whole way. I didn't think my ribs were broken, but they were definitely bruised. Even the thought of breathing hurt.

I opened the door and met with a steep staircase. The voices got louder.

Climbing up, I found myself in a space three times the size of the one I was in. A panoramic wall of windows told me exactly where I was—on a boat in the middle of the ocean.

"What the fuck?" I croaked, stumbling on the same black-and-white carpet. Pressing against the window only provided more proof of what I didn't want to believe.

I was not in Regalia anymore.

"Luna."

I turned slowly, meeting Leon Dumont's gaze.

He was seated at a small, diner-style table across from a man I didn't know. I stared at them, not moving or breathing.

What was I supposed to think of this situation? Rafael's dad clearly didn't kill me, despite being ordered to by Everleigh Starling.

Everleigh Starling.

For the rest of the life she didn't take from me, I'd ask myself how I was so incredibly wrong about her. There was no sign—*none*—that lurking beneath the surface of the pretty, pampered princess was a twisted maniac.

Leon stood up, making me step back. "My debt to you is paid," he told the man.

The stranger nodded. "In full."

Leon left through a side door, leaving the two of us alone. The man smiled at me.

"You must be hungry," he said, crossing over to the kitchenette. "Please, sit. I'm useless in the kitchen, but even I can handle a turkey sandwich."

I didn't so much as twitch. "Who are you?"

"There's plenty of time for that," came the calm response. He was a handsome man with auburn hair flecked with silver; a hooked nose; and a strong jaw covered in stubble. I put him at midforties. He reminded me of someone, but my fuzzy head wouldn't supply the image.

"Sit, Luna. I know from experience that rubber bullets still pack a mean punch."

Rubber bullet? Is that what Mr. Dumont shot me with? He truly wasn't going to kill me, even though Everleigh threatened—

"Rafael," I cried. "Cato. Lucien. Wilder. Where are they? What did she do to them!"

"She let them go shortly after your home on campus was reduced to a pile of charred wood and melted appliances."

The man pulled various items out of the fridge and began preparing my sandwich. We looked to be in one big living room—complete with couches, television, kitchenette, and eating area. Outside, there were lounges, a hot tub, and no signs of how far from home these men had taken me.

"Leon confirmed they were safe before bringing you to me."

"Why would he bring me to you?" I snapped. "Why would he bring me anywhere? Take me back!" The shout was a knife through my sore chest. "I need to see the guys. I have to make sure they're okay."

"Okay is exactly what they won't be if you get near them." He set to work cutting avocado, slicing tomatoes, and chopping red onions. "Think it through, Luna. They were spared because you died. If it's discovered you're still alive and Leon didn't keep up his end of the deal, Starling has no reason to keep up hers."

"Everleigh's not going to touch them because she'll be too busy having her head bashed in. Now, whoever the hell you are, stop messing around with avocados and turn this boat toward Regalia. I'm going home. Now."

He smiled through my berating, his eyes getting softer as my voice climbed higher. "Goodness, you look just like your mother."

I started, moving back again. Was there a better way to trap someone than by boat? "You don't know my mother."

"Don't I?" he asked, amused. "Pretty sure I know Eloise Sinclair better than anyone."

"I'm pretty sure you're nuts."

He laughed. "Don't know a single person who isn't. Mustard, mayo, or both?"

My glare drilled a hole in his head. He laughed harder.

"Definitely Eloise's daughter." My sandwich done, he made one for himself and brought it to the table. He gestured again for me to join him. "You saw me make it yourself. It's safe."

"Doesn't mean you are."

He shrugged, taking a bite. "Leon wouldn't risk everything to save your life just to bring you to someone who meant you harm."

I tried to wriggle out of that logic, and couldn't. Moving slowly, I claimed the seat across from him and picked up the sandwich. My stomach was growling too loudly for me to protest further.

"Who are you?"

"Haven't you guessed? Leon heard what she said to you before he fired."

My voice was calm. "You're going to say you're my father."

"I am your father, Luna."

I gazed out the window—quiet as I ate my sandwich. A moment like that, a million thoughts should go through your head with even more questions. Who are you? Where have you been my whole life? Why did Mom refuse to tell us anything about you? Why were you here now?

All of them good questions, but there was only one I needed to know.

"Why weren't you at the funeral?" I asked flatly. "Do you not care about us? Did you not care about Winter?"

His smile melted away, and in its place was naked pain. "Of course I care about you. Both of you. You're my daughters."

"So why weren't you there?"

"Your mother decided it would just be family. If I showed up, she'd have to explain who I was to you, and she wasn't ready to do that. She allowed me a private moment before the funeral to say goodbye, and I'll forever be grateful."

"Why didn't she want us to know you? Is it because you rack up the kind of enemies who plot and murder and burn people alive to get to you?"

He sighed, giving up all attempts at finishing his food. "The answer to that isn't as simple as you think."

"Didn't you bring me here to give me answers?"

"I brought you here because you're in danger, and I won't lose another daughter. If there was any other choice, I'd still be a question mark in the back of your mind."

"Oh, gee, sorry, *Daddy*. Didn't mean to inconvenience you." I shoved away and stormed off, making for the windowless room I woke up in.

"Shit. Wait! That didn't come out right. Luna? Luna, please," he cried. "I'll tell you everything."

I slowed, pausing on the first step.

"The whole truth. If by the end of it you still think I'm an asshole... then it's no more than I deserve."

I froze—torn between leaving and staying. I did deserve an explanation, but I wasn't stupid enough to believe it'd be a happy or positive one. How many more awful truths was I supposed to handle, one after the other?

My sister was driven to suicide because of a purple fucking flag? The person behind it was staring me in the face for months. There was still so much I didn't know about my guys, including if they were truly okay. Wasn't the smart move to just crawl in bed and stay there until the world wasn't so impossible to handle?

When would that be? I have a feeling if I crawled under those covers waiting for my life to change, I'd be under there until the seas dried up and the moon fell out of the sky.

"Okay," I said. "I'm listening."

"Please, sit. I know you're in pain."

I did, but not next to him. I stretched out on a plush white couch—holding a pillow to my aching chest. He—my father—came to me anyway. He pulled the armchair closer and made like he was going to take my hand. Changing his mind, he drew back.

"I guess I should start with my name. I'm Alistair."

I cracked an eye open, brows snapping together. "Alistair? Don't meet many of those."

"My family has a tradition of unique names. There's an Osvaldo and a Seven lurking in the family tree."

"Seven? Yikes. I thought Winter and I had it bad, named after how we were conceived."

He smiled. "Your mother and I chose those names for a reason. You both were named to remember the best moment of our lives—the days you both came into it."

I dropped my gaze, not able to handle the tenderness in his eyes. This guy spoke like he loved me. But how could I be loved by someone I didn't know?

"You make it sound like you and Mom were in a real relationship."

A frown twisted his features. "What do you mean? Of course we were."

"Mom said she loved you, but your relationship was forbidden," I explained. "I figured you were married, and the beautiful blonde housekeeper was your secret."

"No, Luna, I've never been married. It couldn't work with your mother *because* she wasn't my secret."

Alistair dropped back, head tilted to the ceiling. "I met Eloise by chance. Woke up early one morning to surf and she was there on the beach, lost in her thoughts as she watched the sunrise. I left her to it—not bothering or sparing her a second glance. Then, I wiped out," he said. "Board smacked me over the head and knocked me out. I was dead..." A smile stretched his lips. "Until I woke up on the beach with this sand-covered vision staring down at me."

"Sounds very *Little Mermaid*."

"It does, doesn't it?" He laughed. "Your mom always said we were something out of a fairy tale. After she saved me, I refused to go to the hospital, so she insisted on staying with me. Making sure I was okay and didn't have a concussion. We spent the whole day together, and by the end of it, I knew she was the only one for me."

I sat up and scooted farther away, pressing my back against the armrest. But I didn't leave.

"But if you loved each other so much, and your relationship wasn't a secret, why was your relationship forbidden?"

"You've been in Regalia long enough to know about its twisted medieval caste system. There are those at the bottom and those on top. The Royals."

I nodded. "You're a Royal."

He didn't answer, which was answer enough.

"So, you couldn't be together because Mom was a *Dreg*? Was it different back then?" I asked. "Plenty of Royals marry Dregs. Victor is marrying me."

"For most Royals, it doesn't matter who they marry. They're low enough on the hierarchy that no one cares. But for those at the top of the line, their marriages aren't about love, they're about power. How to get more so that you're lifted even higher than the desperate hands trying to tear you from the throne.

"My father picked out a match that would do just that. She wasn't a Royal in that she'd never been to Regalia before. She was the daughter of a Japanese business tycoon," he explained. "Marrying her and merging our companies would've given our business global recognition the likes of McDonald's. Didn't matter that I didn't know a thing about his plans until after I introduced Eloise to him. I was expected to break up with her and marry a perfect stranger for the good of the family and company."

My brows blew up my forehead. This shouldn't surprise me after Adonis was kicked out of the family because his fiancée left him, but I didn't think I'd ever stop being shocked by the bonkers things the Royals did. Ordering your son to leave the woman he loved to marry someone he never met? What era did the Royals think they were living in?

"That's rough," I admitted. "But I still don't see why Mom couldn't tell us all of this. We didn't know you our whole lives because your dad is a douchebag?"

"This is only the beginning of the story, Luna."

I quieted, tipping my chin for him to finish.

"My father's disapproval of Eloise and her part in me turning down his handpicked fiancée is why you don't know him or anyone from my side of the family—despite them being so close your whole life." Alistair balled his fists, muscle ticcing in his jaw. "Your mother didn't want you and Winter to be rejected or looked down on by your own family, and it's my greatest shame to admit that you would've been. My family would not have treated you well."

My eyes narrowed to slits. "Why won't you say it? Who is your family and— And why do you look so familiar!"

"Can't help it. The Burkhardt family resemblance is strong."

The air whooshed out of my lungs. He said the name, then I saw it clear as day. The shape of her eyes. The curve of her nose.

Saylor Burkhardt.

"No. No, no, no, no, no. No!" I cried. "You're lying."

"Afraid not."

Tossing my head, my mind rebelled. "I'm not related to Saylor. I can't be."

"You can be," he said mildly. "She's your cousin."

"No!"

I choked on the word. After everything that's happened between us. The horrible things she's said about Winter and done to me, and the vicious things I've done in response. After all that time, we were... family?

"That just can't be true. Me? A Burkhardt? I refuse to believe it."

"Why?" he asked, cocking his head. "Haven't you been asking why Martha and John Wilson are so eager for you to marry their son?"

I opened my mouth, but nothing came out. *Martha and John? The whole time... this was the answer?*

"They know who I am?" I rasped.

Alistair shook his head. "Martha knows who *I* am. We were good friends. She knew Eloise and I were together, and she was the first person I told when we got pregnant. Of course, I had no clue she was dating John at the time. Next thing I knew, she was marrying our rival family and sitting on information that turned out to be incredibly useful twenty years later." He gestured to me. "Burkhardts don't marry within the Royal line, and they definitely don't marry Wilsons."

He chuckled. "I'd be furious with her, and I am, but this is typical Martha. She used to be a cheerleader. They always find their way to the top of the pyramid."

My head spun. I threw up my hands. "Hold on. You're saying that all this time, Martha wanted me because she knew you were my father? But that still doesn't make any sense. How could she benefit from a secret everyone was keeping from me!"

"I've gotten off track again. This will make more sense when you've understood who I am—"

"A Burkhardt," I sliced in. "Where exactly are you in the family tree?"

"I'm the youngest son. William Burkhardt, the head of the family, is my father. Your grandfather."

I rejected that title as I was rejecting all the new slots in my new family tree. "Senator Burkhardt is your brother?"

"Yes."

"Saylor is your niece?"

"Yes."

"Then why have I never heard of you? I've read the bios on the senator. There's no mention of a younger brother."

Alistair got up and rescued my half a sandwich. He placed it back in front of me, silently encouraging me to continue eating. I did—occupying my mouth long enough to let him continue.

"There's no mention of me because I was cast out before Dario took the political stage. Since then, my family's undergone great pains to erase me, but not, as it happens, to erase you." Again, his soft smile unsettled me. "You didn't know my father or brother, but they know you. They've kept your inheritance intact despite disinheriting me."

"Why would that matter to me? I don't want anything from the Burkhardts."

Alistair gave me a long look. Suddenly, it clicked.

"But Martha does," I said slowly. "This is why she hasn't been straight with me, isn't it? She wants me to be clueless and indebted to the Wilson family. Once the truth comes out, I'd love the family who accepted me and hate the family who rejected me for eighteen years. Then she'd use my inheritance and position in the Burkhardt family to elevate hers. The Wilsons finally stop being second best."

He tapped his nose. "Got it in one."

"Fuck's sake," I cried, not caring I was cursing at my father. "You call this woman your friend? What kind of conniving witch uses a grieving teenage girl and her own son like—?" A thick, sludgy panic coated my heart. "Wait. Does Victor know all about this?"

"I can't be sure what he knows, Luna, but I doubt it. Martha was always one to play her cards close to the vest. Wouldn't do for her son to fall for you and spill the truth before she got what she wanted."

"Again, why don't you sound upset about this? The daughter you supposedly care about is being used for her inheritance."

He shrugged, boiling my irritation. "I'd be quite the hypocrite if I was. If the positions were switched, I'd use Victor Wilson in the same way without losing a wink of sleep. Matter of fact, you'd be a hypocrite too." Alistair cocked a brow. "Aren't you using Martha too?"

I tried to hold his gaze and couldn't. I flicked away, flushing angrily.

"And if I'm being more honest," he continued, "Martha is being kinder to you than I would in her situation. My information says she hasn't made you sign any contracts or prenuptial agreements that would ensure everything you *didn't know* you have remains with the Wilsons, no matter what happens between you and Victor. If it was me, I would've tied your share of the Burkhardt empire in so many legal knots, I'd own my half of your DNA too."

"Why would you do that?"

Another shrug. A bigger smirk. "I've never been one to play fair."

I didn't know what to make of that, so I put it aside for the moment. "But why disinherit you and not me?"

"My old man isn't one for sentimentality, so I assume the decision is a preemptive strike. Eloise can't sell a salacious story to the media about the illegitimate Burkhardts who were abandoned and cast out. They always knew about you and were willing to provide for you. It was our choice to keep you away. In every version of this story coming out, we're the bad guys."

My head bobbed, taking this in. It was a smart play, especially for a man who planned to become president of the United States. He wasn't ashamed of the housekeeper's daughters. Look, here was the proof he was happy and willing to welcome them any time. It was their parents who didn't tell them the truth, so there was no mark on the Burkhardts' shining reputation.

"This does explain a lot... but none of it explains Everleigh Starling."

His smirk disappeared. "In a way, it does, Luna. There's a reason why my family erased me. None of the Royals mention my name. Saylor only has the vaguest recollection of a man who used to blow raspberries on her belly and carry her around on his shoulders. I chose the wrong side. When you're a Royal, there's no worst sin."

"The wrong side? What does that mean?"

Getting to his feet, Alistair paced in front of the television, using the chance to break my probing stare. "By now, you know there are three factions in Regalia, yes?"

"Yes," I replied. "The Royals, Rogues, and Dregs."

"What do you know about the Rogues?"

"My guys are the Rogues."

"Did they tell you anything else? As in, why they're called that and why it sets them apart?"

"No." A thought occurred to me. "Does it have anything to do with purple flags? They freaked out when they saw it."

"It has everything to do with that flag." Alistair stopped before the window, looking out at the endless sea. "What you must understand, Luna, is that Regalia isn't just home to a bunch of rich families. It's where the king-makers live. Every business, every town, everyone traces back to one or more of the Regalians. They are each of them responsible for making the country what it is today, but the truth is, a country isn't shaped by heroes and do-gooders alone.

"From the slavers who soaked our country in shame we've yet to fully amend, to the explosion of organized crime during Prohibition, the bad guys leave their mark on the country just as wide as the good."

"What does that have to do with my guys or the flag?"

Alistair finally faced me. "I've been vague till now, so let me finally be blunt. The Rogues aren't a cute name for a bunch of teenage fixers. The Rogues are the largest, oldest, and most dangerous criminal empire in the country. The shadow faction of Regalia, their legacy is woven through every business, every town, and everyone too."

My mind wiped blank. "The Rogues are... what?"

"We go back to the very founding of Regalia. Elmer Wilson commanded the militia that slaughtered an indigenous tribe on the orders of Ansel Burkhardt. Elmer never trusted Ansel, so he kept his militia handy. This turned out to be the wise choice because Ansel tried to have him killed mul-tiple times to hide the truth of what they'd done to get the land.

"Elmer greatly rewarded the men who saved his life. Based on their blood-soaked secrets, they formed their own ties—"

"—becoming a band of men called the Rogues," I finished. "A group of fricking monsters. So Elmer Wilson was the first Rogue?"

"He didn't call himself that, and at the time, I doubt he realized he was the start of something bigger. The men who chose his side and protected him automatically became the enemies of the Burkhardts. Ansel Burkhardt was a wealthy robber baron and had all the privileges an unequal society gave him. He had the means and money to bring the full weight of his displea-sure against the militia members, so they had to get creative and underhand to protect themselves," Alistair said. "Only Elmer received two thousand dol-lars for the atrocity. They didn't."

"They banded together in protection and fought just as dirty and under-handed to stay alive in their new home, Regalia," I said. "Sounds familiar."

"Exactly," Alistair said, inclining his head. "Some chose to thrive in this town by following the rules and climbing the ladder only when tapped to rise. Others have moved their pieces in the shadows."

"Why haven't I heard of this? Why didn't the guys say it was more than just them?"

"Because they value their lives," he dropped, blowing me back. "The Rogues don't advertise who they are. The members of the organization are a secret. Your boyfriends announced themselves because, for various reasons, they can't rely on their families.

"No money, no home, and no other skills, they linked up and started offering their services. I don't need to tell you that even with safety in numbers, that was a dangerous move. This was the second time their home was burned down."

I didn't want to go there. "It's supposed to be a secret. That's what Victor meant when he said he couldn't publicly throw in with the guys. No one can know that the Wilsons are Rogues."

"They're not."

"But you just said—"

"I said it started with Elmer Wilson. The Rogues aren't like the Royal line. You're not born into it. It's a choice."

"A choice?"

Alistair tipped his head. "Well, I say choice. There are certainly some within our group who've raised their children to be one thing and one thing only. But you can be a Royal who chooses to become a Rogue. The same as if you're a regular citizen who chooses a life of crime. Bad choices aren't owned by anyone."

I slowly stood up, moving behind and putting the couch between us. "Is that what you did?" My voice was barely above a croak as I looked into his hooded eyes. "Is that why you keep saying *we* and *our*?"

"You're in no danger from me, Luna. I would never hurt you."

"How do I know that?" I demanded. "Who are you? Why does Everleigh want you dead? Why did she kill my sister to do it!"

Alistair winced like my shout slapped him. "This is what I'm trying to explain. The Rogues are a secret criminal organization with ties that spread across the country and overseas. Knowing the members of the organization is valuable currency, but running the entire operation..." Alistair trailed off, whistling. "It was just a game to us at first—me and Everton Starling."

My spine stiffened. "Everton Starling. Everleigh's biological father."

"Yes," he said, turning back to the window. "Growing up, we were best friends. The only one wilder and more reckless than me was him. We wreaked holy terror on Regalia and no one could stop us. I could wipe my boot on someone's back and they'd bend down and ask if I'd like to do the other one. No one told us no. That kind of power goes to your head fast."

"I've seen it," I said, tone flat.

"Everton and I liked being on top, but we never would be. We were both the youngest sons. Our older siblings were going to inherit the companies while we were left with whatever scraps they tossed our way. We wanted more. We wanted the Rogues."

I frowned. "Isn't that a bit of a leap? You can't take over the company, so you join a criminal organization? If you couldn't reach the cookie jar back then, did you burn the house down?"

He chuckled. "I was quite the brat, but I stayed away from the matches. Listen, I know how it sounds, but it wasn't a tantrum that made me seek out the Rogues. I was always... different... from my family. Everyone around me played the game. They smiled, schmoozed, and oozed doublespeak, back-stabbing, and point-scoring.

"All of it seemed pointless to me. It's like... say, there's a playground that's taken over every night by inconsiderate shits who smoke and drink and leave their trash and broken bottles for little kids to stumble over. Dario's way of solving the problem was writing a letter to the city council, organizing a volunteer cleanup, and posting a sign that said, *please don't litter*.

"My way was beating the shit out of them and promising to do worse if they came back. I know this because that's exactly what the two of us did all those years ago when Seven's daughter cut her leg open on a broken beer bottle in the sandbox." He met my wide eyes. "It didn't occur to either of us to try the other's method. Dario was always peace. I was the chaos."

"But... why does that mean you had to become a Rogue? You're a Burkhardt. You could've done anything."

"I couldn't, Luna. The more I rebelled, the more my father tightened the chains around me. He refused to pay tuition for an out-of-state school. I got an internship in London, and he bought the business and shut it down just to stop me going. The more I tried to get away from him, the closer he held me."

Understanding tried to trickle in. "I'm guessing it's not easy to break free of a man like William Burkhardt."

"It's impossible. He's tied to everyone in Regalia, but no one was bound tighter than his children. At least Dario would take over the company until he was ready to follow his political aspirations up the ladder. The only thing I had to look forward to was endless days of filling my boredom with booze and women because my father made it clear he wasn't letting his trouble-making son out into the world to embarrass him and blacken the Burkhardt name," he said. "I was looking for a way out, and the Rogues were it.

"They were the bane of his existence. All the time and money my father put into trying to find and stamp out the Rogues, and he'd gotten nowhere. As a young, brash kid, I saw them as my way to break free. What they did didn't bother me as much as it should. Like I told you, there was always a darkness in me. I was falling in with the right crowd, not a bad one."

What he said should bother me, but that would make me a hypocrite too. I said so many times that I belonged with the Rogues. Sounded like Alistair found where he belonged too.

"What about Everton?"

Alistair came back to the armchair and motioned for me to sit. I did—needing to hear the story too bad to hear my warning bells. "It's not as simple as announcing on a street corner that you want to be a Rogue. You didn't find them. They found you," he said. "There are plenty of low-rent delinquents running a dozen rackets.

"The Rogues don't need that. They want talent. They want something only you can do. They want connections only you can make. Didn't matter that we were both rich or our places on the Royal line. Plenty of people have money, but not everyone can bring those people to their knees."

"What did you guys do? How did you get in?" Yes, it did occur to me that I wasn't having the most normal conversation with the father I just met, but it had been an abnormal week. This fit in perfectly.

"Everton's family owned a string of private law firms all over the country. Everton used his name and access to get into their clients' private information and sell it to the highest bidder."

My mouth fell open. "That's way past unethical! It's disgusting."

"It was a serious line to cross," Alistair agreed, "but it worked. Rogue members lined up at his door to buy the information. He was in."

"And you?" I asked, bracing myself.

"Me," he drew out, gaze tipping to the ceiling. "I took another route."

"You can tell me. It's not like I have the right to judge anyone after all I've done."

He smiled. "Everything you've done was for your sister. Your intentions were always good."

"Do you know everything? What I've done to Wesley, Levi, Ashton, Owen, and indirectly, Giovanni?"

His smile didn't waver. "Leon knows a lot of things about a lot of things, as he likes to say. He brought me up to speed. My question is how? How did you know to go after those five? I exhausted all my resources to find the bastards, but the bullying came from almost everyone and everywhere. Why those five?"

"Winter named them in her note."

He stilled. "But your mother showed me her note."

"Winter sent one to me too. I never told Mom about it. In it, she told me everything."

It was impossible to read his face as he took that in. "You didn't tell your mother because you decided from the moment you read the letter to take them out one by one. You didn't want her to suspect you when they turned up dead."

He said it so plainly, I flinched. "So what if I did? They took the life of the best person in the world. They deserved everything they had coming to them."

"I'm not criticizing, sweetheart. Just the opposite. I'm so proud of you, I want to dress down my father again for suggesting I get a paternity test. You are definitely my daughter."

"You're proud of me? I basically took a hit out on Owen. I tortured Wesley. I got Ashton Scott stabbed."

"Well, yes," he said, inclining his head. "You went easy on them, but that's to be expected. You're new at this."

If there was something to say in response to his casual dismissal of murder and mayhem, I didn't know it.

"I've shocked you," he said. "Understandable because I haven't gotten to the end of the story. What did I do to get the Rogues' attention? I hunted them down, Luna.

"I did what my father, his father, and his father's father tried to do for decades. I found every Rogue and either took over their rackets or shut them down. Within two years, there wasn't a single one who wasn't owned... by me."

"But how could you do that? How could that be possible?"

"Money, deception, favors, bribes, informants. Whatever it took. You see, I wasn't looking to be one of the Rogues. My goal was always to make the organization *my* organization. The thing about Burkhardts is we're not joiners—"

"We're leaders." I didn't realize I chose *we* until it was already out of my mouth. "You're the leader of the Rogues."

"I am," he said, the picture of nonchalance. "Over the years, I've made many changes to the organization. I got us out of the kind of vile businesses that founded us and brought order to a disjointed group of felons used to doing what they wanted, whenever they wanted. There was one such change that brought us where we are now, Luna. In this room."

"What was it?"

"The Dumont brothers told you about their mother, yes?"

I nodded.

"What they may not know is that her killer taunted Sasha and Leon for months before they struck. They led them on a chase of random attacks and twisted clues that led to exactly what they wanted. That day, Leon thought he was cornering them—when it was actually a trap to get him out of his home. The plan all along was to kill his family."

I squeezed my eyes shut, bearing the pain for my boys. "That's awful."

"It is awful. It's even more awful that Leon and Sasha went through all of it alone. I don't know if I could've made a difference to the outcome. Saved those boys from losing their mother. But I would've tried.

"As it was, all I could do for my friend was create a new system of protection for the members and, most importantly, for their kids. I hired people like Vanna O'Rourke to take an active, instead of passive, approach to tracking down threats against us before they get close. And if that failed, I told the Rogues to hang a purple flag. Anywhere and everywhere, hang the flag and the organization will know you're in trouble. Help will come."

"Everleigh made me hang the flag to get you to come," I said, putting it together. "But I still don't understand why it had to be me. Or Winter. That monster could've done it whenever she wanted."

"She could, and…" He frowned. "I'll bet anything she has. Over the years, we've had a few false flags in Regalia. The purple flag was hung, but when one of the members investigated, no one was in danger or knew a thing about it. Might very well have been her attempt to lure me out.

"It didn't work because I never answer the call myself. I value my members, but they're all a bunch of fucking criminals."

I barked a laugh, startling me.

"The king who blindly comes running when summoned will have a short reign."

"It made sense that you didn't. You avoided exactly what she was trying to do—lure you into a trap. But because that didn't work…" My voice faltered under my swimming eyes.

"She went after the people I wouldn't ignore. If my daughters hung the flag, asking for my help"—Alistair knelt in front of me, taking my hand—"I'd come running even if I knew it was a trap."

"But Winter wouldn't do it." I squeezed his hand unconsciously. "She wouldn't hand you over to that psychotic bitch just to save herself. I knew Winter was protecting our family. In the end, she was stronger than Everleigh. Stronger than Levi. Stronger than Ashton. She never gave in and let them force her to do something she knew was wrong. She beat them," I whispered. "It was me who failed."

"You didn't know." He wiped a stray tear from my cheek. "Your mother and I thought we were protecting you. Me staying out of your lives. Her keeping the secret of who I am and what I did. It was all to protect you from my enemies, but all it did was leave you both vulnerable. The only one who failed is me."

I shook myself, letting go of his hand. This wasn't the time for a father-daughter bonding moment. I still needed an answer to the most important question. "All this to get revenge for Everton Starling. Why? What happened to him?"

He rocked back on his heels, leaning against the armchair. He was quiet for so long I thought he had changed his mind.

"I told you what he did to get into the Rogues," Alistair said, speaking to the ceiling. "I knew why. He was desperate to claw out from under his father's thumb, the same as I. He bargained with the only chip he had... then, a kid died."

I sat up straighter. "What? Who?"

"This was before you were born. Attorney-client privilege didn't exist within the Starling Group while Everton was selling it all to the highest bidder. There was a case—not even well known at the time. A Royal couple, low on the ladder, did what many of us do when love turns sour. They jumped to hate with quick and alarming speed.

"There was a spousal abuse accusation that turned out to be fake, and child abuse that turned out to be very, very real. Because Everton sold their entire legal strategy to the lying fake, their side shredded an innocent man on the stand and got him sent to prison for ten years. His pleas that it was all lies and the true abuser was his spouse were ignored. Three months after he was sent away, his son was beaten to death."

"Oh no." My eyes rimmed with more tears. "That poor boy."

"It was an unconscionable tragedy. Of course, people weren't buying what he was selling for noble reasons, but that a Rogue played a part in locking away an innocent man and trapping a child with an abuser? That couldn't stand, Luna.

"When I took over, I told Everton he either found a new racket or he was out of the Rogues. The thing is, the Rogues aren't an after-school math club. There's only one way to leave—in a body bag."

I shook my head. "I'm guessing Everton didn't like being threatened."

"Didn't like it one bit, but I had to make myself clear. What he was doing had to end. No discussion."

"Did he stop?"

"No."

"I knew before you answered," I said, dropping my chin on my knees. "We wouldn't be here if everything went well with you two."

"Everton didn't believe his childhood friend would kill him, and he was right. I had a moment of weakness," Alistair confessed. "I punished him instead. I outed him and destroyed the reputation of the Starling Group in the process. Every case they tried was overturned, and countless people were able to demand a retrial. Including the father of that young boy. He got out of jail, leaving an empty cell for Everton."

"Everton was arrested?"

He nodded. "Arrested, disowned, reviled. He lost everything, and believe me, it did not soften the blow that he didn't lose his life too. All he saw was that I betrayed him. It sealed his hatred of me."

"You were trying to do the right thing. You were doing what Everton should've done himself. Why would he want to continue after someone used him to destroy an innocent man and kill a child?"

"Everton took the approach that all he did was sell the information. It wasn't on him what people did with it."

I scoffed, feeling less and less sympathy for the guy by the second.

"Everton wasn't on trial for long," Alistair continued. "He fled in the middle of the trial and lay low among his many undisclosed properties. During that time, he plotted how to take me down."

"He wanted you dead?"

"He wanted me dead *and* he wanted my throne. Everton secretly spread division among the current and former Rogues. Weren't they chafing under my new rules? Didn't they hate taking orders from a twentysomething upstart? Didn't they want a return to the old ways? Join with him, put him on top, *kill me*, and he'd give them everything they wanted and more."

Even all these years later, I saw the pain in Alistair's eyes clear as day. "This set off a wave of assassination attempts that'd make a president quake in their boots. Old and new enemies came after me relentlessly—spurred on by my oldest friend."

"Wow." I tried to imagine my old friends from Catholic school hating me so much they sent assassins after me. Alistair was right. It was a frightening thing when love turned to hate. "Were you with Mom while all of this was happening? Did she know the truth about you?"

"Your mother knew everything about me, from the mundane to my deep, darkest secrets. I never lied to her and never will," he said firmly. "She knew everything and didn't judge me. All she wanted was to be with me and raise our family together. The only thing I wanted more than leading the Rogues was to give you, your sister, and your mother everything.

"I was stupid to think I could do both. The day my brakes failed and I crashed the car with the three of you inside ended my silly fantasy."

My lips went numb. "A car crash? But... I don't remember that."

"You wouldn't. We were bringing you home from the fucking hospital," he forced through gritted teeth. "You were three days old. Winter was only one. I had no idea someone had gotten close enough to your mother to watch and wait until she went into labor. Everton knew I wouldn't miss your birth, so that's when he told them to strike."

Oh yes, my sympathy for the man was nonexistent.

"After that, your mother and I agreed to split up for your safety. She took you girls out of Regalia"—emptiness bled into his eyes—"and I killed my oldest friend."

That was the only way this story could end.

"You did it?" I asked softly.

"I say this all like it happened quickly. I didn't realize Everton was behind that attempt and the many others that followed for quite some time. It took years of following money trails, listening to whispers, speaking to this broker who received a call from that blocked phone that was prompted by this email from a dummy address. All that time, I didn't consider Everton was behind the many assassination attempts that drove me further and further underground, farther from my family.

"When the trail finally led back to him, it was riddled with unforgivable betrayals after nearly a decade of us having no contact. There wasn't a friendship left to fight for."

He stared off into the distance, eyes glazing with memories I didn't want to know about. The emotion within them said it all.

"It only seemed right for me to end the war between us. I wouldn't pawn his death off like some coward. He deserved to look in my eyes and say his piece before the end. And he did before he left behind a nine-year-old girl so consumed with hatred she made my girls pay for her revenge."

I drifted off him, staring unseeingly outside. "She killed us both to get you here. The only reason my death didn't take is because she chose a hit man with principles. Anyone else, and I'd be gone."

"That's what she wanted. For me to come running at you hanging the flag, but I was always meant to be too late. She likely thought I'd stay in Regalia to search for who killed you. To search for *her*. Finally, her target would come to her."

A chill climbed my spine. "That's exactly what she said while smoke filled the room." I locked on to him. "But I'm not dead, and I'm not going to play dead now that I know the whole truth. Winter was innocent in all this, and she tortured her to get to you. All to avenge a monster who got one child killed, then tried to soak his hands in the blood of two more.

"I get that he was her biological father, but the nut didn't fall far from that sack. She's no less a sociopath and she's not getting away with it."

"She won't get away with it, and she won't get what she ultimately wants either." Alistair got to his feet. "Starling thought she could lure me out into the open, but now you're here and safe. In the meantime, my associates are in the process of making sure she's arrested for arson, kidnapping, and murder. They'll plant the evidence if they have to.

"Once she's safely behind bars, you can go back to your life, Luna. Winter will have justice. It's finally over."

The weight of that settled on my shoulders. *It's over?*

But he was right. Everleigh lost her last bargaining chip. She couldn't use me to get to my father, and she couldn't hide anymore. I had four Rogues, but Alistair had all of them. He'd get the revenge I'd been seeking. He'd give Winter the justice she deserved.

"But I don't want that." As soon as I said it, the truth of it pressed harder than the weight. "I don't want the pretty princess to sit behind a wall of lawyers, batting her dreamy eyes and fake crying while they spin the world into believing she was framed. I don't want to watch her cut some kind of deal for a slap-on-the-wrist sentence. I don't want to bite my lip till it bleeds when she pulls the same move as Everton and disappears the way only the mega-rich can do.

"Prison sounds like justice, but it's not. Because in or out of a cell... she's still alive."

"I understand how you feel, but that's not an option. Leon's policy of not killing teenagers is one shared by me and everyone in my organization. We don't kill kids." He reached for my hand again, and I pulled away. His arm dropped by his side. "If there's any benefit to her being so young, it's that she'll spend that much longer pondering her actions in jail."

"You're not hearing me." I stood up, facing him down. "She's not going to prison. Everleigh doesn't feel an ounce of remorse for what she did to Winter. She said the goal wasn't to kill her, but that didn't stop her from laughing and taunting me.

"She will die for what she's done. She's going the same way as her father. Outed, disinherited, reviled, then dead." I folded my arms, shrugging. "If you don't want to be a part of it, that's fine. Never asked for your help anyway. Now, is this ship pointed toward home? It'd better be. The guys are waiting for me."

Alistair patiently waited for me to stop. "My dear, it's you who isn't hearing me. Your guys will be in danger again the minute she finds out you're still alive. Leon risked his life and their lives to save you. Are you telling me you're going to repay that sacrifice by making it all worth nothing?"

Guilt panged my chest.

"Everleigh Starling has countless resources at her disposal, and you have four teenage boys. How will you stop her, Luna? She's always seen you coming."

"I don't know how. Yet." Why lie? After all my scheming, tricks, and hacks, the only revenge I'd gotten against Everleigh was what she allowed me. I had zero dirt on her other than the Book Lady, and she didn't give a shit about that.

I didn't have a lot of options. What I had was four guys and a wayward father to protect. How did I do that while killing the bitch?

"Alistair, if you understand, then you know I need to do this. For Winter."

His face hardened. "You can't ask me to put you back in danger, Luna. Your mother would never forgive me. I would never forgive myself if something happened to you. I already lost your sister. I won't lose you too."

I flung away, making it as far as the staircase, then doubling back to say... what? I didn't know.

Think, Luna. Think. There's nowhere to storm off to on a boat in the middle of the ocean. The only way back is to convince him you need to do this. Figure out how.

"What if there was a way to guarantee my safety?"

"Then I'd patent it, sell it, and become the richest man in history. No one can guarantee their safety." He frowned. "Particularly because of this club Leon was telling me about. Do I have it right that there's a secret dare club that makes people's lives a misery?"

"Yes, and—" The truth hit me in the face. "Everleigh is one of the monsters behind the scenes, running things. That's how she knew she was talking to the right people when she sent Giovanni, Wesley, and the others after Winter," I said. "They're a threat, but thanks to me, they're not a secret anymore. I've got the whole campus talking about them."

"That doesn't protect you."

"The guys will protect me, and I'll protect them. It's what we do."

"Like they protected you from Starling?"

"That's different." I went to the kitchen and poured myself a drink. I didn't know how much time had passed since Mr. Dumont pulled me out of that fire. It was long enough that my throat was sandpaper. "We got into that mess because we couldn't be honest with each other. Now that everything is out in the open, nothing like this is going to happen again."

"You don't know that. If you're so worried, I'll allow them to join us where we're going. That's my best and final offer."

"But—"

"Feel free to explore the boat," he said, walking out. "Nothing is off-limits to you."

"But, Alistair!"

He left, leaving me fuming at his retreating back. Eventually I dropped the scowl, and then myself in the armchair. How could I blame him? No one could deny Everleigh Starling was dangerous. She tried to have me killed and would've succeeded if she hadn't chosen the wrong hit man.

I was asking to face her again with the odds uneven. She had enormous wealth, influence, the Royal line, and the T.O.D. Club at her disposal. What did I have to go against her? Alistair wouldn't help me kill the teenage daughter of his former best friend. I only had my guys by my side, and that's assuming they weren't planning on dumping me for getting them in this mess.

Groaning, my head dropped on the cushion. Victor refused to throw in with the Rogues. Wilder was preoccupied with the mysterious threat from his brother. Rafael and Cato were being used to control their father, and me...

I was no closer to figuring out how I would take down Everleigh since before I started my thought train.

"Think," I said out loud. "Eventually, Everleigh will realize her plan to draw Alistair out into the open failed. She's waited ten years for this. She won't just give up. So, if I was her, what would I do then?"

My brain didn't have answers for me.

Chapter Two

"You have to take me back."

Alistair munched on a piece of toast, paying me half a mind while he scrolled on his laptop. "I only have to do what someone has the power to force me to do. That's not you, sweetheart."

"Stop calling me that," I snapped. "I'll admit I'm a Burkhardt when the paternity test comes back."

He laughed. Three days, and we'd been having the same argument. Three days I'd been on a luxury yacht with the father I never knew, and it turned out he was a massive jerk.

He teased me, walked out in the middle of my pleas, laughed at my taunts, mercilessly beat me in every game we played, then hugged and kissed me good night even when I yelped and wriggled away from him. One didn't become the leader of a criminal organization by being a pushover, and Alistair Burkhardt didn't give an inch.

"My guys must be going out of their minds thinking that I'm dead. I can't put them through that. It's not fair to them."

"That's a nice sob story. Shame a violin wasn't playing in the background."

"Ugh, you're such an asshole! What did Mom ever see in you?"

"I'm fantastic in bed."

I blew back. "What in the hell. Are you trying to make up for eighteen years of not mentally scarring me for life!"

"Course. Now we're together, I've got to make up for lost time."

Groaning, I gave up and ate my eggs. The guy insisted that we eat breakfast together. Lunch and dinner, he was off making phone calls he wouldn't let me overhear or tip-tapping away on his laptop that he wouldn't let me near.

But for breakfast, he'd track me down wherever I was and eat with me. The day before, I locked myself in the bathroom with my spinach and egg white omelet, and the guy parked outside the door and ate on the floor, chattering at me the whole time.

"Tell me about your mother," I mumbled.

"Excuse me?"

I lifted my shoulders, picking and nibbling on my breakfast. "You've talked about how terrible your father is. What about your mom? What's she like?"

Alistair smiled. "You can just say that you want to know about this side of your family."

"Paternity test," I reminded, earning another laugh. "But I am curious about what goes on inside the Burkhardt mansion, that they've turned out one criminal mastermind and one succubus."

Amusement was all over his face. "It was mentioned to me that you and my niece do not get along. Something about you selling her text messages for a couple hundred a pop?"

"How do you know all of these things? You're floating in a rich man's version of a prepper bunker in the middle of the ocean."

He tapped his laptop. "See this thing? It's a magic box that receives communications from anywhere in the world."

"I hate you."

"I love you," he rebounded, enjoying himself entirely too much. "On a serious note, the highest collection of Rogues live in Regalia. I make it my business to know what they're up to at all times. If my employees pick up other interesting information—such as my daughter striking the first significant blow against a Burkhardt in fifty years—they pass it on."

"The highest collection of Rogues. Really? Who are they?"

He looked down his nose at me. "Why even ask? You know what I'm going to say."

"Why wouldn't you tell me? I'm a Rogue too."

"The hell you are."

I goggled at him. "What are you talking about? Of course I am. Me, Rafael, Cato, Wilder, Lucien—"

"They aren't Rogues either," he sliced in. "They're the children of Rogues who were groomed to one day join. In the future. When they're older. If I wouldn't go after a teenager, why would I let them in my organization?"

"Fine. I'm not a Rogue, but I don't see why you won't tell me. You mentioned that anyone can be one—including a Royal." I thought of Victor. "It'd be good for me to know who my secret allies are before I face Everleigh."

"Sweetie, your eyes are open. Stop dreaming."

It was everything in me not to throw my chocolate chip muffin at his head.

"You asked about my mother," he continued, returning half his attention back to the laptop. "That I can answer. She's the coldest, most unforgiving taskmaster that ever wielded a Mastercard. She stopped speaking to me the day I turned down the arranged marriage. Literally walked out of every room I entered. Once, I sliced my hand with a kitchen knife and she didn't even look up from her paper.

"That said, I love the old broad. Wouldn't be where I am without her."

I wasn't sure if that was a good or a bad thing, considering the whole criminal situation. "It sucks that she punished you for wanting to be with Mom though. Seems like no one in your life supported or trusted you to make your own decisions. It's tough when our parents refuse to stop seeing us as children." I flashed him a mirthless smile. "I know what that's like."

"Nice try. I'm more than happy to be a hypocrite if it keeps you safe. I've lost one child to a ten-year-old revenge plot. I won't lose another." He gestured to his laptop. "Trust me, Luna. She's not getting away with what she's done.

"My people are the best at what they do. I'm sure Starling was smart enough to cover her tracks. Ronin will uncover them. Every piece of evidence found, he'll make sure it leads back to her. Faking or planting it if necessary. I've got friends in the RPD to bring the investigation the rest of the way."

I took a deep breath and let it out slow. As frustrated as I was, I understood where he was coming from. Everleigh in jail for the crimes she committed was justice to ninety-nine percent of the planet.

"Look, I know you think I'm blinded by revenge. That I can't see past what she did to Winter, but it's not that I don't see past it. It's that I didn't see anything." Pushing my plate away, I leaned over the table, as if my words needed a shorter distance to reach him. "The whole time I was looking for the Phantom, I didn't see Everleigh right in front of me.

"She's too good, Alistair. The only reason I know she's behind this is because she told me," I admitted. "The whole time, she's worked through puppets too scared to rat on her, and when they tried, she was ready for that too." Sighing, I rubbed tired eyes. "You know what you do when you have ten years to plot revenge? You prepare for every outcome.

"You believe she can't be ahead of you because you're you and she's a nineteen-year-old coed, but underestimating her is a mistake I won't make again. She did what you did," I said. "She created an anonymous army willing to do her bidding. I've seen how far they'll go. I've experienced how far *she'll* go. Whatever is coming next... she's ready for it."

Alistair squeezed my hand. For some reason, I let him. "I don't underestimate her, Luna. Royal or Rogue—doesn't matter. We all receive a very different education growing up. People will take advantage of us for money or favors, so we're taught not to trust. Our future is boardrooms and political dealings. We're raised not to give an inch, always look for the angle, and in every situation, make sure we're the one who walks away from the table with everything we want.

"I know Everleigh is more than a coed because she's Everton Starling's daughter. And Winter was mine," he said, giving me that soft look that I couldn't take. "I'm leaving nothing to chance. She will pay for what she did. Within the next twenty-four hours, we'll get word that she's been arrested."

He let go of my hand. "After that, we'll talk about you returning to Regalia. First, we have to make sure she can't use her money or secret club to get back at you."

"I may not have had ten years, but I've spent the last three days thinking about how to get to her before she can get to me. I have a plan." It was me who held his hand. "If you trust me, I can do this. I can give our family peace."

He stared at our grasped hands as the silence stretched. "Do you know why I stayed away? Yes, your mother and I agreed it was best I stayed out of your life, but I didn't have to shroud myself in mystery. There could've been phone calls or emails. You could've known my name."

"Then why?"

"Because I'm not a hypocrite, Luna. Whatever route you took in life, it had to be your choice and your choice alone. The Rogues are seductive. Living life by your own rules, taking what you want, beholden to no one, the most powerful person in the room. We wouldn't have laws, courtrooms, or police if crime wasn't so tempting.

"I knew that if I told you the truth about what I do, I'd edge you slightly off your path and onto mine. For eighteen years, I fought my instincts to give you a chance at a normal life, then, as a result of my actions, it was taken from you both anyway.

"You're smart, Luna. Smart, resourceful, ruthless when you need to be, but kind always. I know you could face Everleigh and come out on top, *but you shouldn't have to*. Would you have made the choices you have in the last several months if Winter was still here?"

My jaw clenched. I didn't answer.

"Exactly. You wouldn't have fallen in with those guys, planned murders, or had to be dragged out of a burning building. You don't have to live this life anymore. I'm here to do what I should've done." He tipped my chin, smiling into my eyes. "Protect your shot at a normal life."

"Maybe this isn't what a bitter, abandoned child should say, but you don't have to put that much regret on your shoulders. I had a good, normal life before all this happened. Beach summers, crushes, staying up late roasting marshmallows in the backyard with Winter. I did normal, but it isn't what I miss. Winter i-is." My throat clogged. "All the choices I've made since then, I don't regret them because they led me to the Rogues. It's only when the worst happens that you find out who is truly there for you.

"An average, normal boyfriend wouldn't hang a guy off a ceiling or blow one up for me," I said. "A parent is supposed to protect their kid's childhood, and you did. But you're not supposed to settle my scores. She tried to kill me. She threatened to kill my boyfriends. She destroyed my sister.

"This is between me and Everleigh."

"Luna— Hold on." He flicked to the screen. "Well, it looks like this discussion has been decided. Ronin's gotten in touch with an update." Alistair let go and clicked the email. "I'm sorry, Luna, but this is for the best. We need... to..."

He stopped, eyes narrowing on the screen. I watched his eyes scan all the way down, fly up, and then read it again.

A terrible snarl split his lips.

"What? What is it?"

Alistair's reply was to turn the laptop around and let me read. Leaning in, I read it for myself. A boulder-sized pit lodged in my throat.

"Confessed?" I rasped. "Someone named Connor Langston confessed to arson and the murder of Luna Sinclair-Bowden? I don't even know who that is."

"It's someone who's going to receive a reduced sentence and a hefty reward when they're released from prison. Fuck!" Alistair slammed his fist on the table. "Their investigation is over. They have their guy, there's no reason for them to keep looking."

"This is Everleigh." We both knew it, but it had to be said. "This is the T.O.D. Club."

Alistair shot to his feet. "No, it's not over. Ronin will get to this kid. He'll offer Langston more than Starling could ever give him. He'll recant and—"

"I don't think he will," I said softly, lips trembling. "I've seen the kind of blackmail they hold over the members' heads. Their every little secret from black to light gray. Whatever Everleigh has on Connor, it has to be terrible for him to confess to a crime like this. I'm sorry, Dad."

He snapped to me, eyes wide.

"We lost."

Alistair dropped to his knees, holding his head. Every emotion cycled across his face, each more heart-wrenching than the last. I felt everything he was feeling inside, though it didn't show. I was horribly used to being outmaneuvered by Everleigh Starling.

"No."

It took me a minute to realize the hoarse croak that came from him was a word.

"We haven't lost." Alistair pushed up to his feet, eyes heavy with a darkness I'd only seen from one other person. Me when I looked in the mirror.

"Tell me your plan."

***

I stepped onto the dock, shading my eyes against the piercing glare. I turned and there she was, giving me a smile that every mom perfected—laced with equal parts love and worry.

We took off running.

I jumped in Mom's arms, smothering in her peach perfume and the scent of fresh laundry. She hugged me so tight my bones creaked.

"Oh, my baby. My sweet girl." She peppered my face with kisses. "Even though I knew you were okay, it killed me seeing the news reports the last few days. It brought e-everything back."

I squeezed her just as hard, breaking under the same grief.

"I'm so sorry we fought, baby. I never meant to shut you out. I was struggling with your choice to stay, and I didn't know how to speak to you and not beg you to reconsider every time."

"I know, Mom," I whispered. "I understand more than ever now all that you've given up to keep me and Winter safe."

"Eloise."

We turned, facing Alistair as he stepped off the boat. He lit on my mom like she was the only one there.

"My goodness, woman, you're gorgeous."

My mother did something she's never done in my eighteen years of life.

Burst out giggling.

I suddenly found myself off to the side, staring at the shocking spectacle of her neon-red cheeks.

"Oh, Al," she said, patting her perfect bun and straightening her dress. "It's good to see you too."

"When are you going to stop all this and run away with me?"

More giggling. More needless fussing with her clothes.

"Behave," she said in a tone that was supposed to sound scolding but wasn't at all. "I'm a married woman."

"True. Better hop on the boat quickly before he gets here."

Her husband in question was coming down the dock after parking the car, moving fast like he heard my father's comment. Unlike my first meeting, he looked at Alistair with recognition—which made sense. Jack knew he could make a marriage deal with Martha that would protect me and give her everything she wanted. He had a lost Burkhardt heiress eating pancakes at the dining table every morning.

"Hello, Alistair." Jack fell in beside Mom, snaking a possessive arm around her waist. "Thank you for taking care of our Luna."

"No need to thank me." Alistair's smile was predatory. "She's my daughter. I'll do anything for her."

Was it just me, or were sparks shooting out of their eyes?

I didn't know the full history between these three, but I was getting the feeling Alistair wasn't joking about that offer to run away with Mom.

Mom cleared her throat. "Yes, thank you for getting Luna out of Regalia. But I don't understand why you're both back. You told me you'd be away for a while and that you'd send for us when you arrived in Crete."

So that was the plan. Whisk me off to Greece where I'd live safely with Mom, Jack, and Alistair—likely in the luxury my father could clearly afford. So much of that would've been perfect. When he wasn't irritating the mess out of me, Alistair made me laugh, think, and wish that I had a different life. One where he was there.

But there was a problem with that happy scene of a blended family in Greece. Winter wasn't with us. And neither were my guys.

Moving on wasn't possible while Everleigh Starling ran free. When I put her in the grave she had picked out for me, then I'd spend my time getting to know the father I just met, alongside enjoying life with my guys—who I hoped looked at me in twenty years the way Alistair still looked at my mom.

"That was the plan," Alistair said, "but circumstances changed. Luna has unfinished business in Regalia."

Mom's eyes narrowed. "I see. I thought we agreed that our children weren't you."

"She's not me, El. She's the best of both of us. She can end this horrible nightmare and bring closure to our family. Or," he said softly, "the person who killed our Winter can live free, rich, and unpunished. The choice is yours. We agreed."

She flew to me, and I nodded. "No more fighting, secrets, or silent treatment. I can end this if you'll trust me."

Mom was quiet, flicking from me to Alistair. She settled on her former love. "Will she be safe?"

"She's got the help of a couple of guys who were trained by the best. She's also my daughter. She's more than a match for what's coming."

Lips pursed, Mom's face was unreadable. "I'll think about it."

I knew better than to push. It wasn't like I was going to kick Everleigh's face in right that minute. There were other people I needed to see first.

"Where are my guys?"

"Their home was burned down, and a cache of weapons was found in the remains."

My eyes bugged, remembering that horrifying detail.

"Starling was good enough to drop them off in front of the police station after she released them."

"And you didn't tell me this!"

He shrugged, completely unfazed by my rage. "I told you Ronin was handling the situation. He arranged for their release from custody. They're suspended from school but not under arrest while they sort everything out."

"I need to see them. Now."

"I'm told Victor Wilson put them up in his beach house. I'll take you."

I took off, then halted. "Wait, should you? Everleigh did all this to get you here, so here is the last place you should be."

Alistair sidestepped me and strode off. "Did you think I was going to drop you in danger, then float off in my prepper bunker?"

"What else have you been doing for the last eighteen years?"

"Luna!" Mom cried.

Alistair howled. "Don't worry, El. We have the lovingly antagonistic relationship only a father and daughter can have. She's got to give me shit to make sure I don't get too comfortable."

"She has to do no such thing." Mom towed me in, resuming her tight hug. "We'll talk about everything tonight. Alistair, the Burkhardts, everything I wanted to tell you but couldn't. Alistair isn't at fault for any of this. He was only respecting my wishes."

I rested my head on her shoulder. "I want to talk, Mom, but Alistair does have to go. You both know how dangerous it is to have a Starling after you."

Mom stiffened. "Starling? Alistair, what is she talking about?"

"We also need to have a conversation tonight, El," he replied. "But first, we should get out of the open. If we don't want her to know I'm here, let's not broadcast it."

We got into separate cars—my mom and Jack agreed to go home and wait for us after much coaxing. She didn't want to let me out of her sight.

I shot glances at the back of the driver's head during the ride, wondering if the shaved gentleman with a black dragon inked on the side of his head was Ronin.

Alistair reclined on his seat, focused on his phone in place of his laptop.

"Will you let your family know that you're here?" I asked.

"I won't have to. The Burkhardts own this town. They know everything that happens on its soil."

"Not everything. Saylor didn't know Everleigh was her long-lost evil twin."

"How can you be sure?"

"Because I read her texts." I pressed my forehead against the cool glass. "The Royal Wenches held nothing back. Every twisted, cruel thing they've done. Every sex secret. Every deep, dark thought. They slung it all back and forth, except for Everleigh. She joined in, but she never gave away anything that could be used to bring her down.

"I should've noticed that." My fists balled. "I should've noticed that *Jezebel12* offered up the Book Lady site a little too easily and a little too quick. I should've noticed that Everleigh was working too hard to separate me from Victor.

"That day I went to Martha about my tuition, she told me the Starlings came to her with a serious, eye-popping business merger if she agreed to dissolve our engagement and have her son marry Everleigh instead."

Alistair nodded slowly. "You're harder to get to, holed up in Wilson Manor, and the Wilsons are a powerful enemy. Of course she wanted to separate you from them... before she killed you."

"It's all so obvious now. Just like it's obvious Saylor doesn't know what's going on under her nose. She's done a lot of cruel, manipulative things. That's why Everleigh knew to keep her real secret to herself."

"Hmm."

"What?" I asked, facing him. "What is it?"

"Nothing. I just find it humorous that you and Saylor don't get along."

"Why?"

He gave me a knowing look. "Because you'd both make good Rogues."

"I'm your daughter. Don't compare me to Satan."

"That Starling is acting alone doesn't make her less dangerous," he warned. "No one with an unlimited bank account is. Especially when she uses it to run this T.O.D. Club."

"Why didn't you know about it? Mr. Dumont did."

"I was informed of a dare club, but not that it went this far. I assumed it was a bunch of college students blowing off steam and getting high off mildly risky behavior. If I had known the members would go as far as running a kid over..." He shook his head. "I've been away from Regalia for too long. Secondhand information isn't good enough to run an empire. The peasants always misbehave when the king's away from the throne."

I did not comment on him referring to himself as a king and everyone else as a peasant. He was a Burkhardt. That kind of arrogance was in his DNA.

Your DNA too, a voice reminded. *You're heir to the throne. You'd sit right alongside Saylor.*

I shivered, grimacing at the thought. The fact that we were family changed nothing. We hated each other and made no secret of it. Blood didn't make someone any less a bitch.

"Does that mean you're coming back when all this is over?" I asked the passing trees. "You're going to... stay for good?"

"Do you want me to?"

I pressed my lips together, looking anywhere but at him. He holed up in his floating bunker to prevent the next assassination attempt. I couldn't ask him to move back to where he'd always have a target on his back.

"Is it possible?" My voice was getting smaller and smaller. "When Everleigh's done, will it be safe for you to come back?"

"I didn't stay away because I was afraid of anyone here. I stayed away because I was afraid for you. Now, you need me here." A warm hand settled on the back of my head. "I won't leave you again, Luna. I promise."

My cheeks warmed, but I didn't let on. Like he said, I couldn't let him get too comfortable. "But you do have to go for now. The T.O.D.ers could be anyone and anywhere. For all we know, she has them on the lookout for you right now."

"I'm not going anywhere. Might as well make me the leader of the pantywaist club if I run scared of a teenager. Don't worry," he said, returning to his phone. "I'm making arrangements for the final move now. Time for Alistair Burkhardt to return to Regalia."

I held off on arguing with him—for the time being. Seemed there would be a big family talk that night. Mom and I would have a better chance of convincing him as a team.

We were quiet for the rest of the drive. Alistair was busy making his arrangements while I was busy coming up with an explanation for the guys.

Alistair asked Mr. Dumont to not tell them that I wasn't dead. All that time they've spent grieving, and now I was going to burst in with not a scratch on me and tell them my father was the shadowy head of the organization that claimed their parents. Where did I begin? It all sounded crazy to me too.

All too soon, our driver turned off the paved road and onto a tree-lined path leading to the beach. Recognition smacked me in the face. Why didn't I realize when he said Wilson beach house?

I swallowed hard at the wraparound porch and chair swing. Victor put Rafael, Cato, Lucien, and Wilder up in his brother's house.

The car stopped before the driveway. I froze with my fingers around the handle, willing them to pull, let me out, face what was coming.

"They won't be angry."

My head snapped up, fixing on Alistair's smile.

"When someone you love comes back to you, anger is the last thing you feel."

"I was in way over my head. I got them sucked into a situation that never had anything to do with them, and it almost got them killed. Now I'm going to waltz in and ask to kick the war off again? They're going to tell me to get the fuck out of their faces."

"They won't." His gaze flicked past my shoulder. "Trust me. I haven't lied to you yet."

Turning slowly, I watched Wilder, Rafael, and Victor step onto the porch, glaring suspiciously at the random black car sitting in front of the house.

I reached for the handle again.

"But if they do let you down," Alistair continued, "I'll kill them. So it's good for me either way."

I snorted, barking a laugh. It gave me the strength to open the door.

"Hey, guys."

The three of them didn't move—each staring at me with varying degrees of shock.

"I'm so sorry," I blurted. "I swear I couldn't contact you before now, but I'll explain everything and—"

"Luna?" Victor jumped off the porch. "Luna!" He scooped me in his arms, spinning me off my feet. I couldn't catch my breath under his onslaught of kisses, so I stopped trying.

Cupping his cheeks, I kissed him back hungrily, desperately, freely. What I had with Victor was so new, and Everleigh almost cut it short permanently.

"I can't believe you're alive." Victor squeezed the breath out of me. "When they told me you didn't make it out of the Gallery..." Wetness dripped on my cheek. "Don't ever do that to me again."

"I'm sorry. I love you so much."

The confession was barely out before I was torn from Victor's arms and Rafael buried me in his chest.

"I knew you weren't gone," he whispered. "I knew you wouldn't leave me."

My heart melted like ice cream in the sun. I couldn't believe I wasted a second in fear of what they'd say when they saw me. These guys were my hearts. They beat for me. I lived for them. We were together again. Everything was as it should be.

I broke from Rafael only to end up clinging to Wilder. He kissed my forehead, cheeks, lips, everywhere.

"How?" he gruffed. "I scoured the ends of cyberspace for a trace of you. How?"

"I didn't have my phone or internet access."

"My doing." Alistair's voice stole their attention. "Hello, gentlemen. Aren't you going to introduce yourselves?"

I slipped out of Wilder's suddenly stiff hold. He gaped at my father in open-mouthed shock.

"Sir."

Sir?

"What are you—? Wait, we didn't hang the flag, sir." Wilder snapped me behind him, making me yelp. "It was all a misunderstanding. Luna didn't know what it meant."

"I know the circumstances. I'm not here for punishment, though I do respect that you anticipated it and put yourself between me and my daughter to protect her. Brings you a tad higher in my estimation."

I couldn't describe the look on Rafael's face. I'd never seen it on him or anyone else before. "Daughter?"

I knew the look on *Alistair's* face. It could only be described as predatory. "Daughter," he said firmly. "What are your intentions toward Luna?"

"I—I—"

"We are— I mean—"

I gaped at a stuttering Rafael and Wilder. I'd never seen these two as anything less than confident, and here they were, looking like they already shit their pants and were trying to cover it up. Who was this guy that he made my bomb-juggling boyfriend nervous?

"We love her—"

"—never hurt her—"

"Their intentions," I sliced in, "are the same toward me as I'm sure yours were toward Mom."

"Then I'll definitely have to kill them."

Rolling my eyes, I stopped when I saw my guys pale. "He's kidding," I cried. "Alistair, are you staying?"

"Ronin is." He nodded at our silent driver. "He'll keep an eye on you while I check into my accommodations. I'll be back in a few hours to pick you up.

"Behave, boys." He winked. "If you don't, I'll know."

I don't think Wilder or Rafael took a breath until he got in the car and drove off.

"Gorgeous," Rafael said. "You have explaining to do."

"I'll tell you guys everything. Let's go inside."

It was my turn to hold my breath as we entered Adonis's place. Victor knew about us, but I hadn't told Rafael, Wilder, Cato, or Lucien. His job was at risk. It didn't feel right to tell a secret that affected him more than me, but it also felt terrible not telling my guys.

Especially when they were living in his house.

Walking in, I didn't make it two steps before Cato was on me. Growling, he snatched me off my feet, tossed me on the nearest couch, and pounced. It was impossible to tell if he was kissing me or devouring me.

I didn't care which. I kissed him back twice as hard—tongues battling and moans filling the room. Warmth melted my stress. Explosions set off in the back of my mind. Finally, I was where I was supposed to be.

When we finally broke apart, I was hot and dizzy. I pushed myself up on the couch but couldn't go farther than that. The guys pushed in around me instead—each holding a hand, stroking my leg, and resting my head on their shoulder. I relaxed being surrounded by their love.

"Where's Lucien?"

"He had a meeting with his lawyer," Wilder said.

I glanced at Victor. "And Adonis?"

"He's in class."

"Of course he is. I forgot it was a weekday," I said. "So much has happened, it blows my mind that the world has carried on."

I traced a fading bruise on Rafael's cheek. "What happened? What did she do to you?"

"Kept us blindfolded and bound in some hole for eighteen hours. No food or water."

I clenched my teeth hard to stop myself from summoning the devil and exchanging my soul for Everleigh's eternal torment.

"We got beat up fighting the goons that came to take us, but afterward, they didn't touch us. After we were released, Dad called, told us Everleigh Starling was behind everything, and that he'd tell us more when he had the chance. We've been here waiting for him to show up ever since."

"I'll tell you what he was going to."

I spilled everything from beginning to end. I told them about my parents meeting, falling in love, and how the Burkhardts' rejection of her was the final straw that ended Alistair's life as a Royal and sent him to the Rogue side. I told them about the feud between him and Everton Starling and that it led to where we are today.

Victor dropped on the beanbag chair, brows blown up his forehead. "Killed his best friend because said best friend sent assassins after him that nearly killed your family when you were a baby? What the fuck!"

"I couldn't have said it better myself," I replied. "The whole situation is so fucked. Everton put my father in an impossible situation, and then Everleigh did the same to Winter. She refused to lead him into a trap, but she was too scared to bring us into her battle with Everleigh and make us targets too." My lids tipped, heavy with tears. "We've continued a war that's gone on longer than twenty years. It goes all the way back to Elmer Wilson and Ansel Burkhardt. Rogues versus Royals.

"Alistair is trusting me to end it for good, but I admit, I can't do it alone." I took a deep breath. "I want your help, but I won't demand it. If you don't want any part of this—"

"Let me stop you before you say any more nonsense," Rafael broke in. "I'm yours. Whatever you need, just name it."

"Me too," Victor said.

"Obviously, I'm going to help you take her down," Wilder added. "From what you're saying, it sounds like your fight is our fight anyway. If Everleigh is running the T.O.D. Club, then she's in bed with Wolf. The two of them together..." He shook his head. "You need me, Luna, but even with me, I don't know if we can take them down."

"Why?" I asked. "What makes your brother so dangerous?"

"Before we get to that," Victor spoke up. "How can we be sure your brother is working with Everleigh? The new T.O.D. Club was started six years ago. Everleigh was only thirteen. The girl's diabolical, but I don't buy that she started this blackmail and murder club in middle school."

"That is hard to believe," I admitted. "But no matter how I look at it, everything that happened with Winter's bullying and Jezebel12 only makes sense if Everleigh has more access to the members' information than everyone else. She must—" I bolted upright. "Hold on. Wilder, what did you just say?"

"I said I don't know if we can take them down."

"No," I breathed, mind racing. "You said if she's in bed with Wolf... That's it! The Book Lady. Everleigh told me she became the Book Lady to get secrets from horny idiots that they won't give up clothed.

"That's how she found out about my mother and Alistair's daughters. I bet everything in Victor's bank account that's how she found out about the club too. One of the actual members tried to impress her by bragging to the Book Lady about bringing T.O.D. back and making it stronger than ever. With that knowledge and a little blackmail, access to the members is hers."

"Then she has access to Wolf too," Wilder confirmed. "I can't stand up to his hacking skills. If she has him on her side, her phone, computer, and entire online life are bulletproof."

We stared at him, waiting him out.

Sighing, Wilder tugged my feet onto his lap and rubbed them. He looked down rather than at us as the story poured out.

"Wolfgang O'Rourke is my mother's first son by a different guy. His father split when she cheated on him with my dad."

I winced. I'd bet the first strike of sibling rivalry started there.

"I told you that in my family, nothing is given to us," Wilder continued. "There are revolutionaries, rebels, and intelligence agents going all the way up my mother's family tree. Every generation made deadly enemies that drove us further into hiding and made it more necessary for each member of the family to know how to take care of themselves.

"My mother's way of doing that was to make Wolf and I compete." An edge crept into his voice. "Every Christmas, she bought one present. Just one. It went to whoever passed some new test or challenge. Wolf won every year."

"Oh my gosh," I said, stroking his hand. "Are you saying you never got a Christmas present growing up?"

"I never got any kind of present. Not even on my birthday."

My heart broke in two.

"In my mom's head, she was making us—me—stronger. Preparing us for what it meant to be a Rogue and live a life where you always had to stay ahead of your enemy. One mistake can cost your life. So," Wilder said, "the winner was given a reward... and the loser was punished."

I didn't ask him what the punishment was. The look on his face screamed it loud and clear.

Wilder's light eyes gazed down at me without seeing. "I don't blame Wolf for never letting me win. But I do hate him for how much he enjoyed it when I lost."

"Oh, baby." I kissed him slow and deep, sending waves of comfort. "On a psychopath scale of hamsters to Everleigh, what are we dealing with?"

"Wolf is Everleigh's soul mate."

"Then him coming here is bad for us," I confirmed.

"He'll fuck with me just because he can. He'll ruin everything I touch just for the laugh," Wilder gritted. "It's bad, Luna."

"But you said you have a plan," Rafael spoke up. "Hopefully one that doesn't rely on hacking or computers."

"I have a plan. Not sure if it's a good one yet. Don't know if it'll work. But I do know it'll cause Everleigh Starling the maximum amount of pain non-stop until one of us is taken out permanently. I'll make sure that one is her."

"Lay it on us," Wilder said. "All my shit is in a charred pile—again. And I've got the cops threatening to put me on a terror watch list because of the stuff in my second room. The maximum amount of pain is too little."

"The first step is simple..."

Chapter Three

The bell chimed, welcoming me into a pine-scented lobby. My purple wedges sank into the memory foam mat, drawing my brow up. Between the cucumber and orange slices floating in the water cooler, antiquey chairs in the waiting area, and a plate of cookies with a "Take one!" sign by the receptionist, I could honestly say this was the nicest police station in America.

"Hello." The receptionist waved. "How can we help you, ma'am?"

"My name is Luna Sinclair." I closed the distance and helped myself to that cookie. "I'm here to report an attempted murder. Mine."

***

Tap. Tap. Tap.

I followed the rapid rise and fall of her pen while sipping on my cucumber water. If I thought the lobby was nice, it had nothing on the captain's office. Ornate desk, upholstered seats, and photos of the captain beaming alongside every important person in Regalia.

"This is quite an allegation, Miss Sinclair."

"It's not an allegation. It's what happened."

"Are you certain you're recalling the details correctly?" She leaned back, pressing her tight chestnut bun into her high-backed chair. The wrinkles around her gray eyes deepened. "We have a confession. Connor Langston admitted to setting the fire. Clearly, the body we recovered in the wreckage wasn't you."

For as long as I lived, I'd wonder how Mr. Dumont was able to get his hands on a spare corpse so quickly. Wonder was all I could do since he smoothly dodged all questions about it during the three days we were on the boat.

"But that means you weren't there," Captain Capaldi finished. "Why should I believe your version of events over Connor's?"

Scoffing, I shook my head. "Aren't there courses and seminars available on how to talk to victims? You really need a refresher."

The lines around her mouth hardened. "Excuse me?"

"You should believe my version of events because I'm the one who was electrocuted, woke up to flames eating the room, and was treated to Everleigh Starling crowing about how she drove my sister to suicide and was now going to kill me. Langston wasn't anywhere near the place."

"Why would he lie and confess to such a serious crime?"

"I'm sure a peek in his bank account will answer that question. You could also drop by his house and join the party his family is throwing now that they're moving up the Royal line."

Saying nothing, she scribbled something short in her notebook. I noticed she didn't ask me what the Royal line was.

"So you're claiming Everleigh Starling set the fire to kill you?"

"She tied me to the furniture and said she was going to kill me, so... yeah, that was the goal."

Tap, tap, tap, tap.

I gritted my teeth as her pen did another dance on the mahogany.

"Why would she do such a thing?"

"For the same reason she paid monsters to bully my sister. She thought that by tormenting his daughters, she could drive my biological father out into the open and kill him."

"Your biological father would be...?"

"Alistair Burkhardt."

A vein in her forehead jumped. Alistair laughed when he said she'd remember him. She was a regular uniformed officer the many times she arrested and then was forced to let the rich boy go, but he said she'd remember him fondly.

I noted her curled lip. *Not so much fondly as furiously.*

"Alistair Burkhardt went missing eighteen years ago. He didn't have children."

"He had two, and the guy you're shaking hands with in that photo will confirm." I gestured to a picture of her and Dario Burkhardt. "They set aside an inheritance for me and my sister."

More tapping, then some scribbling, then tapping again. The captain stared at me like she was trying to x-ray my head and figure out my angle. "I'll need time to verify these claims."

"You mean you're going to investigate the very serious crimes committed against me. Everleigh Starling tried to kill me and covered it up. She's extremely dangerous."

"How did you manage to get away?"

"I was rescued," I replied. "I don't know by who. I passed out. But someone pulled me out of the fire.

"I lay low for a few days because I was afraid she'd come after me. Then, I saw on the news that someone named Connor Langston confessed to murdering me, and I had to do something."

"I see." The captain pushed her chair back, standing up. "I applaud your bravery. Thank you for coming in today, Miss Sinclair. You can leave the rest to me."

I shook her hand and left without another word. Walking out, I'd describe my mood with one word: unsatisfied.

I thought it'd be a great moment when I went in there and ripped Everleigh's sweet little heiress mask to shreds, but Captain Capaldi could not have been more obvious in her disbelief.

Everleigh wasn't supposed to be arrested. I was very clear on this ending one way—with her dead and disgraced. The disgrace part started with openly revealing she was a murderer and psychopath. Even so, it was highly disturbing having a police captain blow off serious crimes.

It wasn't that she'd eventually take the bribe to look the other way, like she did when William Burkhardt paid her to drive her son home instead of the police station. It was how obvious it was she wouldn't even get that far. She wasn't going to investigate. She wouldn't talk to Everleigh.

Captain Capaldi didn't believe a word that came out of my mouth.

Plan B.

Hopping in one of my stepdad's cars, I took off.

The night before, Alistair, Mom, Jack, and I had that promised talk. It all came out. My parents' past. Their decision to split to keep us safe. Jack and Martha's true arrangement. How sorry they were for lying to me my whole life.

It was a lot to take in, and I had four days to do it. Truthfully, I may never fully come to terms with everything that happened. It'd always be a wound in my heart knowing that if they'd been honest sooner, Winter might still be here.

I drove across town, lost in my thoughts. What did Winter think when she found all this out the hard way? Did she see a long, terrifying life where our father's enemies used and abused her to get to him? Was that the life facing me now?

Alistair agreed that staying out of my life to protect me didn't work, so there was no reason to keep doing it. He would stay as long as I wanted him to. And I did want him to.

Everleigh had taken enough from me. I wouldn't let her take away the chance to get to know him and answer the questions that have been dragging down my heart my whole life. I wasn't the dirty little secret of a married man. Our father loved us. He wanted us. Everleigh's hate would not get in the way.

I arrived at the restaurant, parked the car, and climbed out. I didn't have a network of T.O.D.ers to do my bidding, but I did have the Instagram-loving Katie and her minute-by-minute updates. She was currently at Toussaint's, "finding her peace at the bottom of their endless grapefruit mimosas."

I found her exactly where social media said she was, sharing a table with Dean, Piper, and the person in her background shot that brought me there.

"Hello, Everleigh."

She froze with her saltshaker hovering over her plate. I rounded the table to see her—

I smirked.

—jaw-dropped, wide-eyed panic.

"Surprise, bitch. I'm not dead. You had your puppet confess to your crime too soon."

"Wha— I— You—"

I said a while ago that seeing Gabriella tackled and arrested was better than sex. I was wrong. Looking at the woman who stood over me laughing while she shrugged off driving my sister to suicide—gaping and bug-eyed like a dead fish... I nearly came on the spot.

"Shocked to see me? You would be after you *tied me up, set fire to the Gallery, and left me to burn alive*," I half shouted through the restaurant, snapping all eyes to me. "All this after you bragged about bribing Wesley,

Levi, Giovanni, Ashton, and Owen to torture my sister and then killed Giovanni and Wesley before they could give you up."

Everleigh tripped over her chair, scrambling up.

"Luna?" Katie said. "What are you talking about?"

"Nothing! She's spouting bullshit, as always." Everleigh rushed me. She stuck her mouth to my ear. "You keep your fucking mouth shut, or I'll—"

"Keep my mouth shut, or you'll what?" I was practically screaming. I had the attention of the entire restaurant. "Try to kill me? Again. I'm sure you're going to do that anyway, which is why I told Captain Capaldi everything. Enjoy those oysters, Starling. The food in prison isn't made by a five-star chef."

"What's going on?" Katie pushed back her seat. "Are you saying Everleigh tried to kill you?"

"You'll hear the echo of her maniacal laugh in the burned-out remains of the Gallery."

"That's a lie! I never touched her," Everleigh cried, whipping around. "First, Saylor. Now me. She won't stop until she's destroyed all the Royals—"

"Uhh, it wasn't me who killed Giovanni and Wesley. If anyone is destroying Royals, it's—"

"Enough! Get out of here, Sinclair. We're done being harassed by you. I'm taking out a restraining order. If you come near me again—"

"Your plan failed," I said under my breath, just for her. "My father knows you tried to set a trap for him, and he won't be springing it. How's it feel to know you failed your deadbeat, child-killing daddy?"

She flushed an angry red, eyes narrowing.

"If you ask me, he deserved everything he got. They say you lose control of your bowels when you die. How fitting that a disgusting shit stain like him died bleeding and crying in a puddle of his own—"

Everleigh swung, punching me in the face and popping me off my feet. I landed flat on my back, bouncing my skull off the floor. I'd be a liar if I denied it. That hit *hurt*. Everleigh wasn't all minions and sitting-in-the-background-doing-her-nails. She dealt a solid punch.

Gasps went up around us.

"What the hell?"

"Did she say Everleigh killed Giovanni?"

My secret smile rimmed with blood. "Help," I screamed. "She attacked me! Call the police."

"What? No! She's the one who—"

"What's going on in here?" One of the waiters ran in, landing on the sight of me moaning on the floor while Everleigh stood over me—fist raised. "Oh, dear. I have to get the manager."

"Get the police! She's dangerous."

"I didn't— It wasn't like that." Everleigh backed away, breathing hard like a trapped animal. "It was her! She's the one who attacked me." She tripped over the waiter. "She leaked the website and—and— She killed them! She's trying to make it seem like I did it, but it was her! Her! I won't stand here and be accused of—"

I couldn't hear the rest. She was already out the door and beating it fast across the parking lot. Talking to Captain Capaldi wasn't satisfying, but chasing Everleigh out of her favorite restaurant under a cloud of whispers and suspicion definitely was.

Stumbling to my feet, I kept up the act, playing like I was calling the cops as I made for the door.

"Not so fast." My phone was plucked out of my hand. "You're going to tell me what the hell's going on." Katie spun me around. "Now."

Straightening, I wiped the blood off my chin—dropping the act. "How much time you got?"

"Loads."

"Not here," I said, walking off. "Let's go back to your place. I've been dying for your chef's popcorn shrimp."

Katie didn't argue with me. She went back to tell Dean she was leaving, then followed me out to the car. I was treated to her judgy, suspicious stare the whole ride to her place. I was too busy clocking Ronin's car trailing behind me to give it thought.

When did he start following me? Was he following me all morning?

Ronin slowed and pulled off the road when I approached Katie's gate. It seemed he would stay and wait until I left.

Katie let loose the minute I stepped inside the pool house.

"What the fuck, Luna! I get it, okay. Everleigh, Piper, Gabriella, and Saylor were complete bitches to Winter, and it's horrible that they kept throwing her suicide in your face, but how much more revenge do you need?

"Piper can't walk across campus without someone shouting 'cousin fucker' at her. Gabriella's on parole. Today's the first day Everleigh's gone out since the Book Lady site went wide, and no one's seen or heard from Saylor." She came at me so fast I backed up and tripped onto her chaise. "Now you're accusing Everleigh of being a killer? These are my best friends you're fucking with. I'm not—"

"—their best friend," I sliced in. "You're *not* their best friend, Katie. However you see them, it's not how they see you. I'm sure it was different when you guys were little, but the five of you grew up and changed. Saylor became a manipulative carrion beast who fed on the weak for fun. The other girls aren't as lucky as you to be free of the Burkhardts' power. They learned to play her game to survive."

I shot up, getting in her face. "I've read the texts. I know how they talk about you when you're not around. I know what they really think of you. It's envy, resentment, superiority, and a little nostalgia, but there's *no* loyalty. So before you hear what I have to say, you need to know that you've only seen the fakes. Now I'm going to tell you what's real."

Katie leaned back, a storm brewing on her face. I couldn't tell who the darkening eyes or flared nostrils were for, but I knew what I said cut deep. Katie always stood a little outside of their group. The Royal Wenches roamed campus as a foursome, not a fivesome.

"Okay." She flung herself down beside me. "I'm listening."

"This will go a lot quicker if you tell me what you know about the Rogues. The *real* Rogues."

Her face shuttered closed. "You first."

I hesitated, then gave in—telling her everything except that Alistair Burkhardt was the leader of the Rogues. My father didn't let the world think he was missing and dead because he wanted the truth broadcast.

"She was behind it all, Katie. She dared Levi and the others to torture Winter. She killed Giovanni when he tried to tell me the truth. All this because she blames my father for her father's death."

Katie didn't speak throughout my whole explanation. She didn't look at me either. She turned away, staring at the window around the time I told her about the text chain where her friends laughed about her mom getting cancer—saying it was karma for raising a slutty, sanctimonious bitch.

I couldn't be sure she heard the rest after that, but I kept going—telling her the truth for the first time since we met. After I finished, we sat there—crumbling under the air, heavy with all our regrets.

"Katie?" I squeezed her shoulder. "Are you okay?"

"My mom." Her voice was barely higher than a croak. "Did they really say that about her?"

Saying nothing, I pulled up the screenshots and handed them over. I didn't make everything available when I sold Saylor's texts. The worst I held back, including things no one had a right to know, even in the name of revenge on Saylor. Katie's mom kept her cancer diagnosis private. I respected that. I also wouldn't stand for people to throw what Katie's friends truly thought of her in her face.

Katie was quiet as she read. Her expression gave nothing away... almost. My heart constricted, seeing the tiniest tremble on her lips.

"We grew up together."

"I know," I whispered.

"They were the only ones I knew weren't using me for money, attention, or a ride up the ladder. The only ones who knew what it was like."

I thought of a young Victor who could only call his brother a friend because the guys he thought were friends almost drowned him in a lake. It was true what they said: It's lonely at the top.

Straightening, Katie cleared her throat and handed the phone back. The tremble fled when she turned on me, replaced with a curl I knew well.

"What do you need?"

"What?"

"You heard me," she snapped. Katie stalked over to her desk, yanked open the drawers, and started throwing things out. "You're going to take the bitch down, yes? Saylor and the others hid a lot from me, but I know plenty of their secrets. Those texts are just the things Saylor wrote about. I know so much more.

"And Everleigh. If she's truly done all those awful things…" She stopped, doubling over and clutching her stomach. She was visibly sickened. "Let's take her down."

I smiled. It was still rimmed by dried blood, but it wasn't hidden. "I'm very happy to hear you say that, Katie, because you're the biggest part of it. Everleigh's not going to let me close after today. But she thinks you're her friend."

"Where the hell is—? Here!" Katie flung her last marker, then picked up a small, leather-bound book. "When we were in elementary school, we started writing in this book. Each of us would take turns writing about anything and everything. It was pretty much how we texted before we got phones.

"Everleigh talks a lot about her dad. Her *stepdad*, Grant. She hated the guy." Katie tossed me the journal. I ripped it open without hesitation. "Her mom slept with Everton and got pregnant as revenge against him for cheating. The spiteful woman even named her Everleigh, so Grant would hear the 'fuck you' every time he said it. And trust me, he got that message loud and clear.

"I honestly don't know why they stayed together. They made each other's lives miserable after that, and Everleigh got the brunt of it. Her mom ignored her, and Grant treated her like shit as if that was the next best thing to getting back at his brother.

"Lately, Everleigh's gotten closed off. She doesn't talk much about home or anything real actually," Katie admitted. "I used to try to get her to open up, but she always said she didn't want to talk about the messed-up shit in her life when the five of us were together. She just wanted to have fun.

"I respected it and figured she'd open up when she was ready. Now I know why she shut us out." Katie reclaimed her seat next to me. Taking the journal, she turned to a specific page, then passed it back. "Everleigh loved Everton and he loved her.

"Sometimes, she wouldn't come home for days because they went on a trip together, or she was staying at his place. Her parents didn't even notice." A trace of sympathy crossed her face till she stamped anger down on it. "Anyway, I'm telling you this because Everton kept this up even after he ditched his trial and went on the run.

"He rented a property nearby under an alias and sent for her whenever he could." She tapped the page. "Everleigh made us promise not to tell."

It was true. Written in the bubbly, honest speech of a nine-year-old, Everleigh gushed about her daddy's secret cabin in the woods. I read a short, sweet little paragraph on how much fun she had roasting marshmallows, curling up in sleeping bags under the stars, and fishing for pike.

"Do you see?"

"See what?" I asked.

"Pike, my sweet little dummy." Katie would always be Katie. "It's a freshwater fish and we're surrounded by ocean. There's only one freshwater river that cuts through the forest. Everleigh doesn't live on campus, but she still blows off going home for days or weeks at a time.

"I told you she stopped being real with us a long time ago, so I don't know where she goes, but it did cross my mind that the cabin could still be there. Everton left everything to her when he died, so..."

"So if she inherited this cabin, she'd never sell or give away a place that was special to both of them. A home where she was actually safe and loved," I finished. "I bet it's also the place where she plans everything. That's where the dirt is. Not in HapApp or on the T.O.D. web server, but in that cabin. Katie, you're helping already."

"I have to," she replied. "I don't have to tell you that Captain Capaldi isn't going to arrest her, do I?"

I shook my head.

"It's not that she's corrupt, though she is. It's that she knows a lost cause when she sees it. Connor already confessed to burning down the Gallery, and you already confessed to sabotaging and attacking Royals to get revenge for your sister. If Capaldi tries to put Everleigh in a courtroom, not a single charge will stick."

"I know this. I assume Captain Capaldi had the same thought when she refused to take Winter's statement and took the dean's word over hers when she reported her rape."

Katie's eyes widened.

"I just announced to an entire restaurant that I reported Everleigh to the captain. When it all comes out and no one can deny the truth anymore, the first question they'll ask is why the cops did nothing. Our friendly neighborhood corrupt captain is going down with her."

She squeezed her eyes shut. "About Ashton Scott... Please tell me Everleigh didn't use the club and paid him to do that to her."

"I can't be sure what she told him to do, but Everleigh blackmailed my boyfriend's father to shoot me and leave me to burn. I don't think there's any line she won't cross."

Katie went to her desk again. She was trying to hide it, but I knew she mourned the friend she thought she knew. "We should try to find that cabin. Satellite view on the GPS should narrow it down."

I joined her. An hour passed while we used the flimsy details in the journal to narrow down the list of cabins close to the river. Between that, I flipped through, reading the passages in Everleigh's unique handwriting. I didn't have to ask anymore how she became such a cold, heartless person.

The abuse was never physical, but the wounds from her parents' neglect ran as deep. Ignored birthdays. Vacations where she was left behind with a nanny. Constant taunts and insults from her stepfather. Cold indifference from her mother. The only time the nine-year-old Everleigh wrote with any joy was when she talked about her time with Everton.

It was clear he was the only parent who loved her. I understood that losing him shattered her. I even understood her wanting revenge against the man who killed him. But what I'd never understand or forgive is that she hurt Winter—an innocent person—to get that revenge. Some lines should never be crossed.

No matter how much I hated Saylor, I removed all the secrets about other people that she shared in the texts. I wasn't about to step on innocents to bring her down. The Royals may have been raised to believe everyone was fair game, but that was just another lesson they'd pay for when I brought the Royal line crumbling to its knees.

"Twelve cabins along the river, but only five that aren't beneath a Starling," Katie announced. "Start with these."

"How will I know if I got the right place? Everleigh's smart. She'll catch a tail right away."

"You're right." Katie chewed her lip. "You can't follow her there, and you can't be sure of her car because Grant has a dozen of them. She drives whichever one fits her mood. She's rarely home, so I guess you could wait until late at night, check each one, and you'll know you've got it when you peek through the window and see her eating ice cream in her pajamas on the couch."

"Yeah. Seems like that's the only way."

My phone buzzed, drawing my attention.

Alistair: Got plans for dinner tonight? I want you to see where I'm staying. You'll know where to go if anything happens.

Me: Don't think I can tonight. I've got a list of out-of-the-way cabins that I have to creep around at night, looking for a murderer.

Alistair: If you had sent that to any other father...

I laughed. It was weird how easily we fell into our own kind of rhythm. At first, it was hard for me to picture my serious, straitlaced, type *A* mother falling for the reckless troublemaker that was a young Alistair. I told him as much, and he scoffed and asked me what my Rogue boyfriends were like.

"No one wants to date a copy of themselves," he had told me. "Average person has too much self-loathing for that."

Don't know that I'd put it that way, but it did make me think of what it'd be like to date four versions of the old, boring, boarding-school me.

I'd take my paranoid, explosive, bitey, growly assholes any day of the week.

Alistair: It's important, Luna. We promised your mother last night that you'd be safe and wouldn't do anything reckless. Stowing away in that beach house with single door locks, regular glass windows, and no alarm is the definition of reckless.

I wasn't going to ask when he clocked Adonis's security measures.

Alistair: You've got to get the pass from security for them to let you through the door. Let's do that tonight so that after you run away in terror of the murderer in the woods, you can beat it straight here and be safe.

I audibly sighed. It'd still be nighttime after dinner. I might as well handle things with Alistair, then I'll take up my disturbing task of creeping around the woods, looking for a killer.

Me: Cool. What's the address?

Alistair: Ronin will drop you off. You done with the Langford girl?

"I've got to get going." I gave up the journal and traded for the list. "I'll check these out tonight. Here's hoping you're right about Everton refusing the other cabins."

"I am right. I didn't know him like that, but Everleigh wouldn't shut up about him back then. He once threw out a pair of brand-new, five-thousand-dollar shoes because he got a scuff on them. He wouldn't have locked himself away in any less than a mini-mansion."

"Okay. Thanks for this, Katie."

"Don't underestimate me." She met my surprise with a hard look. "I can do more than read old journals and mess around with GPS. Everleigh got Winter raped and tried to murder you. Because of what she did to Giovanni, Mom is so freaked she doesn't want me farther than her shadow. She'll pay for what she's done."

"I trust you, Katie. Don't know why," I muttered, "but I do. The main thing I need you to do is stick close to her, let her think you're her friend, and give me inside details like this." I gestured at the journal. "Everleigh's too careful. I only found her Book Lady site because she gave it to me. Since I can't rely on Wilder's skills to find out what she's up to, you're perfect."

"Always was, always will be. Now go." I suddenly found myself being pushed toward the door. "I just found out I've wasted my life with a bunch of fake bitches. I need my man to come over and fuck the stress out of me."

"Your man? Are you finally admitting Dean is your boyfriend?"

"Nope." She deposited me on the porch and flicked the door closed. Just like that, I was dismissed.

Shaking my head, I left and met up with Ronin, who idled ten feet from the front gate. I tapped on the window, a shiver going up my spine when it slowly dropped down and revealed him.

The dragon tattoo needled into his skull was intimidating enough. Ronin had to build on his aura of mystery with dark, impenetrable shades; unsmiling, thin lips; and a crooked nose that told of a break—or three.

"Alistair said you're taking me to his hotel or something. What should I do with my stepdad's car?"

"Drive it back to your place." A deep, bass tone flowed from his lips. "We'll leave from there."

"Sounds good."

I did as he asked—driving back to Bowden Manor, dropping off the car, then walking out to slide in the back seat. Ronin took off, whisking me away to my father.

Ronin didn't take the street that would carry us out of the mega-rich neighborhood my stepfather and mother were lucky to call home. He turned right, carrying us up a hill that brought us deeper into Royal territory.

Wonder if Alistair has something in common with his old friend. Looks like he refuses to hide away in anything less than a mansion. Plenty of those whisked by, each grander than the last. *Maybe he's holing up in a vacant home like you hear people do.*

I frowned, immediately throwing away that thought. Alistair said I had to go through the security process so they'd wave me in without a problem. Wouldn't make sense to post security outside a house that's supposed to be empty—unless you want to give yourself away.

"Where are we going?"

"There." He motioned in the direction of something too fast for me to catch it. "Five minutes."

I got the sense Ronin wasn't much for chitchat. Sitting back, I got out my phone and texted Lucien.

Me: Busy tonight? What do you think about sneaking through the woods after midnight?

His reply was immediate.

Lucien: I think I love you, and I'm so glad you're back. It's about time we finished our date.

I loved that this is what passed for a date between me and my Rogues. What did people with normal boyfriends even do? From watching Katie, it was just a lot of hooking up in random places and eating at Toussaint's. I'm betting the two of them never shared empanadas and conversation while exploding cars and ratting out cheaters.

Me: I want more than anything to finish our date, but I was thinking of something a lot less sexy for tonight. Katie told me Everleigh used to visit Everton in a cabin in the woods somewhere. We've got a list of five possible places. We need to see what she's got in there, because I'd bet everything in Saylor's bank account on that being the one place Everleigh lets her guard down.

Again, his reply came back in an instant.

Lucien: Send me the list.

I fished it out, flicking back and forth to type the first one in.

"Here."

Glancing up, I landed on a familiar insignia and froze. "No."

"Give your name to the guard." Ronin unlocked the doors. "He's expecting you."

"No, he's not."

"Get out."

"The fuck I will!" I slammed the lock down. "What kind of game are you playing? Did they pay you off? Take me to Alistair now."

Ronin's impassive face didn't crack. "That's what I've done. He's inside waiting for you. He said the surprise would be... funny."

My lips peeled back from my teeth. Why did that sound like exactly what my jerk of a bio dad would say? I was starting to understand him too well.

Glaring through the window, I gazed up at the gold insignia woven through the gates—Burkhardts.

Alistair Burkhardt has returned home.

"I'm calling him," I warned. "If you're messing me around, now's the time to drive off."

Ronin didn't move. That was a bad sign.

Dread filling my bones, I called Alistair—tensing as the call rang out.

A buzz sounded in my ear.

Alistair: Come inside already. I'm starved and Laura made truffle risotto with lemon butter scallops to celebrate your homecoming. She can't wait to meet my daughter.

Me: No.

He couldn't be an asshole in person, so he shot me half a dozen laugh emojis.

Alistair: There's no safer place for a Burkhardt than within these gates. Come inside. It's past time you met the other half of your family.

Me: No.

Alistair: If you try to run, Ronin will chase you down and haul you inside.

I shot narrowed eyes at that dragon tattoo.

Alistair: Might as well take the easy way.

Me: Why do you do these things to me? As far as I know, I've done nothing to piss you off.

Naturally, that reply received more laugh emojis. Why was it parents could legally give up their children for adoption, but I couldn't unload this guy on another eighteen-year-old?

Me: I thought you hated these people. They rejected the woman you loved, ignored your children, let everyone think you were dead, and unleashed Saylor Burkhardt on the world! Was everything you told me a lie?

Alistair: Discuss over scallops?

It was so very obvious he wasn't taking my anger seriously, which meant if I wanted to yell at him...

I threw another glare at the gate.

...I had to go inside.

"Be honest. Alistair has to make up for a lot every year on Employee Appreciation Day."

No reaction from my silent companion. I wasn't even sure he was listening to me.

"You're a part of a criminal organization. Any chance I could bribe you into letting me walk away?"

"Try it."

Okay, time to go.

Climbing out, I forced myself to walk the path under Ronin's watchful eye. The same guard who greeted me on my first and only visit to the Burkhardt mansion waited for me in the booth.

"Luna Sinclair. Remember me? You confiscated all my concealed weapons."

He cocked a brow. "Will I have to do so again?"

I shrugged, throwing my hands up. "Would you believe me if I said no?"

The answer was no. I endured two pat-downs and him thoroughly checking everything in my bag. Made me glad I left the list of cabins in the car.

He handed my purse back. "Inside," he said, motioning at the booth. "I'll need to fingerprint you, copy your license, and run through a few basic questions."

"Come on. This isn't the White House. It can't be that serious."

"I also need a photograph to keep on file."

All right, it was that serious. I fought the urge to turn tail and walk away. I believed Alistair when he said Ronin wouldn't let me get far.

The guard, Frank, put me through the whole routine. I swallowed my tongue through the fingerprinting but ended up bitching through the rest of the process. None of this was necessary. After I chewed out my father, I was never setting foot in this place again.

The guy weathered my protests until the final snapshot. Yes, he made me turn side to side like I was being arrested. The Burkhardts didn't play.

Finally, he opened the gates to let me through. "Your friend in the car is not allowed in. You'll have to walk."

"Walk? But it's like half a mile to the mansion."

He slid the booth door shut in my face. Frank was done with me.

Steaming, I stormed through the widening gates and stopped. Alistair waved from a tiny little silver Toyota Sports 800. You learned how to pick out cars when your stepfather supplied their tires.

"Explain yourself, Burkhardt." I dropped into the passenger seat. "You spun a whole tale about being estranged from your family. Now you're bunking down in your old room."

Alistair started the car, taking off. "I am estranged from my family. If you think you're about to walk into a happy family reunion, let me deflate that fantasy now. I'm here for one reason and one reason only. There is no place in the whole of Regalia that's better protected than this piece of property.

"I told you the largest concentration of Rogues lives within these city limits. As soon as you hoisted the flag and my boat sailed into the marina, they knew I was here. More than a few of them will take their shot at the king while I'm in town."

My eyes bugged. Who talks about assassination attempts this casually?

"At least this way I won't have to sleep with one eye open."

"Won't you? Can you trust"—I looked to the grand palace in the distance—"them?"

"My family doesn't want me dead. They just want me to keep pretending I am." He beamed at me. "I promised not to go to the media with my harrowing tale of love getting me kicked out of the family, and into the arms of a gang, as long as everyone lets bygones be bygones."

"To sum it up, you blackmailed your family."

He mouth-shrugged. "Yeah, that about sums it up."

"Advice, Pops... sleep with one eye open."

Alistair cracked up. Joking around with him distracted me... for two minutes.

He parked before the grand entrance, pulling up beside two attendants waiting to bow, open our doors, help me out, and take his keys. My getaway drove off, leaving me and Alistair on the front steps.

The butler led us inside. Each step was a rope around my heart—binding tighter, dragging me deeper.

"Did you invite me to dinner with all of them? What am I supposed to say?"

"No, Luna. I wouldn't do that to you."

We passed into the foyer. The butler took our shoes and replaced them with warm, elegant house slippers. He bowed again, for no reason that I could see, then led us past the staircase and into the bowels of the mansion.

"Dinner is for the two of us. Just us," Alistair continued. "Although my father would like to meet you."

"We've met." I thought of the split-second encounter when he patted my head on the way out the door. "Did he know who I was then?"

"He's always known who you were, Luna."

I quieted, looking down. I was that close to my grandfather and didn't know. But he knew me. William and Dario knew where to find me my whole life, and they didn't bother to sneeze in my direction. More than that, they knew about Winter, but they didn't so much as send an anonymous bouquet after her death. What was I supposed to make of that?

"He didn't rant, rave, or chase me out when he saw me," I admitted. "I guess that's something."

"William means you no harm." He placed a warm hand on my head. "By now, you know the power he has. If he wanted you gone, he would've sold Bowden Manor out from under your stepfather and burned him from the Royal line. Burkhardts don't go after Burkhardts. It's the one good thing about us."

I nodded, taking that in. To say I had mixed emotions would be an understatement. They didn't attack me or my mother, and they kept my inheritance intact. Was pretending like I didn't exist what passed for familial kindness around here?

"In here."

Alistair veered off, heading for a door on the right. I followed him into a space I would not have expected of the Burkhardts. Nothing like the over-the-top displays of wealth in every corner of the mansion that I'd laid eyes on. This room was, dare I say it, cozy. More than that, it was simple.

Yes, that was the word that came to mind as I took in bookcases, comfy white couches, and a small table set for two placed before the window-paned doors. Alistair turned a cozy little reading nook into our dining room. As promised, risotto and scallops waited for us.

We sat down, making small talk and trading stories about our childhoods while eating the most delicious meal I had ever put in my mouth. Of course, I didn't expect the Burkhardts to hire anyone less than the best chefs in the world, but it still had to be mentioned; the food was damn good.

"Wow. If you'd told me you left Mom so you wouldn't have to live without Laura's cooking, I'd have understood."

His laugh rang out through the terrace and into the garden. "I offered Laura a blank check to get her to come with me. The woman was frustratingly loyal."

"Where's the bathroom?"

"Turn left down the hallway and it's three doors down on the right. Want me to show you?"

"No, I've got it."

Pushing back, I walked out with a weirdly warm feeling. I was back in Regalia with my guys. Mom was on her feet, doing better than she had in months. Alistair was here—protecting and spending time with me. I'd forgotten this feeling, but it was coming back to me. I think I used to call it happy.

Turning the corner, I skimmed my fingers over the embossed wallpaper, thinking of what I'd say to William Burkhardt. I didn't want to hold on to a twenty-year-old grudge. In the end, my parents split up because of Everton Starling, not because of him. Besides, Alistair's childhood stories made it sound like it wasn't all bad times. Movie nights, fishing, camping, and driving lessons. He might not like the comparison, but William sounded like his counterpart, John Wilson. He tried to be a good father. William just didn't realize that the trade-off for good parenting isn't the right to run your children's lives forever and make all their decisions for them.

I lit on the third door, already picturing what passed for a bathroom in Burkhardt paradise.

I bet there're gold toilet seats, pearl bidets, and a bathroom attendant who wipes my butt for me.

A door flew open, jarring me out of the fantasy. Saylor stepped out, carrying a food tray. Our eyes met and we froze.

I scanned her up and down, biting my lip hard. There was no other way to describe her. Saylor looked *terrible.*

Her normally sweet-smelling halo of blonde loveliness hung in greasy hanks around her face. Puffy, red-rimmed eyes blew up at the sight of me, cracking the dried crust around her lids. Gone were the designer clothes. In their place were stained sweatpants and a blue tank top that had a streak of something orange across her stomach. I think it was Cheeto dust.

Saylor goggled at me, clearly not informed that I was dropping in for a visit. She flicked down to her tray. I followed her gaze, both of us landing on the steak knife. Her eyes narrowed to slits.

Oh, shit.

"Saylor," I said slowly. "No. Whatever you're thinking—"

Crash!

She snatched up the knife. Glass and porcelain shattered at our feet. "Argh!"

"Nooo!" Twisting around, I hauled ass—screaming my head off.

"You evil bitch! You ruined my life!" I felt Saylor on my tail like the breath of Hades scorching my neck hairs. "Did you come here to rub it in? Big mistake!"

"Alistair! Alistair!" Lucien was teaching me self-defense. Unfortunately, we hadn't gotten to the lessons on how to evade a knife-wielding lunatic. "Dad!"

Alistair shot through the door. Snatching me off my feet, he threw me behind him and swung up, blocking Saylor's wild jab.

I tripped over my feet, clutching my chest and gasping. *Holy fuck, she swung. She really tried to stab me.*

"Let go of me! Let go!"

Alistair wrestled the knife from her grip, then restrained her when she dove for it again.

"You don't know who that is," she shrieked, "or what she's done. Let me go!"

"I know who she is. She's my daughter and your cousin."

I don't think anything could've stopped her from trying to kill me... except those words.

Saylor went limp, her eyes huge. "Excuse me?"

"Luna is your cousin." Alistair set her on her feet, tossed the knife in the room, and shut the door. "I thank you for bringing this up so quickly. The war between you two stops now. I'm sure you'll find you're on the same side."

Saylor looked from me to him, back to me, and then to him. "No."

"I had the same reaction," I snapped, stepping out from behind him. "I don't like it any more than you do, but—"

Saylor pounced—seizing the chance I stupidly gave her. We went down in a screeching flail of punches, kicks, and scratches.

***

"Let's try this again."

Saylor and I glared at each other from opposite sides of the room. She nursed a fat lip while I held an ice pack to the lump on the back of my head.

Alistair sat beside me on the couch. He didn't have to be my human shield. Dario Burkhardt claimed the spot next to Saylor, ready to hold her back.

I was less than dazzled by being in the room with a sitting senator. Don't get me wrong, I had nothing against the guy. I was simply distracted by the fact his devil spawn was still looking around for a weapon.

"Fresh start," Dario said, flashing me a smile. It was wild how much he looked like my father. Same auburn hair. Same whiff of mischief in his grin. "That's exactly what all of us"—he placed a hand on Saylor's arm—"my family and I are hoping for. A fresh start with my brother and with you, Luna. We're glad you're here."

"No, we're not," Saylor barked. "That bitch isn't my cousin. I don't care what either of you say."

"Now, now." Dario's tone was mild, even fond, as he addressed his daughter. Seemed I'd found the only person on the planet who liked this monster. "No need for that kind of language. I'm aware this is an adjustment for both of you. I've come to understand your relationship has been antagonistic up to this point."

"Understatement of the century," I said. "That hellbeast started this war. She's just mad I won."

"You—!"

"It stops now," Dario sliced in, giving us stern frowns apiece. "Today is cause for celebration. My brother has returned home. I have a chance to get to know my niece. No more fighting. No more *wars*. We're family."

Cause for celebration? Didn't his precious brother blackmail him to get through the door? And seeing as he ignored me for eighteen years, that didn't sound like someone hurting to know his niece.

Had to hand it to the senator. You didn't get where he was without knowing how to spin bullshit.

"She is *not* my family," Saylor said. "She ruined my life. My friends won't talk to me. I had to shut down all my accounts and block almost every number in my phone. The whole town hates me. Throw her out of here, Daddy. She can take the random, long-lost uncle with her."

"Fresh start, sweetheart. Everything you and Luna have done to each other is in the past. You didn't know you were family then. Now you do. We live by one rule and one rule alone." The sweetness dripped out of his tone. "Burkhardts don't go after Burkhardts."

"Tell her that, not me."

Dario turned to me.

I sighed. "Here it comes."

"Luna," he began, "about that website—"

"And there it is," I groaned. "Want to know why your precious hellbeast—"

"Stop calling me that, Dreg!"

"—had to be punished? She tried to strip me in front of a party full of people. She got me jumped, punched me in the face, threatened to kick my stepdad out of the Royal line, and she's thrown my sister's suicide in my face over and over since the first day we met.

"I've met rabid squirrels with a kinder personality. Obviously, Saylor's life of privilege didn't teach her about consequences. I took it upon myself to give her the lesson. Why would I take the site down? This greasy, Cheeto-covered look is the best I've seen on her."

She launched off the couch. "You're dead, Sinclair!"

I jumped off. "I'm taking you with me!"

It took another twenty minutes of grunts, shouts, and wrestling to get us back into our respective corners. I was proud of myself for finally bloodying that fat lip. Although Saylor was clutching a healthy bunch of my hair in her grip, so I didn't get out unscathed.

"Enough," Alistair barked. "The website comes down tonight."

"I'm not—!"

"Doesn't matter if you do or don't." He tsked. "You know who I am. Think I can't shut down a little website? My contact is already in the process of removing every trace of it from cyberspace. She's also following the credit card trail to everyone who downloaded a copy. They'll be hit with a nasty computer virus that'll crater their hard drive."

My jaw dropped.

Alistair nodded at his brother. "I hope that will suffice, Dario."

"Thank you. We appreciate it."

"I can't believe you," I hissed. "You're supposed to be on my side."

"I am on your side, Luna. You didn't know she was your cousin before all this happened, but now you do. I've broken every rule that exists, love, except one. Burkhardts don't go after Burkhardts." His eyes hardened, turning on her. "Agreed, Saylor? The website is down. Anyone who has a copy won't by morning. You will not retaliate against Luna. You most certainly won't try attacking her again. As your father said, the war ends now."

She sniffed, folding her arms and looking away. But I noticed she didn't disagree.

"Good," he said. "Now that's settled, let's get you back to your mother."

"Back to Mom's? But you said your father wanted to meet me."

"Check the time, kid. It's after midnight. That old man's been asleep for hours."

He was right. Between all that fighting, arguing, and running for my life, I didn't notice how much time had passed. I was supposed to meet my grandfather, then tromp through the woods looking for Everleigh. Instead, I was tromping to the nearest bed and passing out.

"Unless you'd like to stay here," Alistair offered. "I can have any empty room done up for you. Take your pick."

"Like hell," Saylor said before I could open my mouth. "Get out of my house, Sinclair. No one wants you here. No one ever will. You'll never be a Burkhardt."

"Promise?" Rolling my eyes, I grabbed my stuff and made for the door. "Oh, one more thing."

I twisted around, phone up, and snapped her picture. "Your new look is gonna be fire on the next website I put up. The Royals will love guessing what all those mystery stains on your sweatpants are."

Saylor shrieked, trying to cover herself much too late. "Daddy!"

"Luna!"

"Alistair!"

"Buh-bye," I sang, beating it out of the room. Saylor was hot on my heels.

Again Alistair had to chase her down to stop her from killing me. Again we both received a lecture on Burkhardts never making other Burkhardts their enemy. Again, my phone was taken from me and the picture deleted.

It was past two in the morning when Alistair dropped me off at Mom and Jack's house. I waved him off, then went immediately for the garage. I loved sleeping in my old room after all that time I wasn't welcome in it. My room would be even better if my guys were curled up on my bed, waiting for me.

We also spent too much time apart. That night, I was sleeping with them.

The ride to the beach house gave me thirty minutes of true alone time to think. I did have a plan to take down Everleigh, and it was a good one. The only problem was I had no idea what she was planning.

Purple flags, fires, and blackmailing Leon Dumont won't work for her, so what would Everleigh do now? I had no delusions that she would give up on killing my father. The question was, what options did she have left?

I underestimated her once and it nearly got me and my boyfriends killed. This time, I had to be five, ten, twenty steps ahead of her, or I wouldn't make it out alive.

My thoughts scattered throughout the whole ride, fighting to come together and form something sensible through the late-night, early-morning fog clouding my mind.

I turned onto the dirt path, driving up to the cute little bungalow and parking next to Lucien's car. Seeing it reminded me that I never finished sending that text. It also reminded me the list was in Ronin's car.

Groaning, I trudged up the sandy path. How did my day start with chasing Everleigh out of Toussaint's with her tail between her legs and end with Saylor beating the shit out of me? I wouldn't lie, it rocked my confidence a bit. This fight with Everleigh was one to the death. It required all my attention. Fighting Saylor at the same time was a distraction I couldn't afford.

Burkhardts don't make enemies of Burkhardts.

Saylor didn't give the impression that she'd trade that promise for her first one—that she'd make me regret the day I was born.

I snuck the spare key out from under a porch chair and let myself in. A sweet smell of sand and cedar washed over me. I didn't notice how good Adonis's place smelled the first time I was there. I was too busy internally freaking out at the two of us alone in his place while I nursed a massive crush on my professor.

But his place did smell nice. And it was warm. And cozy. And the kind of place I pictured living in when my life returned to a semblance of normal. On my craziest days, I pictured living in exactly this place... with him.

My guys were scattered all over the place. The bungalow had four rooms, which left one for Adonis. One for Victor. One for Wilder, who would only sleep behind locked doors. One for Lucien, who didn't mind sleeping on a foldout couch in Adonis's office. The couch for Rafael. And Cato slept outside.

My muzzled love started a fire in the bathroom two hours after moving in. Adonis promptly kicked him out, and Cato made it as far as the hammock on the back porch.

Who will I curl up with tonight?

I crept through the hall, tiptoeing to the kitchen. The whole thing with Saylor took so long there was no trace of my delicious dinner left in my stomach. Rafael took over cooking since moving in, so the fridge should be filled with restaurant-quality leftovers.

I popped open the door, already salivating at all the containers. "Score."

"Seriously."

I jerked, whirling around.

"If they turn his suspension into an expulsion, he'll have a job as my personal chef, no problem."

Adonis leaned against the kitchen counter, eating out of a container. Boxers concealed the most tempting parts of him and nothing else. Fridge light chased back the shadows on his bare chest, skating over him like my hands did that day in his office. Was it really such a short time ago since we had sex? So much had happened since then. It felt like another lifetime.

"Hey," I whispered, mindful of my sleeping boyfriend on the couch. "What are you doing in the dark?"

"Didn't want to wake anyone. Try the smoked salmon pasta," he said. "The first bite made me cry."

Chuckling, I took it out and stuck it in the microwave. I couldn't tell what Adonis was thinking behind his calm and steady eating. I wished I could peek into his mind.

I felt his presence all around me like a living thing—teasing me, seducing me, comforting me. I missed him while I was floating around in my temporary prison.

I couldn't admit it and tell my father I wanted updates on my English professor, but the whole time I starved for news of him. Was he okay? Did whoever stalked me and discovered our secret blab it to the rest of the school? Did Wesley carry it to the grave? Did I mess up his whole life? Was he mourning for me?

Dozens of questions haunted me while I was gone. Finally, we were together, and I could voice none of them. What could I say when I didn't know where we stood?

"Sorry about this," I muttered in the direction of the stove. "The Gallery was burned down because of me, and now you're in an awkward position.

Professionally and otherwise. I didn't mean for you to meet my boyfriends this way."

"They're an interesting bunch for sure." His tone gave nothing away. "They love you. When they thought you were gone... never seen people so utterly destroyed."

I almost asked if he was destroyed too. Almost.

"Victor knows about us." I spoke so softly I competed with the hum from the microwave. "I don't know if he told you, but he knows everything."

"He passed that on when he gave me this."

I found myself spun around and trapped between his arms. Adonis bent over me, granting me a proper look at him. What I thought was a shadow was a black eye.

"One shot for fucking around with his fiancée and lying about it, then he clapped me on the back and said we were all good." He chuckled. "Don't know when my little brother got so mature, but he put me to shame. I should've manned up and told him how I felt about you from the beginning."

My heart thumped audibly in my chest. I was certain Adonis could hear it.

"I missed you, Luna." His fingers skated over my mouth. "When I lost Catalina, I was crushed. When I lost you, it broke me."

"Adon—"

He bent and captured my lips. Moving fiercely against mine, his kiss was rough. Insistent. Hungry.

I pushed back twice as hard, driving him back against the island. He twisted and laid me flat, fervent kisses and hushed moans heating the room as he climbed on top of me. Apparently, all it took was me dying to make the sexy, commanding, self-assured professor that took me in his office return.

"Where were you, Luna?" Adonis kissed my lips, nose, chin, eyelids, everywhere. "Why were they saying you died in that fire? Why didn't you let me know you were okay?"

"I'm sorry. The person who saved me thought I'd be safer if everyone thought I was dead, but I couldn't do that to you guys." My fingers curled on the nape of his neck. "There's so much I have to tell you. There's so much you don't know."

I tried to wriggle away. Adonis scooped me under the tailbone, crushing my middle against him. He ground his hardness between my legs, chasing away any delusion about getting away.

"Please," I moaned—either to get him to listen to me or for him not to stop. Maybe both. "I dragged us all into a war I didn't understand. Because of me, someone found out our secret."

Adonis stopped mid-kiss. "What are you talking about?"

I closed my eyes, thankful Adonis couldn't make out my shame in the dark. "The T.O.D. Club. Wesley Hill dared one of the members to dig up dirt and get me to back off. It had to be a private dare because I would've seen it on the page otherwise. Somehow, they got their hands on the paper I wrote describing all the things I wanted you to do to me.

"Wesley's gone, but whoever stole the paper for him is still out there. Plus, I have no idea if Wesley told other people before he died." I cracked an eyelid. "Please, don't hate me. You said over and over that we couldn't do this. I didn't listen, and now someone knows—"

"—that you liked to be spanked. Good thing because I very much like spanking you."

My vision adjusted, granting me a clearer look at his grin.

"That paper is nothing, Luna. It doesn't prove a relationship. I didn't mark or grade it, so there's no proof I read it either. There's nothing that mystery blackmailer can do to hurt us." He cupped my cheek. "And I wouldn't care if they tried. I thought I lost you. Now that I have you back, I'm not wasting a second worrying about what-ifs. We can tell the world tomorrow that we're dating. I don't care what happens as long as I have you."

Giggling, I laced my fingers through his. "Slow down, baby. I don't want you losing your job. The whole professor thing is ninety-nine percent of the reason I'm into you. Take that away, and what do we have?"

Adonis nipped my bottom lip, making me squeal.

"Okay, okay. Ninety percent your job, and ten percent your cute ass. I guess we could build a relationship on ten percent."

"You're really trying to get another spanking, aren't you?"

I shivered. "So badly. Gonna make me beg again, or are we going back to your room now?"

"We're going back to my room." The shadows whirled as Adonis lifted me up, swinging me bridal-style in his arms. "You'll do your begging in there."

Yep, I was very glad I skipped back out the gate and drove here. Adonis was about to turn a terrible night into the best.

"Wait," I said. "Bring the food. Bet it tastes even better when I'm the plate."

"Fuck's sake, I missed you."

"This"—the lights flicked on, snapping our heads around—"explains so much." Rafael stood in the entrance, smirk heavy on his lips. "You're fucking your professor and fiancé's brother. No wonder you couldn't tell us." His smile vanished. "Luna, what the hell? Who did that to you!"

Rafael's shout and Adonis's sudden horror shocked reality back into me. I forgot what I looked like.

"No one," I blurted. "I mean— Not no one, but it wasn't like that. Alistair invited me over for dinner at the Burkhardt mansion, but he forgot to lock Saylor in her cage. To be blunt, she kicked my ass."

No point beating around the bush. I had scratches all up and down my arms and face, a sore head, a bald spot, and a limp I almost covered by letting Adonis carry me.

"Good news is I kicked her ass too." I climbed out of his arms and kissed Rafael. "I didn't mean to wake you up, then scare you with this face. Get some sleep, baby. We'll talk about everything in the morning."

"You didn't wake me up, although you're right about the scare." He was gentle, tracing a particularly vicious scratch from my forehead to my top lip. Saylor took all the skin off on the way down. The bright-red spot on his finger said it was still bleeding. "*This* woke me up."

Rafael handed me his phone. Stark at the top of the screen was a number I didn't recognize.

787-555-4978: If you help your shared slut come after me, I'll bury you alive in the next hole I put you in. The Rogues are closed for business.

787-555-4978: Permanently.

Rafael and I looked at each other and burst out laughing.

"Good," I said, deleting Everleigh's nonsense off the phone. "She's scared."

Chapter Four

I thought my first day walking onto this hated campus was uncomfortable. It was nothing compared to the dropped jaws, whispers, and half a dozen actual screams that accosted me as I headed for the dean's office first thing the next morning.

Someone had to tell him I wasn't dead.

"—can't believe it—"

"It's really her."

"Told you. Tiffany texted me that she blew into Toussaint's last night and accused Everleigh of trying to kill her."

Iris snorted loud. "Everleigh? I would've put my money on Saylor after the shit she pulled with the texts. Creepy little stalker."

Victor squeezed my hand tight, tugging me past the early-morning café crew. He said we should go the long way to avoid the crowd. I wished I listened.

"I swear, Everleigh could shoot me in the face in the middle of the café, and the Royals would say I imagined it and gave myself the hole in the head. It's terrifying the way you guys band together and defend each other."

"Not *you guys*. I'm not with those shits. The only thing terrifying about me is how violently and brutally I'll defend you." He tugged me in and kissed my forehead. Victor had been all over me since I walked out of his brother's room that morning. He didn't even blink at my messy hair, hickeys, and eau-de-sex parfum. I wondered if loving both brothers could truly work for us.

Victor stopped messing around with my forehead and kissed me hard.

It was working just fine.

"I hate that I gave Everleigh a whole night to calm down, send nasty texts, and plan her next move," I said. "Tonight, I have to find that cabin."

"Why do we have to do this at night? Rafael and the others are suspended. They can check out the cabins while Everleigh is in class. No chance of getting caught."

"Because that's the last time I'm an unconscious clueless dummy while you guys are in trouble. We don't have to wait until night, but we do have to do this together. Don't forget..." I glanced back at the crowd, wondering who among them was in T.O.D. "We're outnumbered."

"Wish we could figure out who's in the club or how many. It's disturbing to think anyone we pass by could be biding their time, waiting to carry out a dare from Jezebel12."

"Disturbing is a nice way of putting it. I'm completely blocked from the site." I blew out a breath. "I'll see if Alistair has better luck. If he wants to go around shutting down websites, he can shut down this one."

Victor winced. "Can't believe he stopped you selling Saylor's texts after everything she did. I know the Burkhardts have that family rule, but she fucked with you plenty over the last few months. She could've served her punishment for longer than a week at least."

"He's not stopping at taking down the site. Alistair said everyone who bought a copy will wake up to a black vortex of death where their hard drive used to be. Once they figure out that's because of the texts, I'll be public enemy number one. Again."

"Shit." Victor craned his neck, swinging around like the angry mob was about to descend. "Didn't he think of that? He just landed you in it."

The administration building loomed ahead of us.

"I assume he has a plan for dealing with all those angry customers because I'm just as pissed as they are."

"Bright side," he said, "the damage is done. My rugby guys don't care that I'm not interested, they've been updating me on every juicy detail from her texts. Saylor really fucked over a lot of people just because she could. She won't recover from this."

"And yet she blames me for ruining her life." My head still throbbed from where she smashed it against the wall. "Didn't occur to her that none of this would've happened if she wasn't such a poisonous, soul-sucking monster."

"Who happens to be your cousin." Victor drew ahead and held the door open for me. "Luna Sinclair-Bowden is actually Luna Burkhardt."

"I love you, but I will leave you at the altar if you call me that again."

"No, you won't," he said, grinning. "You're stuck with me for life. But speaking of our eternal commitment, do you think my parents knew you're a Burkhardt?"

The smile froze on my face.

"It would explain a lot," he mused. "Why they picked you, and why they threatened to disinherit me if we don't go through with the match. Burkhardts don't marry within the Royal line because they'd never know for sure if that person loved them or was using them for a quick ride to the top of the ladder. If a Wilson and Burkhardt got married, it'd change everything."

I studied his face. Deep down, I didn't believe Victor would've gone along with Martha's plan—using and deceiving me to get his hands on the inheritance I didn't know I had. Gazing at him then, I knew I was right.

He was as open and honest as he was every day since we met. Victor wanted me for me.

I took his hand, tugging him down to kiss his cheek. "A Wilson and a Burkhardt *are* getting married, and damn right it's going to change everything. We're taking over, baby."

His grin was wicked. "Our parents will regret this, but I won't. This is going to be fun."

I dropped my head on his shoulder, snuggling his arm as we headed to the dean's office. Finally, I understood why Victor had to be careful about his association with the Rogues. The best layer of protection that a Rogue had was their anonymity, and my guys gave that up when they were forced to go it alone. That put them in danger, but they were willing to accept the risk.

On Victor's side, he'd be taking that risk on for his whole family—making them a target like Winter and I became targets in a fight we didn't know about. I understood why, after we got married, we could only be Mr. and Mrs. Wilson in public, even if in private I was committed to all of my guys.

I understood, and that's why I had to burn the Royals, and now the Rogues, to the ground.

Sorry, Pops. I smiled sweetly at my man. *Anyone who stands in our way has to go. But don't worry, I'll set you up with a nice retirement package.*

"I'll wait here for you."

Victor grabbed a seat in front of the dean's office.

I glanced at the receptionist's empty desk. "It's seven thirty. That's what time he said to be here. Think I should just go in?"

"Pretty sure he doesn't start work until eight," Victor replied, jerking a chin at the desk. "Go in. If he's not there, fuck with his stuff and make it look like an accident. He's got a vase in there worth half a mill." Shrugging, he winked. "Payback for not believing Winter."

"My gosh, I'd marry you right now if there was a priest in this building."

"Don't think there is, but I'll take a blow job when you're done."

"Jerk," I said, though it was fondly, and he was definitely getting one.

I knocked once, then pushed into the dean's office. It was as grand as I imagined it to be. An office in one of the wealthiest, most prestigious schools could be nothing but.

My soles sank into the expensive blue-and-silver Persian carpet. Book-shelves surrounded me, every shelf filled with old, rare tomes. In the corner sat the sitting area, and its centerpiece was the very vase Victor talked about. It looked old, extremely priceless, and obviously a wordless brag. Everything in the office was, from the antique furniture to the oversized portraits of past deans in their ornate frames.

I took a step toward the vase. The desk chair squeaked, spinning my eyes in their sockets. The back of the chair swayed side to side, confirming I wasn't alone.

"Dean Simmons," I said. "You wanted to see me?"

"I did, but you don't have to call me Dean." The chair spun, and a man who was certainly not the dean smiled at me. "Wolf will do."

I flicked from him to the door. I could make it and get out before he rounded that desk.

"Thinking about running?" Wolf kicked his legs up on another man's desk. "I kindly ask that you don't. I went through the trouble of getting you here so that we could talk. Ten minutes of your time. That's all I ask."

I took a step toward the door, then another. Just to be sure he wouldn't try to stop me. "Where's the dean?"

Wolfgang O'Rourke let out a gusty sigh. Seeing him in person, he was nothing like the face on the screen.

He was even more gorgeous.

Wolfgang was Wilder's dark twin. Where Wilder's hair and eyes were light and soulful, Wolfgang was nothing but ebony locks and enigmatic black orbs. The resemblance between them was strong from the same nose, curve of their lips, and wide forehead, but somehow it still made sense to say they were nothing alike.

I looked at Wilder and felt safe. I looked at this man and felt... scared.

"Cars are so much better these days. They've got computers in them now. The esteemed Dean Simmons is currently shouting his head off, calling for someone to get him out of his car," Wolf sang, grinning away. "Mysteriously, the door locks engaged and won't open. Here's a hint. Deans call and leave a message. They don't summon you through email."

"You did go to a lot of trouble," I said mildly. "Why would you be so desperate to speak to me?"

He clapped. "First things first, take a seat. Can't have a proper conversation if we're shouting across the room."

"I'm good here."

"Why?" His grin widened. "Don't trust me?"

"No."

That cracked him up. "I see you've talked to my little bro, Wiley. What did he tell you? That I'm evil incarnate. The mean big bro who never let him have his way? We all do what we must to survive, Burkhardt. My mother was no easier on me than she was on him."

"He mentioned that," I said, trying to cover my flinch at hearing that name. "I think the real problem is what's making me hate you right now... how much you're enjoying yourself."

"Ooh." He pouted. "That's not very nice. I could be putting on an act to hide the frightened, wounded child inside. Did you ever think of that? Give a survivor the benefit of the doubt."

I gritted my teeth. Was this the kind of smiley, twisted mind games he put Wilder through his whole life? I no longer wondered why Wilder cut himself off from connection and saw everyone as a threat. No one born in a den of vipers ever felt safe.

"Why are you here, O'Rourke? What could we possibly have to talk about?"

"Nothing." Wolf dropped his feet and crossed to the dry bar, pouring himself a healthy amount of scotch.

I couldn't be sure if he was old enough to drink it. Wilder never specified his age, but they shared the same mature features that concealed their birth dates better than boyishness.

"I came here to speak to Wiley after that little stunt he pulled with the T.O.D. Club. He recognized my code the minute he peeked under the hood but didn't stop there. Your doing, I'm sure." He toasted me, smirking. "Ah, the things Wiley will do to impress a girl. He's a hopeless romantic, you know. Don't let the stoic act fool you."

"Does this have a point?"

"Why yes, it does." He hopped on the desk, gesturing again for me to join him.

I did. Moving slowly, I lowered myself in the seat—not taking my eye off him for a second.

"As I was saying, I came here to have a little chat with my brother about messing around in the wrong person's business, only to find out he learned that lesson the hard way. His place got burned down, and the cops found his stash."

He clicked his tongue. "I'll make sure they know that whatever lies he's spinning aren't truth, and he stockpiled all those illegal weapons and material. You'll send your love letters to supermax. I hear the way the sunlight glints off the rusted, chain-link fence is beautiful this time of year."

The breath knocked out of me. "What? Why would you do that? He's your brother!"

He shrugged, taking another swig. "Doing it out of necessity, not malice. I got a call last night after you showed up in Toussaint's very much not dead. The T.O.D. Club is a little side project a couple friends cooked up six years ago. They brought me on board to lock down the site, but I didn't find out until you did just how much free rein little Everleigh Starling had in the club. The lady knows how to twist a dick around her finger."

I lifted my chin, fighting the weight pressing on my chest. "How tight has she wrapped yours?"

He laughed. "Come now. I meant what I said about feeling sorry for you and your sister. Those guys went way overboard. The club is about having a little fun with Dregs. It's not about driving them to suicide.

"When Everleigh called, I hit record and started working on the computer virus that would deliver her confession to every phone, iPad, and laptop in a hundred-mile radius. I stopped halfway through."

"Why? What could she possibly have said that changed your mind and made you think putting your brother in prison is a necessity?"

"She said she'd make me leader of the Rogues."

I made a huge mistake. I should've walked out when I had the chance.

"Leader of the Rogues?" I forced a laugh. "Don't know who you've been talking to, but the Rogues don't have a leader. Rafael, Lucien, Cato, and Wilder don't take orders from anyone. Definitely not each other. They're friends who work together."

His smile turned nasty around the edges. "I've been calling you Burkhardt since you stepped in the room. Why play dumb when we both know what conversation we're having?

"Everleigh used Winter, then you, to lure Alistair Burkhardt out of hiding. You didn't die like you were supposed to, but it still worked. He's here.

"Problem is the element of surprise is blown to shit. You've already started blabbing to everyone who'll listen about the real Everleigh. Alistair didn't become the longest-reigning Rogue king by being an idiot. He's already weaving a cocoon of protection around you. I only slipped that email through because I sent it from the dean's actual computer.

"The text I spoofed from your friend Katie's number bounced back as undelivered. So much for that little distress call—getting you to run out and help your poor friend whose car broke down on the way back from her hookup's place."

My muscles went rigid.

"I mean, look at me," he sighed, flapping his hand. "Out in the field. I prefer doing my work behind a computer screen. I'm definitely not into Everleigh's suggestion that I kidnap you, hold you for ransom, and force your father to give his life for yours." Wolf shook his head to my growing horror. "Where's the finesse? Any brute can overpower a hundred-pound girl and lock her in a closet. But only a few people in the world can link a trail of weapon purchases, extremist sites, and a manufactured manifest to turn your boyfriends into the deadliest terror sleeper cell this world has ever seen."

"You can't—!"

"It's already set in motion," Wolf cut off. "First step in taking down the enemy is weakening their defenses. With one hit, my brother, his friends, and their resources are gone. All that's left is Victor Wilson and, of course, the king himself."

He winked. "Forgive me if I don't tell you what I have planned for them."

"Why are you doing this?! What kind of monster are you?!"

Wolf's eyes flashed. "The same kind of monster your father is. Do you have any clue what he did to crown himself king of the Rogues? He put a collar around their necks that strangle every generation. No one gets in who doesn't submit to him.

"Everleigh doesn't want to lead the Rogues, even though that'd be her right after she kills Alistair Burkhardt. She's happy to stand aside and let me have the throne as long as I help destroy every trace of him from existence."

"Then why are you here?" I shot out of my seat. "What's the point of telling me? Why go after my guys first? They're not even Rogues. You should know my father doesn't let teenagers in."

"Because, Luna, Everleigh had one thing right." I drowned in his bottomless black pools. "The way to Alistair Burkhardt is through you. Forget ropes, knives, abduction, or murder. I'll destroy everything you love by doing what I do best.

"Daddy will do everything he can to help you. Further compromising himself. Further exposing himself. When he finally comes *to me* and begs *me* to stop, that's when he'll pass the leashes he has on the Rogues into my hands. That's when I'll hand him over to Everleigh."

"Why would you tell me this?" I asked, stepping back. "You know I'll go straight to Alistair and tell him everything."

"I'm telling you this because despite what you're thinking of me right now, I'm not a complete evil bastard. I made a deal with Everleigh, but I could just as easily make one with you— Scratch that." He hopped off and closed the distance so fast my feet tangled stumbling back, and I fell on my ass. "I want to make a deal with you. The way Everleigh handles her business is sloppy. Look at what a terrible job she did tying up your loose end. And making an enemy of Leon Dumont?"

Wolf tossed his head. "She's the succeed-or-die-trying type and I'd rather not get tangled up in that kind of crazy if I can avoid it. You, on the other hand, are clever. The way you infiltrated and used the T.O.D. Club to turn it on itself was genius. Plus, I do take some responsibility for not creating a sys-

tem to flag and remove the kind of dares that pushed your sister to kill herself.

"That changed as of yesterday. From now on, I'll get a warning if more
than three dares target the same person. Also, the words rape, murder, bully,
kill, etcetera will result in an immediate block and admin review."

Wolf held out a hand. "Consider that a gesture of goodwill to prove that
I'm serious. I want to make a deal with you, Luna. I'll hold up my end as long
as you hold up yours."

I eyed his outstretched digits. "What deal?"

"Alistair Burkhardt is a ghost. He runs his entire empire from the shadows, and he does it from a laptop. It's his dark vault."

"Dark vault?"

"Where he keeps his blackmail, account numbers, contacts." Wolf got
tired of waiting. Tugging my wrist, he pulled me in and didn't let go. "It's
where he protects the true names and information of every Rogue in the
world. All you have to do, Luna Burkhardt, is get it for me."

"Get it for you?" I repeated slowly. Visions of that very same laptop float-
ed in my mind. Wolf smirked like he plucked the memory from my head. "I
can't."

"You can. You're his daughter. You're the only one who can get close." His
fingers skated down and tickled my palm. "Get me the laptop, and I'll disappear. I won't hurt you or Victor Wilson. I won't help Everleigh kill your
father. No need after I take his keys to the kingdom."

My thoughts spun too fast for me to catch one and think it through.
What was he saying? He'd betray Everleigh if I gave him a laptop? It's that
easy? "Why did you leave out Rafael, Cato, Lucien, and Wilder? Do you
swear not to hurt them either?"

"Sorry." He let go and spun away so fast I jumped. "It's too late for them, I
told you. Things are already in motion. Cops probably already polishing the
riot gear."

"I don't believe you," I cried. "Wilder's your brother. You wouldn't do
this to him."

Wolf cocked a brow, amused. "Wouldn't I? Who the hell even cares
about that brother/sister stuff? All that means is that we came out of the
same woman. Hardly the basis of a lifelong bond."

Taking a deep breath, I let it out slow. Of course he didn't give a shit about his brother. This guy clearly had a meat grinder where his heart should be. Normal human feelings were sucked in and ground up.

"Okay," I began. "Let's say I'm open to this. You didn't bring me here to make a deal. You brought me here for a negotiation, so let's negotiate. You refusing to help Everleigh doesn't do much for me. She's got more money than the total national student loan debt. She can easily hire another hacker.

"Also, I noticed you claimed you put protections on the site, but I didn't hear you say that you revoked Everleigh's access. Get serious, *Wolfie*. If you want me to steal from my bio father and hand you the keys to the most dangerous criminal organization in the world, you'll have to offer more than getting my boyfriends locked up, then skipping out of town."

Wolf leaned back, his expression shifting. "Respect, Burkhardt. Your proverbial balls are in a vise, and you try to make demands."

I smirked—forcing confidence I didn't feel. "My balls aren't in a vise. You play at being the king, but the actual king is on my side. He already forced you to put yourself at risk, facing me in person."

His lips twitched almost too fast for me to catch his displeasure.

"If you want that laptop, you'll do more than turn Everleigh down. You'll help me put that crazy bitch in the ground. And, oh yeah, you'll undo whatever you fucking did to frame my boyfriends as terrorists!" I shoved him. "I lose them and the only thing you'll get is the honor of being next after Everleigh."

"Uhhh, rude. No need to get physical," he said, making a show of dusting his shirt off. "How many times do I have to tell you there's nothing I can do for your boyfriends? Even without my nudge in the right direction, the cops found those weapons in their place. What exactly do you think I can do to make them forget that? I erase hard drives, not minds."

"There has to be something—"

"Even if I could, I wouldn't," he replied, "because this is not a negotiation. Everleigh's plan gets me what I want too. I'm the one with choices, Burkhardt, while you have one. Get me the laptop, your father lives, and I don't touch Victor Wilson." He brushed past me. "You should be thanking me. I'm leaving you with the richest of your boy toys. Quite generous of me."

"But you can't—"

"You have until midnight tomorrow night to get me what I want," he said. "Or I give Everleigh what she wants."

Wolf blew out the door, leaving me stock-still and speechless.

What just happened? What am I going to do?

***

"You don't think he'll do it, do you?"

I held Wilder tighter. After Wolfgang, I sped all the way from campus to the beach house—half expecting Wolf's horrible prediction had come true. My guys were on their way to a cell.

I arrived and found them in the living room, all present and accounted for.

"He'll do it, Luna."

Wilder traced slow, lazy circles on my arm. Together we swayed in the hammock, warm under a thick fleece blanket. His touch, the ocean breeze, our warm spot for two—all of it was doing too good a job of calming my nerves. Then, more than ever, was a good time to freak out.

"Wolf doesn't lie. Our mother was brutal when she caught us in a lie. She'd say if we were man enough to do something, we were man enough to own it." Wilder gazed up at the awning, tone soft. "Wolf's done everything he's said he's done, and he'll do everything he promised he'll do. Give him the laptop and he'll spare you, Victor, and your father."

"But what about you?" I shot up, and he eased me back down—tucking me snug against his side. I shut my eyes, breathing him in. "What about you? You can't seriously think I'll ride off into the sunset with Victor and forget about my Rogues. I will break you out of prison if that's what I have to do. You're stuck with me."

He chuckled. "I like being stuck with you. I like the future you see for us, Luna, and I hate that I fucked it up. The guys thought it was too risky to keep my arsenal down the hall, but after Levi tried to set us on fire, I wasn't taking chances again. Levi left us the choice of burning to death or running out to get our faces beaten in by him and his boys.

"I figured if the Royals were determined to take us out, we'd go down fighting."

"I know why you had that stuff, Wilder. I don't blame you." I slipped my hand under his shirt. "I also know that you never planned to use any of it except for self-defense. Wolfgang said he was going to make it out like you guys were terrorists. We can't let that happen. We have to do something."

Wilder tipped my chin, lightly kissing my nose. "I'll do whatever it takes to stay with you, Luna. But what will you do? Will you give him the laptop?"

I hesitated. "What will happen to the Rogues if Wolfgang is in charge?"

"He'll modernize. Make them more efficient, deadlier, and hide their identities under so many layers of protection they'll forget they're Rogues themselves. Once he's turned them into an anonymous army, he'll use them to collect all the money, land, and women he wants. And he'll kill anyone who stands in his way."

"Wow," I breathed, working my way up and over his hard bumps and ridges. "He is Everleigh's soul mate."

"There isn't trust, but there is respect between the Rogues. Those who can will drop everything and help a Rogue in need when their flag goes up. It's so serious they harshly punish anyone who raises a false flag. When you truly need one, a Rogue is there."

I kissed his collarbone, lips skating over his chilled flesh. "That's always been my experience."

"In a lot of ways, your father made the Rogues better. He made it so no one under twenty-five could join. He set up the flag system, and he kicked the worst of the worst out of the organization." He tipped his head. "Problem is he did that by bribery, blackmail, crippling businesses, and a bunch of other things that forced every Rogue to obey him. They hate him as much as they love him."

"That's been my experience too." We chuckled. It was short, sharp, and over as soon as it started.

"Okay," I whispered. "I know what I have to do."

Sitting up, I pulled out my phone. Alistair answered on the third ring.

"Luna? Is everything okay?"

"Everything's fine. I was just thinking..." I looked away from Wilder. "Our dinner was ruined last night. Up for giving it another try?"

"Of course. Don't even have to ask," he replied. "Although, fair warning. My sweet niece has informed me in no uncertain terms that she'll kick your ass if you set foot on the property again."

My lips peeled back from my teeth. Cousin or not, I would never like that wench. "Tell her to bring it on."

"I'll do no such thing," he replied. "You free now? I'll send Ronin to pick you up."

"Sounds good to me."

"Perfect. See you soon. Love you."

My heart squeezed. "I love you too."

Click.

I lowered the phone, meeting Wilder's eyes. "Tonight," I rasped. "I'll do it tonight."

"I'm sorry, Luna."

I bent and kissed him slow. "Take my mind off it?"

"I thought you'd never ask."

Wilder tugged me down, matching the slow, gentle pace we created. I sank into his kiss—all traces of duplicitous brothers, scheming enemies, and disappointed fathers fleeing my mind.

Gentle, calloused fingers slipped under my shirt, tracing my bra's underwire like he was asking for permission. An impossible thought because Wilder didn't need permission in bed.

It wasn't that he was rough or demanding. He was simply so confident in what I wanted and how to please me he already had his head between my legs before the thought entered my mind that I wanted him to lick my pussy.

Wilder followed the lace around and freed me one-handed. Impressive. I couldn't even unhook my bra with one hand.

"How many bras did you practice on to perfect that?" I whispered.

He nipped my bottom lip. "If we're counting the bras on the women I've loved... only one."

I couldn't stop myself cheesing. "Good answer, O'Rourke."

Wilder tugged my shirt over my head and dropped it on the porch. My bra followed.

"Damn, Sinclair." Wilder flattened his palms against my stomach and rolled down, taking my pants with him. "Every time I look at you, my heart stops. Why are you so fucking beautiful?"

I ducked my head. For all that I'd done since the Rogues came into my life, I was not as confident as them. My whole life, people praised my prettier sister or got into accidents checking out my mom while she jogged through our old neighborhood. I was the one whose bits of my mom and dad didn't mix together to create a stunningly beautiful kid like Winter.

"You know I mean that, don't you?"

I blinked, startled. I forgot Wilder could do that. Read my every thought like it was written on my face.

"You're the most beautiful woman I've ever seen or will see. It still amazes me that you chose us. No one on this planet would disagree that you could do better."

My fingers teased his lips. "Everyone on the planet would be wrong. I walk around Regalia, and all I see is backstabbing, fake friends, hidden relationships, lies, and deceit. Regular boyfriends would've bowed out of my shit by now—going back to normal lives of climbing the ladder. But you," I said softly. "You're here with me through everything—calling me beautiful even though I'm a puffy-eyed mess. I can't do better than that."

"I'll never be good enough for you," he said, smiling. "But I'm too selfish not to take advantage of the fact that you think I am."

Our lips connected in an explosion of fireworks. My whole body was alive with the touch of him. His hand trailing up my thigh. His chest warm and hard against me. His tongue tangling mine into submission.

I reached between us and helped myself to his zipper. This was only our second time together, and unlike his uncanny mind-reading abilities, I was still learning what he liked and how he wanted it.

I loved that. I loved that there was still so much more to learn about my guys, twice as much in Wilder's case.

Even so, I saw a life with us learning, laughing, loving each other until we were old and gray, and I would have that life. Everleigh and Wolfgang would not take it from us.

Wilder fit warm and hard in the palm of my hand. I stroked him slow at first—teasing out soft, core-clenching grunts.

"Damn, Sinclair. It won't break. Don't be afraid to strangle the fucker."

I giggled. "Makes it sound so violent." I gave him a hard, sharp tug—ripping a pleasured hiss from his lips. "But if I'm going to strangle this cock like I'm mad at it, I expect you to pound this pussy like it stole something."

"It will steal something." Wilder bent and flicked my nipple with his tongue. "My cum."

Thank goodness I was on the pill. Although, I'd be lying if I said I hadn't thought about a little grinning Rafael, mini barking Cato, tiny fighting Lucien, or a sweet chibi smiling Victor. That vision I had of us in the future, it was of a family.

"Ah!"

Wilder took me in his mouth—sucking hard on my poor pebble till his cheeks caved. He rolled his thumb over the other one, rubbing and tweaking it while the other one purred under his tongue.

I melted like butter in the sun, wetness pooling in my middle. My left hand found itself between us too. Slipping beneath, two fingers dipped between my lower lips—matching the pace I was stroking him.

His grunts reverberated through my skin. Mouth warm on me. Fingers rough on me. Cock stiff in my grip. Fingers hitting that spot over and over and over—

My back arched off the hammock, sending us both swinging.

"Whoa," I cried out, dropping my foot to catch us and immediately jerking it back up as my orgasm ripped through my body. We swayed—nearly dumped out on our backsides, but all I could do was cling to him.

"You'll come three times before I let you out of this hammock," he growled. "And the orgasms you give yourself don't count."

"Okay with me."

Wilder slid down, kissing through the valley of my breasts and peppering a trail to my belly button.

Wilder steadied me, strong, firm, and calm, while he braced his foot to keep us still. I brought my knees practically up to my ears, vibrating under the thought of what he'd do next.

A slow, tantalizing lick heated up my pussy, making me half melt into the strings.

"Yes, just like that, baby. Don't rush."

"Oh, so you give the orders now?"

I grinned. "I did escape certain death. I earned a little take charge in bed. Or in the hammock."

"So take charge." Trapping my gaze, Wilder dipped into my well—coating his tongue with my juices. My belly contracted so painfully I let out an embarrassing squeak. "Give me your orders, Sinclair. Tell me what to do. Tell me exactly what you want."

"I take it back."

He laughed. "How can you be shy after all the things you've done with us? You left behind the blushing-virgin bit months ago."

"I did not," I cried, covering my face. "I am still very much blushing. You guys have so much experience, and I only have experience being with you."

"That's all the experience you need. Talk to me," he whispered. "Tell me what you want."

"Okay. Do…" My face heated up hotter than a wildfire. "Do that again."

"Do what again?" Again he held me captive, locking eyes while he slowly licked my pussy like a scoop of ice cream. "This?"

I dropped my head back, eyes fluttering shut. "Yes, please."

Wilder took his time eating every inch of me out.

I came hard—giving him orgasm number one, quick and dirty.

His smirk found me from between his legs. "What do you want me to do next?"

"Fuck me!"

"Whatever you say."

It was awkward having two people in a hammock, let alone the two of them doing what we were doing. That didn't slow down Wilder.

He slid me down and draped my legs over the sides. He didn't mess around with trying to stay in the hammock and rose like a tripod with the third leg…

"Holy shit."

…sliding into me.

I fought against my natural urge to tense, taking him as deep and far as he'd go. Wilder propped on the post, shielding me from the porch light. I don't know why but calm and safety filled me. There, beneath my strong and powerful Wilder, I'd always be safe. He'd never let anything happen to me.

"I love you," we said at the same time, then laughed.

"That's the second time we've done that," I said.

"Second time we've done this too." Wilder started pumping—slow and deliciously deep. "Hope I measure up to the first."

"Only you could compete with yourself." I tugged him down, kissing through a ragged moan. Wilder was striking at a particularly interesting angle, and the swaying swing made sure he hit it on all sides. I was heading for number two fast. "Every time with you is perfect."

Wilder pumped harder. I grabbed his ass, feeling the muscles move and flex with each thrust. Our moans hit the porch roof and escaped, dancing on the night air.

My nails pierced his skin as number two hit me, exploding a million billion fireworks behind my eyes.

Pulling out, he scraped my bottom lip between his teeth, then kissed me sweet. "Lick me clean."

I blinked, my red cheeks coming back fast. "I thought I was in charge."

"You are. It's what you were going to say you wanted next."

"Wow." A grin tugged at my lips. "You are smooth, O'Rourke. No one can deny that. But..." I sat up, looking at him through hooded eyes. "Your cock in my mouth is exactly what I wanted next. Crazy how you read my mind."

I bent at the waist, getting eye level with the oversized beast I was putting in my mouth. People made cracks about guys with big muscles and small dicks, but Wilder put all those digs to shame. There was nothing small about it as it stretched my lips and filled my mouth. The taste of me coated my tongue, and I moaned—feeling his thighs contract beneath my hands again.

My eyes popped open.

It wasn't the two fingers sliding past my folds that startled me. I was quite used to that. It was the thumb gently probing my *other* hole, asking for permission.

This was new. I never thought about trying what he was clearly proposing, but only because my imagination didn't stretch that far yet. Whatever new things the guys wanted to do, I wanted to do.

That's how a girl learns what she likes.

I nodded around him, sucking harder. He grunted short and sharp, sending a bolt of lightning through my core. I loved making him make that sound. It was only our second time and I was already addicted.

Wilder dipped inside me, then teased my juices around my hole. Dear Thor, why was he so sinfully sexy?

I squirmed as he slid inside both holes. Discomfort rocked me, and I bore down around him.

"Easy, baby." He ran his fingers through my hair, soft and soothing against my scalp. "Tell me when you're ready."

I took a moment to get used to the sensation. After a beat, my head started bobbing, taking him in deeper and deeper down my throat. Wasn't that the universal sign for go time?

Must be because Wilder started moving too. In. Out. In. Out. Working three fingers inside me and picking up his pace as he went.

The discomfort disappeared, leaving behind only satisfying pleasure. What kind of naughty triangle did we make? I could only imagine what the guys would think if they looked out the window and saw us. Were they turned on? Were they furiously stroking their cocks and wishing my lips were around them right then? Were they seconds away from making that happen?

A sudden vision of Wilder, Cato, Lucien, Rafael, Victor, and Adonis tag-teaming me popped into my head.

"Hphm!" I bent my back in half, coming so violently on his fingers that I fell out of the hammock, Wilder coming out of my mouth with a "pop." Too late, he was already coming. Hot ropes of cum shot out, doubling him over and ripping all the delicious grunts and moans I collected from him.

I gasped on the wooden slats—too dizzy and humming on the aftershocks of my orgasm to feel any pain.

"And that's three," Wilder said. "How'd you end up down there?"

"Feel free to pick me up at any time."

Wilder scooped me giggling into his arms and dropped on the hammock, holding me close. "How'd I do?" he whispered, kissing the soft spot under my ear. "Did I take your mind off it?"

"Yeah." I burrowed under his chin. "Why are you so good at everything you do, O'Rourke?"

"It's going to be okay, Luna. I promise." His fingertips glided down my spine, rippling goose bumps on my back. "In the end, we'll make it all right."

I didn't say anything. The two of us just swung for a while, holding each other while we hung on to this peaceful, perfect moment for as long as we could.

Lucien, his cane, and a deep-purple vest with matching coattails stepped out onto the porch.

"Luna, are you ready to go? Your ride's here."

Wilder and I untangled ourselves from each other and got dressed. My mind left our steamy, perfect world too quick. It was time to return to the real one—where my sister was dead, and the demon who caused it still ran free.

I kissed Wilder and Lucien goodbye, then left around the side of the building instead of going through the house. Only Wilder knew what I was about to do. I couldn't chance the others seeing my face, reading the misery in my eyes, asking what was wrong, or changing my mind.

This had to be done. The longer this battle with Everleigh continued, the longer my eyes opened to the truth. Choice is an illusion. In war, there is only sacrifice.

Ronin idled in front of the beach house—a silent, intimidating presence that smothered the whole car. Throughout the ride, I stared at the back of his head, wondering who he was in his real life and why he stepped out of it to chauffeur a teenage girl around. My father had to trust him since he entrusted my safety to Ronin.

Was there a file on Ronin on my father's laptop? Was he holding something over him that ensured his obedience until the end of time? Would Wolf O'Rourke use that leverage to put the boot on the throat of this silent, scarred man who was protecting me?

"Ronin?"

A slight turn of his head was the only indication that he heard me and was listening.

"I know a little of what my father has done to become leader of the Rogues. I was told that you guys both hate and love him. Which is it for you?"

His reply was immediate.

"I hate Alistair Burkhardt."

"Oh." I sank back in my seat, head falling forward. Maybe it wasn't a betrayal. How could I betray a man I didn't know?

"But."

Blinking, I raised my head. "But?"

"But," Ronin said, "I'll die for him."

We didn't say more for the rest of the drive. There was nothing more to say.

Ronin dropped me off in front of the gate. Like Alistair wanted, Frank saw me coming up the drive and opened the gate without comment. I was welcome in the Burkhardt mansion at any time.

My ancestral home.

I thought about that during the long walk to the front doors. What would it have been like to be a Burkhardt? Alistair told me that in a family like his, the whole family stays together. Lives together.

I would've grown up right alongside Saylor. My best friends would've been Gabriella, Katie, Piper, and Everleigh too. All those fun, giggly adventures Saylor and her friends talked about in those texts. I would've shared in those just as much as their cruel pranks. Family vacations in Cabo taken together. Fancy private schools, ours to conquer.

An entire alternative life that was so close but out of my reach.

I placed my foot on the first step and the front door opened. Alistair smiled at me from the threshold.

"You didn't have to walk. I would've driven down to the gate and picked you up."

"It's okay. I didn't mind the walk."

"Come in," he said, taking my hand. "Your mom told me your favorite food is breakfast food. I had Chef make us eggs Benedict and chocolate chip pancakes."

"Yum."

"We won't be eating in the same room," he said. "Think it's best we put some distance between you and Saylor."

"Does that mean I can't get the tour?" I forced a smile on my lips. "I've been here twice but haven't really seen the place. I'm curious now since this was supposed to be my home."

"Course you can. Want to start outside with the gardens, three pools, and the greenhouse? Or inside with the two bowling alleys, five home theaters, and off-limits chef's kitchen?"

I laughed. "Let's go off-limits first."

Alistair flicked my nose, eyes warm. "Definitely my daughter."

I ducked my head, hoping he didn't catch my flinch.

I knew the Burkhardt mansion was grand from the exterior and the little I'd seen on the inside, but that didn't stop my mouth from dropping multiple times as he led me through the house. I finally gave up and let it hang open.

One summer vacation, Jack took the whole family to England for three weeks of sightseeing, pubs, and Harry Potter set tours. I'd been inside Buckingham Palace, the home of an actual queen, and I could say without a doubt that Saylor Burkhardt was living better.

Everywhere we went, there was a member of staff offering to do this or get us that. Screamingly expensive furniture, paintings, electronics, and fabrics followed us from room to room. It felt like one big show palace—meant to be looked at but not touched.

"It looks cold and uninviting," Alistair said, reading my expression with surprising insight. We were passing through another endless hallway. "But it's home. Just imagine what it was like playing hide-and-seek."

"I imagine it took hours— no, days for you and your brother to find each other."

He tapped his nose. "Dario never found me."

"Where's your childhood room?" I heard myself say. "Is it the room you're staying in? Can I see it?"

"It is, and you can, but it looks nothing like it did from my teen years. Mother had every trace of me stripped and turned it into another of the many guest rooms."

"That's okay. I still want to see it."

"This way. It's two floors up and in the east wing."

"I thought this was the east wing?"

"It's the northwest wing. The kitchen was in the east wing."

My eyes bugged. "We left the kitchen behind like an hour ago. What kind of never-ending maze is this place?"

Swallowing the rest of my grumbles, we made the trek back to the east wing. My body stiffened with each step, tightening my jaw and leaving me quieter and quieter.

I was stupid before. I acted without thinking or including anyone in the decision. Those choices almost killed me and put my boyfriends in danger. Knowing when to act is everything.

Alistair pushed open the door and waved me in.

My eyes immediately swept around, looking for the laptop, and I hated myself for it. Knowing when to act was important, but so was knowing when to give in. Wilder could not stand up against his brother. Why would I believe Wolf was bluffing about hurting the people I loved? He wasn't bluffing all the times he hurt Wilder.

"It's not much," he said, "but I made do."

I shook my head. Not much?

Alistair's version of not much included a four-poster bed about the size of a small apartment, massive big-screen television, aquarium floors, matching seafoam-green wallpaper, and a roaring fireplace.

I ran over to the aquarium, dropping on my knees. Blue fish, green fish, red fish, catfish—they lazily swam beneath the glass, paying no mind to the gawking human. If this was how the Burkhardts treated their guests, I could only imagine what Saylor's bedroom looked like. Their precious hellbeast must live in luxury itself.

"I didn't know you could put a fish tank in the floor."

Wonder what else they put in the floor. A floor safe, possibly? Alistair wouldn't leave something that important lying around. I swept the place again. *And I don't see it anywhere.*

"How do you feed them?" I asked. Half my mind listened to his answer, the other half mentally sketched out the silver computer bearing a red strip down the middle. I'd seen the back of it enough times when I was on the boat. I knew it on sight, and it was nowhere visible in the room.

Alistair checked his watch. "Food should be ready. Shall we?"

"Okay," I said, leaving easily.

We didn't go far. We went inside a room that was less a small library and more a game room. Billiards in one corner, old-timey arcade games in the other, and going down the middle was the infamous bowling alley.

"Thought we could play after we eat," Alistair said, pulling my chair out for me. The room even had those bolted-down tables and swing-out chairs standard in every bowling alley. "Got time?"

I nodded. "I didn't get my list back until Ronin picked me up, so I'll go hunting for Everleigh's cabin tomorrow." A thought struck me. "Wait. Do you know where it is? Everton used to hide out in a cabin near town to be close to Everleigh. How could someone be such a good father but such a trash human being? From what I've learned, Everleigh grew up in an abusive situation too. You'd think that would've made Everton more sympathetic to the father and child that he helped destroy."

"To answer your first question, no. I don't know anything about a cabin. Everton and I had our final meeting in the Virgin Islands. That's what tripped him up. He got cocky after years of staying ahead of the cops and decided to take a vacation in his family's beach house in St. Thomas. I had all his properties under surveillance."

He gave me a hard look. "If I ever impart any fatherly wisdom to you, Luna, it's to never get overconfident. The moment you think you can't lose, that's when you do. The lion doesn't catch the gazelle when it's running its fastest. He catches that bastard when he slows down."

"I'll remember that." I cast down at the delicious, heavenly-smelling breakfast/dinner my father had made for me. "I really will."

"To answer your second question. It's easy to believe Everton could be a good father." Alistair tipped my chin, surprising me. "Even the worst of men love their daughters."

I pushed back from the table, swinging out till the chair bonked hard against the metal. "Bathroom," I explained to the floor. "I have to wash my hands."

"Second door on the right."

I went out, but I didn't go right. I bypassed photos of Saylor throughout the years. Saylor at the beach. Saylor in Italy. Saylor cheesing at the camera with her arms around her dad. Saylor laughing at me in every photograph.

Snapping my head around, I clenched my teeth as I turned the corner and found myself in front of Alistair's door. My hand shook on the knob, swinging the door open.

I don't have much time, I thought. *Minutes. Ten at the most to search and put everything back where I found it.*

I took a step, then stopped. Squeezing my eyes shut, I allowed the tiniest tear to fall. It was okay to cry when you were breaking your own heart.

But only for a little while.

Taking a deep breath, I bit hard on my lip—the pain chasing away my tears. Here's another lesson my father would teach me. I could cry all I wanted; it wouldn't change a thing.

I steeled myself and went inside. Moving quickly but carefully, I searched the desk drawers, under the bed, around the fish tank, and then the closet.

My heart thumped, seeing my prize waiting for me beneath a rack of coats.

"This is not a negotiation. I'm the one with choices, Burkhardt, while you have one. Get me the laptop, your father lives, and I don't touch Victor Wilson."

"I'm sorry, Alistair," I whispered. "I'm not the one with the choices."

***

Alistair looked up when I returned, smile springing to his lips. "About time. The food's getting cold."

"Sorry." I took my seat, picking at my food. Focusing on my meal gave me an excuse not to look him in the eye. He was still doing it.

Looking at me like he loved me.

"I thought more about Everton's cabin."

That made me raise my head. "Yes? Do you know where it could be?"

"I knew Everton well enough to help you narrow it down. We can call it a cabin, but Everton wasn't one to rough it. That cabin was equipped with the finest amenities. This place would rival the Burkhardt mansion."

I sighed, deflating. "Yeah, Katie mentioned that."

We lapsed into silence. I picked at my food—eating slower and slower, taking smaller and smaller bites.

"One story."

"What?"

"The cabin will be one story," Alistair repeated. "Everton fell down the stairs when he was five. He broke his leg and lay there screaming and crying for two hours before the nanny finally came looking for him. The experience gave him a lifelong phobia. All the years I knew him, Everton either took the elevator or stayed on the ground floor. His old cabin will be grand, but it'll only be one story. I guarantee it."

"Okay," I said, filing that away. "Thank you."

If Alistair was waiting for me to say more, and it looked like he was—I didn't. Instead, I turned toward the arcade games, trying to remember if the satellite photos showed which homes were one, two, or three stories.

"It's the weekend," Alistair said, breaking into my musing. "Turns out my father has upheld the same Friday night tradition of contemplating by the fire with a glass of scotch. You can meet him after dinner if you'd like."

"Can't tonight. Won't be staying that long," I replied. "Maybe another time."

Another silence smothered us.

I dropped my fork, turning to the window. Why keep pretending? The eggs Benedict were sawdust and glue in my mouth.

"Is everything okay, Luna?"

"No," I said honestly. "Everything isn't okay."

"What's wrong? Did something happen today?"

I nodded slowly. "Something did happen. Today, I saw what my life would've been. Walking up to the mansion. Touring your home. It's weird but... I saw it all so clearly. I saw myself growing up in this mansion, playing never-ending games of hide-and-seek, and ruling over the town as another Burkhardt.

"I saw it all, and I realized something," I whispered. "It wouldn't have been me running with Saylor and her crew, cheesing in their vacay photos, or hanging at Toussaint's after school with her, Katie, Gabriella, Everleigh, and Piper. It would've been Winter."

"Luna..."

"You know it's true." The words choked in my throat. "Winter was the same age as Saylor. They were in the same grade. If they grew up as cousins instead of Royal and Dreg, everything would've been different. Like you keep saying, Burkhardts don't go after Burkhardts. Saylor never would've stood by while Royals and Dregs bullied her cousin. She never would've joined in.

"Winter would've been feared. She'd be protected. She'd be alive."

"Luna." Alistair rested his hand on mine. "You can't go there. Losing yourself in what would've been is a sure way to madness."

"Yeah," I croaked. "You would say that. Because it's all your fault."

"Excuse me?"

"You heard me." I snapped up, finally meeting his eyes, and letting him meet the fury in mine. "It's your fault. None of this would've happened if it wasn't for you. You're the one who picked a fight with your psychotic best buddy and passed that grudge to the next generation. You're the one who chose defending your crown as King Rogue over your family.

"You couldn't just let Everton be the leader of the Rogues if he wanted it that fucking much? No. Instead, you told yourself you were abandoning us to keep us safe when really you were protecting what you truly loved. Power."

Alistair reeled back like I tried to slap him. "That's not true. You know that's not true!"

"What I know is that my sister is dead and none of it had to happen," I cried, furious tears streaking my face. "If you didn't make us some damn secret. If you didn't leave us clueless and defenseless. If you weren't such an entitled rich boy who couldn't accept living a regular, disinherited life with the housekeeper and her kids. You, you, *you*!"

"Luna—"

"Winter's dead because of you!" I smacked the dinner plate. Ceramic and eggs burst apart on the floor, zinging sharp pieces that cut my leg. "I want you to leave. Leave Regalia. Leave the continent. You're the reason Winter killed herself and why I was almost killed too. You being here just makes everything worse. Go."

Alistair leaned back—face deathly pale, eyes thunderous. He stared at me without words, a thousand emotions flitting across his face. "Luna," he said, so soft the rasp tickled my ear. "This isn't you. Who is making you say these things? Tell me what happened. I'm here. I'm listening."

My vocal cords squeezed, strangling the lump in my throat.

"No one is making me say this. Winter killed herself because she was lost and alone. Because she was abandoned... by you."

His hands balled into fists, nearly bending the metal fork.

"None of it had to be the way it was. You could've had another stalker like Ronin following her around, keeping her safe, but you stopped thinking about us the minute you sailed off on your floating throne.

"Remaining a blank so you didn't push us into the life of a Rogue? That's a thin excuse and you know it. We needed you, and you weren't there—Worse, you *chose* not to be there." The words kept coming, shooting like bullets from my lips. Each meant to be fatal. "Leon Dumont blames himself for racking up so many evil, twisted enemies he didn't know which one blew up his family and killed his wife. He shoulders the blame for his choices. How dare you do anything less?"

Alistair shot up, making my heart jump into my throat. He dropped to his knees before me, taking my hands in his. "You don't have to do this. Drive me away. Whatever threats Everleigh's made, she's not going to get me too. You won't lose anyone else that you love."

"I don't love you."

The final bullet struck.

"I don't know you," I flung. "You're just a stranger who burst into my life to admit how you screwed it up. I don't want you here, Alistair. We're not family. As far as I'm concerned, you lost two daughters the day Winter jumped off that bridge."

Alistair was deathly pale. Deathly quiet. His eyes roved my face, searching for a trace that I didn't mean what I said. That there was force behind my words and pressure that didn't come from me. He could keep looking, but he wouldn't find it.

"Just get out of here, Alistair. Before you get me killed too."

Hands falling away, Alistair got to his feet. I bit my lip hard when a soft kiss pressed on my forehead. Blood stained my teeth.

"Okay, Luna. If that's what you want."

"It's what I want," I clipped.

He didn't reply for a beat.

"Don't blame yourself." A gentle hand stroked my hair. "Whatever prompted you to say these things—whether it was forced or you truly feel this way—nothing will change how much I love you."

I couldn't see my feet through the tears.

"I'll always love you."

I smacked his hand away, getting up and storming to the door. "Just go. I never want to see you again."

I slammed the door, rattling the priceless crystal chandeliers above. Ripping down the hallway, I ran till I found the front doors. Ran through the gates. Ran outside past Ronin and the car waiting to take me home. Ran and kept running—feet carrying me far away with nowhere to go.

No, I thought, snarl peeling back from my lips. *I know where I'm going.*

Chapter Five

I stumbled over the path, rocks kicking back up and striking my ankles.

My phone claimed I was coming up on the second cabin. I thought my anger would be gone by the five-mile walk over uneven terrain and grasping branches. It fucking wasn't.

My dad was right. I would not see another person I love die. I'd do whatever I had to do to protect him, including break his heart.

I choked on a sob—the vision of Alistair's face when I told him I didn't love him, replaying over and over again in my mind.

It wasn't his fault. I didn't blame him for a thing even though it would be easy to. Even though there was a kernel of truth in every horrid accusation I threw at him. I know he didn't pick power over his family. What he chose was a life of danger and isolation in the name of protecting his family. Of course he had no reason to think any of what happened to Winter and me would go down.

Who predicts a nine-year-old girl with pigtails and a Barbie Dreamhouse would turn into a raging psychopath that would carry out a grudge he buried ten years ago?

The only person at fault then was Everton for shitting on every chance to do the right thing and then continually going after my father until he had no choice but to do the unthinkable. And the person at fault now was Everleigh.

She used brutal, terrible means to force Winter to do what she wanted. She brought Wolf O'Rourke into this. They both made it clear they'd go as far as it takes to get what they wanted.

"So I will too."

A log mansion broke through the trees, its glittering perimeter lights piercing the forest's smothering gloom. The place was truly gorgeous—a wooden mansion fitting for the wealthy community of Regalia.

A river stone path led up to a wraparound porch, complete with warm patio furniture and purple hanging plants. The blue-painted roof set it apart as unique as well as expensive. But none of that interested me. The one thing I cared about was that it was one story.

I crept through the trees, keeping an eye out for... anything.

Cameras, dogs, trip wires, loose dirt over land mines. I didn't put anything past Everleigh.

Someone's there.

Lights flicked on and off from window to window, indicating someone was moving through the mansion. The curtains were drawn on all the windows I could see, stopping me from knowing who.

I had to chance it and get closer. There were three more cabins to check, and it took me hours to get this far. If my trek was finally over, I needed to know.

It has to be Everleigh. I slowly crossed the lawn, cringing under the bright spotlight of the perimeter lights. *Who else would be awake at two in the morning? Everyone knows witches don't sleep.*

Twenty feet.

Ten feet.

Five.

Closer I got to the front steps and no alarms went off. No curtains flung open. No doors banged against the opposite wall.

Maybe I was wrong to think Everleigh outfitted the place like a bunker. It's been years and not even her friends know where the cabin is. Why wouldn't she think she was safe here? She'd let down her guard. Relax. And it'd be the worst mistake she ever made.

My left foot hit the bottom step, and I breathed a sigh of relief. I was right. No insane defenses. All I had to do then was prove this was the right place.

The trail of inside lights led to a big room that I assumed was the living room. I followed them, glancing at the curtains lighting up with multicolor. Everleigh was watching television.

I clenched my jaw—rough pants leaking through my teeth. How nice of the rotted bitch to sit in front of the big screen with popcorn and hot cocoa, having herself a good ole time. Meanwhile, I was forced to say the cruelest things to my father—all to protect him from her.

Again, she's fucked with my family and did damage that may never repair, but why should that bother her? Why should that get in the way of movie night? My plan was just beginning and it already went off track. So far, everything was turning up Everleigh.

I went to the windowsill and strained to see through the slight space between curtains. *Is that...?*

The glow from the television fell over half a foot. It was hard to be certain, but it looked like that foot was encased in a fuzzy white slipper.

A woman. Living in a one-story log mansion. By the river. Where Everleigh and her father used to fish.

What else did I need? This was the place.

I bounced from foot to foot, fists opening and closing. I hadn't been thinking when I fished the list out of my pocket and ran into the woods. The only thing on my mind was making Everleigh pay for destroying my family.

Now I was there. Six feet from the bitch and I had nothing. No weapon. No backup. No clear shot.

I whipped back and forth, looking for something. Anything! I wasn't leaving without taking *pieces* of her with me. Fuck carefully laid plans. Fuck police captains that sat on their asses. Fuck scheming hackers and their twisted deals.

I was ending this tonight.

Twisting around, I landed on exactly what I needed. I darted off the porch and snatched up one of the riverbed stones. Charging the window, I smashed the windowpanes—roaring my fury.

"Ahhhh!"

"Surprise, bitch!" I reached through and yanked back the curtain. "It's your turn to burn—"

I choked, eyes blowing up at the couple screaming in the living room who were not Everleigh and Wolf. I'd never seen them before in my life.

"No! No," the slipper-footed woman wailed. "Don't hurt us!"

The man raced to the fireplace and grabbed a poker. "Argh!"

He charged the window. I spun and bolted.

"Ah!" My feet tangled, pitching me off the porch. I crashed on the river stone path and jarred every bone in my body. I must've blacked out because the next thing I knew, light from their front hallway fell over me.

The man ran out of the house, poker held high. "You messed with the wrong people! How do you like this, bitch!"

He struck—bringing the poker down on my head.

I twisted at the last moment. Snapping to the side, the metal hit the spot my skull had just been in.

He lifted the poker for another try.

Reacting fast, I kicked out and smashed my foot between his legs. He doubled over and dropped the weapon, grabbing his crotch as he went down.

I didn't waste another second. I scrambled to my feet and took off. Their screams and angry shouts jangled in my head long after I couldn't hear them.

***

My feet dragged up the path, moving as slowly as the tears streaking my cheeks.

Four in the morning, I was back at Adonis's place and what did I have to show for myself? Scraped knees, a sore shoulder, no Everleigh, and no father.

Wilder waited for me on the porch. "I'm guessing you went through with it."

I looked at him and burst out sobbing. "The w-way he looked at me, Wilder."

There was only ever one choice when Wolf said they were going to use me to kill my father. Making a deal with that guy was never going to happen. He'd figure that out when I didn't show up at midnight with the laptop. All I could do was make Alistair leave, so the days of our family being used against each other finally ended.

If only I didn't know in my heart that he wouldn't go for anything less than the extreme.

"It's not fair. I just got him back and now..." I trailed off, shaking my head. "I said so many horrible things to him."

Wilder gathered me in his arms, holding me tight. "When this is all over, you'll apologize. He'll understand, Luna. He loves you."

I buried my face in his chest and breathed him in. Wilder always smelled like sunshine after the rain. The hope of something wonderful.

He didn't judge or try to talk me out of it when I told him I wouldn't hand over the laptop and would instead send it and my father out of Regalia.

"Did you run into Saylor after?" he asked. "You're banged up."

I hesitated. I didn't want to lie, but I also didn't want to tell him I acted alone *again* and got hurt *again*.

"I went searching for Everleigh's cabin after." I'd always choose the truth. "I lost it, Wilder. I was— I am so angry I can barely think. I thought I found it, but it ended up being the home of a random couple who really didn't appreciate me bursting through the window and threatening to burn them alive."

Wilder's brows rocketed up his forehead.

"The guy tried to bash my head in with a fire poker and I kicked him in the balls." I clicked my tongue. "The cherry on top of a hellish night."

A strange noise erupted from Wilder, shaking his chest.

Oh my goodness, is he... laughing?

"I'm sorry. I'm s-sorry," he said, straining to keep it in. "It's not funny, but... you kicked him in the balls? Damn, Sinclair. You're spreading that bad night around."

"It's not funny. I busted their window with a rock," I cried.

He snorted, losing control.

"Then I yelled, *surprise, bitch* like I was some kind of badass. They were definitely surprised."

Wilder straight howled, laughing so loud he probably woke the house.

A smile tugged on my lips. Before I knew it, I was howling along with him. Every time I said, "surprise, bitch" we laughed louder.

"Only I can get into messes like this. It's my curse." My smile faded. "Always wrong. Always running. Always late. Always hurting the people I care about."

Wilder lightly kissed the tip of my nose. "That's not how I see it. You're always doing what you know is right. You're always running toward the people who need you. And you're always doing whatever it takes to protect the ones you love. We will win this fight, Luna. Fuck if I know how, but we will."

"Everything's changed now that your brother is working for Everleigh. Because that's exactly what he will do when I tell him to go fuck himself. He'll never get his hands on Alistair's laptop." I sighed, collapsing against him. "We don't have a plan. We don't have my father. We don't have the Gallery. We don't have access to the T.O.D. Club. In one day, everything went to shit. I'd call that unlucky."

"We're not unlucky when we work together."

I almost smiled. "Never thought I'd hear my suspicious love say something like that."

"I couldn't trust anyone before I met Rafael, Lucien, Cato, and you. Now I know what family is supposed to be." He dropped a kiss on my crown. "We've got this, Luna. From the minute you set foot in Regalia University, you didn't doubt that you'd get revenge for your sister. Don't tell me that girl's gone?"

Something in me sparked, lighting a fire in my belly that chased back tears. I glared at him. "Hell no."

"Good." Wilder smirked. "Then, let's go inside, have sex in the shower, then make a new plan."

"You might need to hold me up for part two, then plan with my unconscious body for part three. I don't even know how I'm standing right now."

"Say no more." Wilder scooped me in his arms and carried me into the house. "I've got you, Luna. Always."

***

"We should split up."

Rafael, Wilder, Lucien, Cato, and I were on the couch. Adonis wandered off after dinner to grade papers, and Victor left hours before to speak to his father. Wilson Industries was a billion-dollar conglomerate with its fingers in almost every industry. It was a simple fact that hackers must attack their systems on a daily basis, searching and hoping for a weakness. Victor promised to employ the best in their IT department to help us.

We didn't need them to find Wolfgang. We knew exactly where the guy was and that he was coming to us. What we needed was to stop him playing ring-around-the-rosy in our devices like he did to Wilder's computers.

It was a scary world when we couldn't trust our phones, laptops, Apple watches, Alexa, or anything with an internet connection. All those machines-take-over-the-world movies suddenly didn't seem so far-fetched.

My guys and I gathered in the living room that night, making a plan to find Everleigh's cabin that would hopefully go much better than my adventure the night before.

"The five cabins are now down to three." I absentmindedly rubbed my shoulder. "The problem is the final three are miles away from each other. One is all the way in East Regalia. Cato and I will take that one. Lucien, you take the one closest to the beach. Wilder and Rafael, you two take the one in the middle.

"We'll meet up at Toussaint's after. They're open till late, and after the week I've had, I need three orders of their baklava cheesecake."

"We're not splitting up," Wilder said. "You won't hold back if you're the one to find her, and Cato's not going to stop you." His eyes narrowed. "Bet that's why you want to go with him. You'll say let's go fuck her up, and he'll already have the lighter out and flinging himself through the window like a flaming wrecking ball."

I giggled at the image. Cato would, one hundred percent. "You shouldn't be so suspicious of the love of your life. This isn't a trick to get to Everleigh alone. I learned my lesson from last night. I also learned that I'm not built for tromping through the woods till five in the morning. I want to get this over with quickly," I said. "If I do find Everleigh, I'll get out of there and text you guys right away.

"The last thing I'm going to do is fight her on her own turf. When I come at her for the last time, it'll be in a situation that I control. No more surprises."

The suspicion softened. "Okay," Wilder said. "We'll all go together."

I heaved a sigh. "I will not charge in like a flaming wrecking ball again. I promise. Please, I just want to get through this night, then spend time with my guys. We'll get takeout, then bring it back here and enjoy it, just us."

"All right," Rafael said. "We trust you, gorgeous. Mostly because you've yelled your last 'surprise, bitch' for a lifetime."

I rolled my eyes as they burst out laughing. I told them all what happened, and after kissing me and making sure I was okay, they lost their shit. We'd laugh about this night for a long time. I only hoped that we'd do it with Alistair after Everleigh was gone and I made up for the terrible things I said to him.

A glance out the window told me the sun finished its daily retreat across the sky. "Let's get going. We're splitting up, yes?"

The guys exchanged a look. It impressed me how they did that. Communicated with each other without words. They were a tight-knit unit long before I came along. Four young men given a destiny and then cast out to fulfill it on their own. What kind of fate was it that the daughter of the Rogue king fell in love with them?

Lucien tossed me his keys. "You and Cato take my car. I can walk to my cabin."

I linked my hand through Cato's. "I just hope it is one of these three and that the cabin wasn't sold and bulldozed years ago."

"Katie told you that she avoids her home like it's a plague hospital. She's going somewhere that she doesn't want her parents and friends to know about. The former home of her fugitive father is just as good a guess as any."

All I had was that hope, so I held on to it. "Remember. The cabin will be one story and outrageously grand."

With that, we headed out and went our separate ways.

Cato dropped his backpack in the back seat. The guys lost almost everything in the fire, but somehow my muzzled love held on to a pack full of lighters, torches, and jewelry he maintained wasn't stolen.

The ride to East Regalia felt longer than the forty minutes it took. I kept a stranglehold on the steering wheel, Alistair's face playing on a loop in my mind. I would do everything possible to end the war with Everleigh quickly and make it up to him. Those last few days—talking about our childhood, comparing our uncannily similar likes and dislikes, and telling him all the things I could never say to a normal father. I loved it.

I wanted to get to know this man who already knew me so well. One Starling stole eighteen years from us. The next Starling would not get any more.

My part of town fell away before East Regalia. I didn't spend much time in this part of Regalia, though not for the same reason the Royals didn't. Every part of Regalia was a wealthy town for wealthy people, but not all money was the same money. Or something stupid like that.

Old money like the Wilsons and the Burkhardts claimed West Regalia. That left East Regalia to the new-money families like Dean's. Having new money still made you a Dreg because, like I said, this town is stupid.

I weaved through eclectic neighborhoods with modern homes, game board cafés, clubs, and the infamous Hometown Country Fried. This part of town had less beach and more woods. Likely why the old-money Regalians claimed the west for themselves. They went to bed every night watching the sunset on the ocean while they sipped chamomile tea on the balcony. East Regalians watched crows shit on their lawn.

"I'll take the car in as close as I can," I said, ending the quiet. "Then we'll go the rest of the way on foot."

Cato nodded. "Yes."

I eyed him out of the corner of my eye. "You know that, in all likelihood, this is the correct cabin, right? If I was a two-bit piece of trash in hiding while I tried to kill my former best friend, I'd pick a hideout that wasn't in his backyard."

"Yes."

My voice hardened. "And if I'm right and Everleigh is in this cabin, we're not waiting around for the other guys to get here."

"Yes."

"Flaming wrecking ball?"

Cato turned to me, smirk curling his lips. I didn't notice until then his favorite skull lighter flipped between his fingers. "Yes."

"I love you so much right now."

He laughed. A rich, wild sound that made me feel a little crazy. A little dangerous. "Surprise, bitch!"

And then we were both laughing—loud and unhinged as our car disappeared through the trees.

As promised, I drove in as far as I could, then pulled off on the side of the road. The house I thought was Everleigh's didn't have any security, but her real one might. To be safe, I followed the dirt road as far as I dared. We'd walk the rest of the way to the dim lights in the distance.

Cato was a stalking panther beside me—so silent it was easy to forget he was there. His breaths were whispers on the wind. His steps so light twigs didn't dare break.

The complete opposite to the stumbling, heavy-footed oaf beside him. My foot caught on something and I went flying. Cato reacted fast—catching me before I hit the ground. But not before that *something* screeched and went tearing off into the bushes.

"I don't want to know what that was," I huffed. "Goodness. Is it your father's Rogue training that makes you so good at all of this? Makes me wonder how different I'd be if Alistair raised me. I'd be a lethal weapon too."

"You are." Cato set me on my feet. "One thing would be different. You'd have been mine sooner."

A smile played at my lips. "I would've, wouldn't I? If we all went to school together, guys like Owen and Levi would've skeeved me out with their superiority complexes. Even in Catholic school, I found myself running with the outcasts." I hugged his arm, trying to find his lips in the dark. "Guess we'll have to make up for stolen time."

"There."

The ragged hiss snapped my head around. There in the distance, hazy glows took form, revealing a one-story mansion.

My lips parted. I was deluded the night before. How in the world did I think that rinky-dink pile of logs was the grand mansion worthy of Everton Starling? That place wasn't grand. The vast, gorgeous home of polished stone, columns, twelve-foot windows, and sloped ceilings was where the word grand came from.

"This is the place."

Cato slouched off his backpack. My skin tingled at his smile as he held up a torch and matches.

"It'd be fitting," I whispered, mesmerized by the glittering flame. "Burn down her home like she burned down ours. We can end it all right here. Right now. No more plotting, waiting, hoping, fighting. Just a hollow building with a roasted corpse. The exact end that she planned for me."

I let out a breath. "But we can't. Not yet, at least. First, we have to make sure this is the right cabin. I won't risk destroying the home of an innocent person. *Again*. Also, we can't torch the place before we find her laptop."

His brows drew together in the glow of the fire—asking without asking.

"It's not just Everleigh we have to destroy. We've got to bury the T.O.D. Club too. They were her murder weapon. Fuck's sake, they were my murder weapon." I squeezed his forearm. "It's terrifying what someone with enough malice and money can make the members do. Wolf blocked my access to the site…" My gaze drifted to the cabin. "But he didn't block hers.

"I know her access isn't half as restricted as Giovanni's was. If I can get in through her laptop, I can see all the members, expose the club, and take that weapon away from her and every Royal."

Cato flicked off the lighter. "Break in."

"We have to." My gaze sharpened, looking hard for any sign of cameras or other security measures. "We need to get in there, prove it's Everleigh's place, steal her laptop, then you can burn whatever you want, baby."

Cato kissed me hard, then tugged me along—skirting the tree line leading to the back of the cabin. I said the man didn't need words to get his point across.

"Anything in your pack that can pick locks?" I asked. "Window-breaking doesn't work out too well for me."

No reply from him except to pick up the pace. Cato knew how he was getting in. The question was would his method be anything close to subtle.

"We'll call the guys when we know for sure it's her place," I said—to him or me, I wasn't sure. "No need for them to come rushing out here just to watch another bald man try to bash my head in. When we know, I'll call. The forty-minute drive will give us enough time to find the laptop. It's better to apologize than ask for permission."

Cato stopped dead, making me pull up short. I followed where he pointed, and my eyes bugged.

A window. An *open* window in the back beside glass double doors.

"It can't be that easy," I breathed. "All we have to do is climb in."

Cato set off. He was about to do just that.

"Wait," I hissed, pulling him up short. "It's not that late. Only ten o'clock. She could still be up and chilling in the living room, watching movies in her fuzzy slippers. First, we get eyes on her and make sure we've got the right place."

Cato pointed, then jerked his head in the opposite direction. *Let's split up.*

"You go that way. I'll go this way."

Nodding, Cato backed away and blended into the shadows like they were his playthings. I made for that open window, moving as slowly and quietly as my bumbling feet allowed. The lights we saw through the trees were from hanging fairy lights dotting the roof and a single light on inside the house. Someone was in there, or they forgot to turn that light off when they left.

I pressed against the wall under the window, listening intently. *Nothing.*

Chancing it, I rose on tiptoe and peeked inside.

The fuzzy black outline of a small library awaited me. I fixed on something placed next to the window. After a second, I realized it was a chaise lounge. Everleigh must've kicked back, reading books and enjoying the breeze while outside in the real world, the fire she started blazed out of control. Must be nice to be that carefree.

I would happily put a stop to that for her.

Continuing on, I skirted past the back doors. I rounded the bend and looked right at Everleigh.

I jumped back—heart slamming out of my chest. The hazel-eyed figure poured hot water from the kettle with one hand and scrolled through her phone with the other. She didn't look up as I used the L-shaped wall to duck behind.

All doubt erased before me. This was Everleigh's cabin. All I needed to do was get inside, find her laptop, and make sure I took down the T.O.D. Club along with her. The get-inside part is where it got tricky.

I worried my lip, backing farther away to the open window. Simple enough to pop out the screen and climb in. Not so simple to wander around searching while Everleigh kicked back with her tea.

Should I wait until she goes to sleep?

That could be hours, another voice answered. *Wilder, Rafael, and Lucien will have caught my lying ass out by then. I should call them now. Tell them the truth and that we found Everleigh. Then we can—*

A tap landed on my shoulder, sending me three feet in the air. I whirled around on Cato and held a finger to my lips for no good reason.

"She's in there," I whispered. "If you give me a boost, I can climb in, then pull you up. But how do we make sure she doesn't catch us while we're searching for the laptop?"

Cato held up his bag. "Distraction."

I shook my head. "We used the same kind of distraction on Giovanni and Gabriella—which Everleigh knows all about. If her trash can explodes out of nowhere, she won't come out. She'll go into lockdown." I tipped my head, thinking. "It's good for us that Everton hated stairs. This place is massive, but there's only one floor. She's in the kitchen right now, but she's in pajamas. She's probably taking her tea back to her room."

"Room where the laptop is."

I rocked back on my heels, knowing he was right. Who didn't keep their laptops in their bedroom? No one. We'd have to tiptoe right past her.

"That just means she'll lead us right to it," I tried to say confidently. "Let's go in. Help me up."

Cato bent, grabbed me around the knees, and lifted me up with barely a flex of his muscles. I popped out the screen and carefully dropped it on the soft chaise. This was it. Now or never.

Taking a breath, I widened the window opening and wiggled through. I dropped flat on my cushioned landing pad—hardly believing it was that easy. I was in.

I spun and reached out for Cato. My phone buzzed against my hip. I helped him in, then pulled it out.

An email? I read the address twice and no familiarity bells rang. Who was this? Why didn't spam eat this up?

Time's almost up. Meet me at the Bluffs.

I'm sure you'll do the right thing.

-Wolf

My lips peeled back from my teeth. Everything in me wanted to write a thirty-page reply on what a low-down piece of trash he was, but my not showing up to his little blackmail meeting would get the message across clear enough.

"Let's go," I whispered.

Cato and I padded out of the library. I didn't know what was on his mind. Likely, excitement about how he'd get to commit his favorite crime: arson.

We came out and followed the same bend in the walls leading to the kitchen. Cato left his pack behind. The clanging torch cans would give us away in an instant.

Inside, the mansion was twice as impressive. It had nothing on the Burkhardt mansion and the nauseating boasts of wealth everywhere you looked. On the contrary, there was something warm and homey about the shiny juniper pine walls and cool stone beneath my feet. It felt like a place for a family.

A father and daughter.

My back pressed tighter to the wall. Points for me that I wasn't shaking the whole house with how hard my rib cage was rattling. A shadow moved in the light. Everleigh was still in the kitchen. Cheek touching the wall, I glanced around—

"Luna Sinclair."

My heart jumped out of my throat.

Cato grabbed me from behind and spun. No way she was catching us without a weapon while she stood in a room full of knives!

"A know-nothing little weakling who was smart enough to fuck powerful guys. She's not a threat by herself. She's just very irritating bait."

We jerked to a halt. *What?*

"Wilder O'Rourke isn't a threat anymore. If he could've dug up dirt on me, I wouldn't have had to give up my side project by myself. Wolf will make sure the paranoid freak can't find another way to get at me."

Chancing it, I crept back and glanced around the wall. Everleigh moved around the kitchen, making a late-night snack while she talked to herself.

No— While she took voice notes on her phone.

"She got Alistair Burkhardt here, but now he's holed up in Burkhardt Manor and knows that I'm coming for him. I've already been taken off their allowed-visitors list."

She dropped the frying pan on the stove a little too hard. "As long as Sinclair is running around, I can still use her to draw him out. But as long as *she* is surrounded by those fools, she's impossible to get to. Leon Dumont won't be taken off guard twice."

Cato and I exchanged a silent look. We weren't the only ones plotting that night.

"Wolf can take care of his brother. Cato Dumont is nothing more than a rabid dog. I'll throw something shiny and he'll chase after it."

Cato grinned. Dear Thor, it looked like he loved that description.

"Rafael Dumont, Lucien Calais, and Victor Wilson... they're a problem."

Everleigh gave me her back and faced the stove. I stuck my head out farther, getting a lay of the land.

We were in the center of the mansion. Kitchen, living room, dining area, massive stone fireplace, and another sitting area. On the other side of her and the kitchen was the entrance to the east wing of the mansion.

"Note," she said. "Look through the T.O.D. members for people who have the balls to go up against Calais. Actually, look for ten. If it comes to a fight, I'll make sure he doesn't walk away from it."

My nails pierced my palm. Once a coldhearted bitch, always a soul-sucking, motherfucking, coldhearted bitch.

"Note," she continued. "Victor Wilson has to go. Question is how. Too many people like Victor. He's nice to the Dregs and doesn't use his power over the Royals. No one will want to hurt him for any price. Him, I might have to take care of myself."

Cato tugged my arm, making me turn around. He gestured with his chin.

His unspoken suggestion was right. Instead of standing around listening to her make plans that would *never* come true, we should use this opportunity to search for the laptop.

I backed away, letting her disturbingly sweet voice fade.

"Split up."

I nodded. This mansion was just too big for us to go through every room together. Cato and I traveled to the very end of the house. I went left, he went right. We worked our way down our sides of the hall, and we did it fast.

There was no reason to spend much time. Most of the rooms had nothing in them at all.

It occurred to me that this was Everton's hideout, then it was Everleigh's. There was no one to put a show on for. No one to invite over to sleep, eat, or play in all these rooms. It was just them. Alone. The only one either of them had was each other.

In another universe, I'd feel so sorry for Everleigh, in the universe where she wasn't the reincarnated spawn of Satan.

Cato and I worked our way through the rooms and met back up right where we started. We shook our heads.

Nothing.

My phone buzzed, drawing my attention away from Everleigh. The light was still on in the kitchen, but she stopped talking. I hadn't checked to see where she was yet.

Pressing my back flat to the wall, I opened the message.

Wilder: Our cabin was a two story. Lucien clocked a bunch of photos of an old couple in his. Ours are out. Do I want to ask if you have your foot on Everleigh's throat right now?

Me: You know me too well, baby. We found Everleigh's place. We're inside right now looking for her laptop. She doesn't know we're here, but she will when we burn this shit to the ground.

I wasn't about to lie to the guy.

Wilder: We're on our way. Be careful. Love you.

Me: Love you too.

Stuffing my phone in my pocket, I looked around the wall, then snapped back fast—clapping my hand over my mouth. Flapping a hand at Cato, I warned him to get back.

Everleigh crossed in front of us, moving to the living room. It was only because she was looking down at her phone again that she didn't see us.

We darted across to the opposite wall, keeping out of sight. Everleigh was on the other side of the room, and our way to the other half of the building where her bedroom had to be, welcomed us from the entrance to the kitchen.

I was twenty feet away, but it might've been twenty miles.

The television flicked on, and the rerun of a remake filled the too-quiet mansion with noise. Everleigh settled in with her food and her show, and it didn't sound like she was going to bed anytime soon.

"What do we do?" I hissed. "Just stand around and wait? She's out of her room right now. The last thing we want to do is snatch the laptop when she's in there."

"Distraction."

"But we can't—"

Cato turned and walked off.

"Cato—!" I cut off the whisper shout, biting my lip hard. Stealing, setting fires, giving me orgasms—I'd never been able to get in the way of what he loves to do. That wasn't changing that night.

I just have to trust him. Cato knows how important this is. He wants to bring down the woman who abducted him and threatened his girlfriend as much as I do.

I sat back to wait, breath held tight in my chest. What would Cato do? Lure her outside with a fire? Knock and then attack when she opens the door? Did he pack bombs like—?

The lights flicked out, plunging the mansion in darkness. I smirked to myself. *Or he'd just do that.*

"Ugh," Everleigh sounded in the dark. "Not again."

I didn't waste a second. I moved quickly through the dark, heading for the kitchen. I was begging to trip and fall flat on my face, but I had to get across before Everleigh turned on her flashlight.

The thought no sooner crossed my mind than a light beam pierced the gloom. I dropped flat, pressing my lips together tight when I banged my knee. Ignoring the pain, I crab-walked across the stone—beating it to the other side of the island.

I couldn't stop there, out in the open. If I could just make it to the kitchen, she wouldn't see me from the living room.

"Fuck's sake, this place is falling apart."

I heard movement in the dark, then the front door opening and closing. I could've cried.

Everleigh was going out to check the breaker. That was the gift I needed to get my ass off the floor. I turned on my flashlight, weaved through the kitchen, and walked up to the first door on the right side.

My foot came down on something soft. A bunch of sparkly tulle.

I swept my light over the space, revealing a mass of strewn clothes, a messy bed, textbooks, pictures of a handsome man and young Everleigh, and a laptop.

Jackpot.

Laid out casually on the bed, amid two pairs of tights and a random black dress, was a rose-gold laptop covered in stickers.

I dove for it, tearing it open. *Please, don't need a password. Please, don't need a password. Please, don't—*

The laptop booted up to the home screen. I was in.

You're a cruel, raggedy bitch sometimes, Fate, but then there are nights like tonight when I love you.

"Okay," I said softly. "You pretty much confirmed that you have a way to see the real identities of the club members. I promised I'd bring it all crashing down on your pretty little head. I keep my word."

The lights returned. Everleigh flipped the breaker. She'd be back soon.

I opened the browser and navigated to the history. I didn't have to remember that long string of nonsense that was the club's web address. If Everleigh didn't password-protect her laptop, she didn't delete the history either.

It has to be here somewhere.

I scrolled through the day's history. Then the week's. Then the weeks' before.

"Come on," I gritted. "Where is it!"

Creak.

I slammed the laptop shut and rolled, dropping flat on the carpet. Hallway light spilled into the room, trailing Everleigh inside.

My lungs crawled up into my throat, strangling any chance of making a sound. Of breathing.

I scuttled under the bed, clutching my chest. My heart thundered so loud there was no way she wouldn't hear it.

My eyes followed her bare feet's path. Slowly, they padded around the bed—coming nearer, nearer, closer, closer. They stopped right next to my head.

If it comes down to a fight, I'm ready. Everleigh doesn't know I've got Cato for backup. This won't go down the way she wants.

Everleigh turned and walked out.

I held still, not moving in case it was some kind of trick.

A minute passed.

Two minutes.

Three.

Grabbing a weapon and coming back to attack me wouldn't take that long. I was safe. She didn't see me.

I scooted out from under the bed and reached for the—

My hand fell on downy sheets. The laptop was gone.

I dropped my head on the covers and screamed. I was wrong. Fate was still a fucking bitch.

Shoving away, I marched out the door. I'd had enough of the bullshit. I was trying to get in and get out with the laptop so that Everleigh didn't have a chance to defend herself or even know she was in danger before the fire started.

But that was just me being nice. It worked just as well for me to kick her ass, take the laptop, and leave her out cold on the ground while the fire raged around her. The same end she planned for me.

I stormed through the hall, not bothering to duck down or hug the wall. Let her see me coming and know all her planning, scheming, tricks, and plots were for nothing.

A hand snatched my wrist. I didn't have a chance to think about screaming before I was pulled into the dark.

Cato spun me around and pressed me against the door. "Luna."

I never heard such urgency in his voice.

"Look."

"Look at what?" I asked. "What's wrong?"

I took out my phone and tapped the flashlight again. Lifting it overhead, my eyes bugged.

Right then, I understood the real reason Everleigh kept this place so secret, she refused to let her best friends know about it.

We were inside the mind of Everleigh Starling.

Photos, scribbles, newspaper clippings, article printouts, with blue string connecting it all even from across the room.

I ducked the string, getting closer to the far wall. Of course it drew my attention. Smack-dab in the middle of all the crap she pasted to the wall was a picture of a young Alistair. Below him were pictures of me, my mom, and Winter. I squinted, reading the information she put under our names.

"Fucking hell," I breathed. "She's even got the full names and birthdays of my old friends from Catholic school. There's stalking and then there's this."

"Over here."

I went to Cato, drawn to where he pointed. I scanned the wall up and down, trying to make sense of what he wanted me to see. It was a mess of interwoven string that made it hard to read.

"But this looks like... Oh my gosh." My phone slipped through my fingers. "I need to speak to Saylor. Now."

***

I tumbled out of the car, running to the guard booth. My good friend, Frank, raised a brow at my banging on the glass.

"Can I help you, miss?"

"Frank, let me in. I have to speak to Saylor."

He blinked lazily. "I'm afraid that won't be possible."

"Look, I know it's late, but it's an emergency. Raise the gate."

"Miss, I cannot let you onto the grounds. You're no longer on the approved-guests list." I blew back. What? I was removed that fast?

"Okay, fine." I rebounded fast. "Then, wake her ass up and tell her I need to speak to her. Trust me, she needs to hear this."

"I'm afraid not. The Burkhardts do not allow strangers to disturb their sleep with demands for entry any more than they allow them to wander about their property."

"Stranger?" I gaped at him like he was insane. "I'm not a stranger. I'm Alistair Burkhardt's daughter."

Frank looked me dead in my face. "Who?"

He snapped the glass partition shut, returning to his work. I was dismissed.

I flicked from him to the fifteen-foot-tall gate. How high could I scale that thing before he jumped into action and wrestled me down? How guilty would I feel when my boyfriends killed him for trying?

Stifling a groan, I ran back to the car. Wilder, Rafael, Cato, and Lucien gave me matching "what happened?" looks.

"He won't let me in. Alistair must've left, and the minute he did, his family went back to pretending he didn't exist." I plopped in the back seat, grabbing my head.

Why did I chase him away? Why did I think I could do all this without him? Standing in that creepy room, I saw how in over my head I truly was.

"What do we do? I need to talk to Saylor, but I can't even be in the same room with her without the chick trying to kill me."

Rafael laced his fingers through mine. "Let's go back to the beach house for now. You're not getting in that mansion unless a Burkhardt wants you in there. In the morning, swing by Katie's and have her call Saylor for you. Maybe you can get her to stay on the phone long enough to listen."

I blew out a breath. "That's the only option right now. When will I learn to stop underestimating Everleigh Starling?"

"You learned that tonight," Wilder said. "But she won't learn to stop underestimating you until it's too late."

Wilder started the car and drove away from Saylor's house. I watched it fade in the distance, frustration welling up and having nowhere to go. My showing back up alive started a countdown, and we were running out of time.

An alert on my phone snagged my attention. I got an email.

"Look at that. It's after midnight."

So you decided to do this the hard way. I'm not even mad. It's a particularly shitty person who steals from their own father. I get why you left me standing tonight. But you don't get what a big mistake you've made.

Looks like we're going with plan B, which is cool with me. I'm getting that laptop either way.

P.S. Tell my little bro not to resist. Big guy like him makes people nervous.

Frowning, I repeated that last part to Wilder. "Makes people nervous? What is he talking about?"

Wilder flipped a U-turn, sending us all flying.

"Whoa!"

"What the hell, man!"

"The cops," Wilder bellowed. "The cops know we're at the professor's place. They're either waiting for us, or they're coming."

"Fuck!" Rafael punched the back of his seat. "Haven't met the asshole yet, but I already don't like your brother."

"What do we do?" I cried.

"We can't go back there," Wilder said. "We need somewhere to hide. Lie low until— Until I can figure something out!"

"Where?" Lucien put in. "We wouldn't have been staying with the Wilson brothers if we had anywhere else to go?"

"We have somewhere to go." Wilder white-knuckled the steering wheel. "We're going to my place."

***

Wilder turned off the side street and parked in the drive of a cute, black-painted bungalow. I had a vague idea of where we were.

A couple miles east, and we wouldn't be far from Jack's beach house, where I hid away after losing my sister. Suddenly it made sense that Wilder and I accidentally crossed paths months before we actually met. My love was always nearby.

"Go in," Wilder said. "Take any room you want except the one that's mine. It should be obvious."

Wilder tossed me the keys and we went in, leaving him behind in the car. His brother just framed him for terrorism. He was allowed a minute alone to think.

"Wilder had a whole house that he didn't tell us about." Rafael stepped over the threshold, looking around. "Why am I not surprised?"

I stepped farther in and found a hallway light. Flicking it on, I gave the living room a once-over. It was a rather modest space. Made sense since Wilder didn't live here full-time.

All the living room had to say for itself was one couch, one coffee table, and a television mounted on the wall. Not a lick of decoration graced the beige walls.

I continued on, passing through the dining room—with no dining table. The kitchen—with nothing in the fridge other than a half-empty ketchup bottle. The den that had nothing in it at all.

One after the other, I stuck my head in the rooms. All were pretty modest. Beds, nightstand, dresser.

But which one is—

I stuck my head inside the last room. *Found it.*

Wilder had a distinct decorating style. Computers on top of computers next to computers everywhere I looked. And in the middle of it all, a full-size bed beneath a Faraday cage.

Arms snaked around my waist, drawing me back into warmth and comfort.

"What happened with Everleigh's laptop?"

I shook my head. "No good. She doesn't use that laptop to access the club site. She could have another one. She could use her computer at her parents' house. I have no way of knowing." I screamed in frustration. "Finding the cabin was supposed to solve our problems. Instead, things are worse than ever. How did this happen?"

"We'll make Saylor listen," Wilder said. "Don't worry. We'll stop what's coming."

I dropped my head back, trying to release some of the tension in my body. "We? There can't be a we right now, Wilder. If the cops are officially hunting you down, you can't go near campus. You can't go near anyone. I have to do this by myself." I slumped in his hold. "I let Everleigh and Wolf drive off everyone who could help me fight against them, and I didn't even see it."

"Not everyone." Gently, he tipped my chin and kissed me. "We're not letting you fight this by yourself. Fuck warrants and *most wanted* lists. We're doing this together—even if I have to do it from the shadows. But," he continued, "we're not all in the shadows. Wilson was smart to move out when he did. No one can tie him to my weapons, and they wouldn't dare to.

"Everleigh can't come at you straight as long as you're his fiancée. She doesn't want his family as an enemy."

"Doesn't she?" I thought about what I heard her say in the kitchen... and what I saw on that wall. "She hates her parents, Wilder. If the Wilsons strike her folks from the Royal line, she'll throw a party. Only Saylor can help me now, and I just got through ruining the bitch's life."

"Yeah, that didn't help."

"Wilder!"

He laughed. It amazed me he could do that, considering everything that'd happened to us. "But this might help." Wilder bypassed me and went into the room. "I had another reason for revealing my safe house and bringing you guys here. In the car, Rafael suggested going to Katie and letting her call Saylor for you."

Wilder pulled out a desk drawer, riffled inside, then tossed me what he found. "I installed a spoofing program on that one. It'll let you mask the real number and it'll show up as Katie's on Saylor's phone."

"What? And you were just sitting on this bad boy?" I hurriedly typed in the numbers. "Why didn't you mention this before my freak-out?"

"You've still got to get her to listen."

"Oh, yeah. That part."

Taking a breath, I let it out slow as the phone rang, and rang, and rang. I ended the call and tried again.

Saylor answered on the fourth try.

"What is going on, Katie?" she half snapped, half growled. "It's one in the morning. If you finally called to apologize, do it when the sun's up!"

Apologize? Saylor wanted Katie to apologize for what? Not punching you in the face when she read the horrible things Saylor and the other girls said about her behind her back?

Saylor was such a privileged, entitled monster she actually expected people to apologize to her when she did wrong.

I gritted my teeth, penning in the barrage of insults that immediately sprang to my lips.

"Katie, hello?"

"It's not Katie," I got out. "It's Luna. You need to listen to me, Saylor. It's life or—"

Click.

I called her back again and again, leaving a voice mail each time. On the eighth try, the call connected.

"What! Why the hell are you calling me, Sinclair? We have nothing to talk about."

"We do have something to talk about, and it's important."

"No, we don't. You're not my cousin. I don't care what anyone says. So what, your whoring maid of a mother slept with my uncle a million years ago. I bet she was sleeping with every ass that sat on the toilets she scrubbed. She didn't know which one was Daddy, so she chose the richest one.

"Now you're following her gameplay. Fucking every dick you get your hands on, but when you get knocked up, you'll swear on your life that the kid is Victor's. The whore doesn't fall far from the brothel."

I expected this level of viciousness. Saylor's been saving up to let me have it since our fathers got in the way of her revenge.

"Are you finished?" I asked. "I couldn't give a shit if you believe I'm your cousin. The only thing you need to believe is that I wouldn't call you if I had any other option. This is life or death, Saylor, and you need to listen to me."

"I don't have to do shit, especially if it's your life or death. Drop dead, bitch." Her voice got lower as it did when you pulled the phone away from your ear. She was about to hang up. "The sooner, the better. You'll get to join your pathetic sister in hell."

I thought fast. "That's rich coming from you. You call my sister pathetic, but she didn't run and hide when you guys turned on her. You had one bad day, Saylor, and the first thing you did was hide under the covers until they were slick from your greasy, unwashed hair."

"One bad day? One bad day!" Seemed she forgot about hanging up. "You think you gave me one bad day? You ruined my life, Sinclair! I've been getting hate from everyone. Half the servants quit. Mom and Grandpa won't talk to me. And Daddy is talking about transferring me to a school overseas. My own father wants to send me away! He says it's to give me a fresh start, but I know he just wants to save his political career before this scandal ruins his chances. That's what you did to me!"

I rolled my eyes. "All I did was share the texts. You wrote them. You said and did those awful things. You refuse to take responsibility? Fine. Sit in your room and cry like a little bitch while all your haters grow bolder, laughing about how a few hate texts and the silent treatment pushed Saylor Burkhardt off the throne."

A deep, cutting silence echoed from the other end.

"I was ready for those texts to end the bowing and scraping and make people see you for who you really are. But I had no idea I'd be the one to end your reign and run you out of the university— No, out of Regalia." I let my smirk color my tone. "And with you gone, the Royals will need a new queen. Good thing there's another Burkhardt to take your place."

Her voice was a low, dangerous hiss. "What the fuck did you say?"

"Have fun watching your fifth binge of *The Office*. Maybe I'll visit you in your new French school, cuz."

I hung up, breathing hard. Wilder's expression spoke volumes.

"Didn't quite get to the 'life or death' part, Sinclair."

"No, I took a gamble," I replied, giving the phone back with a hand that shook. "I hope it pays off."

Chapter Six

I sat on the fountain rim, sipping a vanilla mocha latte and watching Saylor's butler open the town car's door. Saylor climbed out, her nose so high in the air birds were in danger of flying up there.

She was night and day from the greasy, stain-covered mess that chased me through the hall with a knife. Gone were the sweats and tank. Saylor wore a satin, forest-green dress covered in cherry blossom branches and buds. Matching green pumps with pink flowers graced her feet, lifting her an inch higher. Her makeup was impeccable. Her hair was washed and combed till it showed.

The queen had come to protect her throne.

I shot up, beating it across the lawn. Saylor's none-of-this-bothers-me stroll was cut short when she found me in her face. "Ugh, get away from me, Sinclair." She shoved me. "If you fuck with my life one more time, I don't care what the rules say. I'll bury you."

"Following the rules, huh? Guess that means you admit we're cousins."

She got a frozen, frowny look on her face, realizing what she admitted. "No. We're not related. Get away from me."

I kept in step with her increasing pace. I didn't care what she said or what I had to do. Saylor was going to listen to me.

"I'm not going anywhere until you stop running your mouth for half a second," I snapped. I wanted her to listen. I didn't want to be nice to her. "If I had any other option, I wouldn't be doing this, but you need to know. Everleigh is not your friend."

"Of course she's not my friend. No one is, thanks to you!" Saylor shoved me again.

I tripped over my feet, nearly going down. That sudden stumble was enough to let her put eight feet between us. I jogged to catch up.

"That's not what I meant. Everleigh wasn't your friend *before* I sold your texts. She's been playing you all this time, Saylor." I was huffing and puffing, running after her. How long had it been since I worked out with Lucien? "The only reason she's put up with you all this time is because she hoped you'd get her closer to Alistair. Everleigh hates him. She's plotted to kill him for years."

"What?" she shrieked. "My gosh, you are insane. Every time you open your mouth, bullshit comes out."

"It's not bullshit! Everything that happened with Winter was because of Everleigh. She orchestrated the whole thing because she found out we're Alistair's daughters, and she wanted to drag him out into the open. Torturing Winter didn't work. Trying to kill me didn't get her what she wanted. The next step... is you."

I grabbed her shoulder, spinning her to face me. "I've never made any secret of how much I despise you, so the fact that I'm here warning you now should tell you something!"

She frowned, brows drawing together.

"Everleigh is determined to get revenge for her father any way she can. She'll hurt whoever gets in her way. She'll keep knocking down the people Alistair cares about until she finally gets to him. This doesn't end unless *we* end it, Saylor. You and me." I forced out the last word. "Together."

She glared at me through slitted lids, but she was listening.

"So?" I asked. "What do you say?"

Saylor punched me dead in the face.

I snapped back, knocked off my feet. I dropped flat on my back—my head bouncing off the earth.

"I'm getting a restraining order, you crazy bitch. Don't ever come near me again."

Pushing up, I swiped the blood from my weeping lip. I didn't try going after her. I knew what was coming. I had a feeling that in the end, Saylor would come to me.

I got up and made for the café. Victor promised to meet me there after rugby practice.

He waved me over when I walked in. My man already had my favorite foods laid out on the table, waiting for me.

"Hey." I leaned in for a kiss and plucked the bacon from his fingertips while I was at it.

"How did it go with Saylor?"

I just shook my head.

"I'm not surprised she didn't listen to you. She and Everleigh have been friends since diapers. She won't believe it... until the knife is in her back." Victor gave up on eating and shoved the rest of the bacon away. "I'm saying that, but she can't really do this, can she? No one in the decades we've lived in Regalia has pulled off what she's planning to do, and believe me, they tried."

"I've seen her plans," I said, teeth gritted. "It'll work, Victor. It'll work all too well."

I grabbed his hands, gripping too tight by his raised brows. "Did— Did anything happen last night? We didn't come back because I got a cryptic message from Wilder's brother that made him think a SWAT team was waiting for us back at the beach house."

I breathed a little easier when Victor shook his head no.

"Nah. Last night was quiet. No one busted in the door or anything," he replied. "But if they were watching the place, they wouldn't have. None of the guys they wanted to arrest were there."

Fear filled my bones again. Of course Victor was right. Why would they bust in and give themselves away until they knew for sure the *terrorists* were inside and clueless?

"Although that's weird, isn't it?"

I pulled out of my thoughts. "Huh? What's weird?"

Victor focused on something over my shoulder. "It's weird that his brother sent you that message," he said somewhat distractedly. "You figured it out and got ahead of the cops. Why say anything at all if he wants to fuck with his brother? He could've just hid out in the woods and filmed the cops hauling his ass to the squad car."

My lips parted, but nothing came out. Why didn't I notice that? It was because of that p.s. that we didn't walk into an ambush. "Now that I think about it, why did he crawl out of his cyberhole and risk himself by taking over the dean's office? He said he wanted to make a deal with me over the laptop, but he could've done that with another mocking email.

"I can tell he wasn't lying when he said he wanted nothing to do with Everleigh, but it's almost like—"

"Luna, look."

I followed his line of sight, twisting around. Saylor strolled into the café—nose up higher in the air if that was possible. It was obvious she was putting on a you-can't-break-me front, but the fact that she was in the café at all proved she'd been knocked down.

Saylor never came into the café. She always had one of her minions fetch her food and bring it to her at the music hall. The queen didn't dare mix with the peasants.

She's mixing today.

She grabbed a tray and stepped up to the line. A hush slowly fell over the café. Saylor didn't need to draw attention to herself. She was getting it without any help.

"You've got to be kidding me," someone said loudly. "How dare you show your face in here, Burkhardt! After what you did to my brother, you don't belong on campus unless you're getting your transfer papers."

Saylor didn't so much as twitch. She grabbed a raspberry scone off the pile and continued to the drinks station.

"Hey! I'm talking to you, bitch!"

Without a lick of rush, Saylor poured herself some coffee, sweetened it with creamer, took a sip, dabbed her mouth with a napkin, went back to grab a knife, then—and only then—did she face the staring crowd.

"I'm happy you're all here."

I exchanged looks with Victor. Why was she talking like we were all sitting here at her invitation?

"Let me make something clear," Saylor began. "You've been fooled. Those texts were not mine. They were faked by a sad, pathetic Dreg who saw a chance to take me down and make some money while she's at it."

Saylor pinned me with a glare. "I've got to hand it to her. It was a good plan. Make a small fortune passing off her fiction as my private texts, then before my lawyers could come after her, she had her Rogue boyfriend infect every copy with a virus that'll crater a hard drive. Evidence gone, money in her pocket, a Burkhardt disgraced."

Irritation strangled my throat. I had to hand it to *her*. She expertly turned everything around and used my father's takedown and computer virus to her advantage.

"I don't blame you all for falling for it, but the disrespect stops now."

Alice pushed out from the pack.

"Anyone who dares to use that bullshit you wasted your money on against me will—"

Alice smacked her tray up, exploding the hot coffee in her face.

Saylor's scream rang through the café.

"Fuck, you never shut up," Alice remarked. "Do you really think anyone is buying your crap? The Dreg made it all up? How could she have done that when she wasn't even in Regalia during half the shit you pulled? I mysteriously fell sick during the Model U.N. trip and you had to take my place. Luna just 'made up' all the texts where you were laughing about spiking my iced tea? How did she even know I drank iced tea that day?"

I couldn't help inclining my head. Alice made a fabulous point.

"What the fuck are you doing?!" Saylor screeched.

I hissed at the angry red burn blotches on her forehead and cheeks.

"We're telling you how it is from now on," said a voice from the other side of the room. I followed it to Iris. "The Royals are done doing what you say. The queen has been dethroned."

Saylor was still puffing and screaming. "You— You can't do this to me! That was the biggest mistake you've ever made. You're out—"

"Out of what?"

I stiffened. Slowly, achingly, my head turned to the door.

Everleigh smiled at her oldest friend in the world. Flanking her were Piper and Gabriella.

"You weren't going to say they're out of the Royal line, were you? Surely you know you don't have the power to do that anymore. Ahhh." Everleigh mock-pouted. "You didn't know. It's cute how deluded you are."

"Everleigh?" Saylor couldn't have looked more confused if she truly was deluded.

"Looks like you need someone to spell it out for you," Everleigh went on. "So, here it is. You're the one who's out of the Royal line, Burkhardt. The next generation is taking over, and they want nothing to do with you. They're ending their business contracts with you. They're moving off the overpriced land you own. And they're definitely not voting for your fake-ass daddy. They're dissolving all their ties with you"—she smiled nastily—"and giving them to me."

"But— But— That's not how it works," she cried. "Who the hell cares what they do a hundred years from now when they take over their companies. All that matters is what I can do today. One call to my dad and—"

"He won't do shit," Gabriella sliced in. "Your power was that you could take out any one of us whenever you wanted. But you never had the power to take out all of us. Grandpa and Daddy Burkhardt need us just as much as we used to need them. More importantly, they need the second and third rungs to support any removals from the Royal line. And you're not getting it."

"The only power you really had over us is fear," Piper said, crossing to the drinks station. "We're not afraid of you anymore."

The lemonade she poured went straight in Saylor's face.

It was a mass exodus, but not a quiet one. The entire café emptied out and dumped their tray on Saylor like she was the new screaming trash bin.

"Bitch!"

"Drop dead, Burkhardt."

"I'll get you back for what you did."

"Get the fuck out of our school," Gabriella said.

"Or we'll do worse," Everleigh finished.

"Piper? Gabriella! Everleigh," Saylor cried at their backs. "Why are you doing this? We're friends. We're best friends!"

The three of them didn't look back. They walked out, leaving the formerly reigning queen of Regalia in a mountain of food trash on the floor.

In the span of twenty minutes, only me, Victor, Saylor, and a handful of incredulous Dregs remained in the café. I walked up to her, not taking any pleasure at the horrific mess that was the great Saylor Burkhardt.

Okay, I was taking a little pleasure, but I didn't let it show on my face.

"Here." I held out my hand.

She looked at it like she didn't know what I wanted her to do with it. It was hard to tell under the smears of jelly and syrup running down her face, though I swore the shining wetness was tears.

"I assume you're ready to listen now."

"Listen? Listen to what?" She tried to snap, but it came out more like a sob. "What the fuck is going on—? Are you behind this!"

"No, Saylor," I replied patiently. "This was all Everleigh. If you give me ten minutes, I'll explain why."

Saylor looked down at the mountain of food and trash, then she glanced at the door where her friends disappeared. A million emotions flashed across her face until she settled on one I knew well.

Pissed.

"Fine." She slapped her palm against mine. "I'll listen."

***

Saylor said that, but it was nearly eight o'clock that night before she deigned to sit down with me.

First, she had to go home, shower, and change, and no, I was not allowed to go with her and step foot inside Burkhardt Manor.

Then, I had to wait hours for her to call and tell me she was ready to talk, but we had to meet in a neutral location with a witness. I got the sense she was still trying to find a way to make everything that happened to her that day my fault. Just in case, she wasn't about to walk into another ambush.

I agreed and told her we should meet at Katie's house. After that, I called Katie, and she said we had to wait until Dean left because they were doing things she unfortunately described in great detail.

Finally, after all that, we were sitting down to plates of stuffed, double-smoked salmon and butternut squash gnocchi in the pool house.

Katie had the full setup with bedroom, living room, dining area, and an entire bedroom she turned into a closet. We sat at the dining table, trading tense looks while one of Katie's staff served us.

"Thank you, Giselle," I said. "One look and I know it's yum. Tell Chef to get ready for my incoming proposal."

Giselle chuckled. "She is always happy to hear her food is enjoyed. Have a wonderful evening, ladies."

I speared a piece of gnocchi.

"No." Saylor snatched my fork and my plate while she was at it. "Don't come in my friend's place, sleaze on her staff, and act like Chef likes or even knows who you are. This isn't your turf, and Katie isn't your friend. She's mine. You're just a housekeeper's worthless cunt droppings."

I hummed, unfazed. "And you're a garbage disposal. Feel free to save me time and dump my food directly on your head."

"You—!"

"Ladies," Katie sliced in. "Enough. That's not what you came here for. Luna, tell her everything. She needs to know."

I did. Starting from the very beginning with two boys that dreamed of becoming Rogues and ending with what I found in her cabin.

"I thought it was just about getting revenge on my father, but Everleigh wants more. She wants everything her father died for," I said. "The T.O.D. Club was about more than using an army of faceless minions to do her dirty work. The strongest tie is a secret. Everleigh planned to use all the secrets T.O.D. Club collected to make the Royals ditch you and obey her. With the way everyone feels about you right now, they jumped on that all too quick."

Saylor said nothing, her expression giving little away. She hadn't spoken through my entire tale.

"I don't need to tell you the power she has now. In this fight, she's got every weapon on her side. Even Victor," I admitted, "can't help me. With Everleigh now at the top of the Royal line, she won't enforce anything he says or does to punish people who go against me.

"It was a brilliant move. I don't know how to counter it, but we have to think of something. She can't win. I don't care what I have to do. Everleigh will pay for what she did to my sister."

Saylor was quiet for a beat. I couldn't begin to guess what she was thinking. "So, if I'm understanding this correctly, I'm getting roped into the drama of some discarded branch of the family tree. Now you want my help to win a fight that you can't."

"If you want to put it like that," I forced through clenched teeth. "Yes."

She scoffed. "Obviously, Everleigh, Piper, and Gabriella won't get away with what they pulled today. Regalia is my town. The Burkhardts own it. As far as I'm concerned, you all are guests who forgot how to act in someone else's house. I'm more than willing to teach a little respect."

I resisted an eye roll. She was saying all the right things. Better not to provoke her.

"But."

"But what?" I said.

"But I'm not doing it for you." Saylor scooped my food on her plate and handed me back nothing. The petty chick even took my apple cider. "I'm doing it because what Everleigh did can't stand. But if you think I'm putting myself in this Rogue-on-Rogue revenge bullshit, then you really are insane."

"You can't take back the Royal line from Everleigh without getting involved in this Rogue revenge bullshit. Everleigh is doing all this in the name of revenge, and she will *kill* in the name of revenge. If you come at her with this 'I own everything, obey me because I demand it' crap, she'll just take out a seven-figure T.O.D. hit on you."

"Oh, please." Saylor speared a piece of gnocchi. "Everleigh isn't going to have me killed. And even if she was that crazy, no one in the stupid little dare club would do it. Messing with some Dreg isn't on the same level as killing a Royal. As killing *the* Royal."

I bit my lip, penning in a hundred harsh responses. One of them being that a club member did kill a Royal because I told them to. Instead, I took out the note I still carried with me to that day and held it out.

Brows crawling together, she took my sister's note and read. I could tell when she got to the part about Owen... then Giovanni... Levi... Wesley... and finally, Ashton. It was one thing hearing about it from me. It was another reading of my sister's torture in her own words.

Saylor refolded the note and set it down.

"I'm warning you, Saylor," I rasped. "If you say anything heartless about my sister's last words, you'll need more than a restraining order. Because I won't stop trying to kill you until the job is done."

She just looked at me. "I don't have anything heartless to say. Everleigh had those guys do all of that to her, including Ashton, just to force Alistair out into the open?"

"Yes."

She nodded slow. "I see. That's... excessive."

It wasn't an apology. It wouldn't make up for all the terrible things she said and did to Winter. But it was the first she acknowledged that anything wrong had happened. Maybe that could be the start of me hating her a fraction less.

Saylor cleared her throat, looking away. "Obviously, this can't stand. I let the Truth or Dare Club survive because I thought it was just a bunch of idiots messing around, pranking Dregs, and throwing lattes. But a rape-for-hire club? No," she said simply. "What's your plan, Sinclair? If it's not completely stupid, I'll consider going along with it."

They both looked at me. This was my cue.

I opened my mouth and said, "I don't know."

"Excuse me?" Kate and Saylor replied.

"I don't know. I had a plan until I snuck into her cabin and saw that room." I sank in my seat, staring up at the ceiling. "I don't know why I thought Everleigh's evil started with Winter and ended with me. Alistair said there'd been a few false flags in Regalia that may have been someone's attempt to lure him out of hiding, but I didn't think about what that meant.

"Winter wasn't the first person Everleigh tortured to get them to raise the flag. She did it herself and no one responded. Then, she figured a Rogue had to do it, so she did some incredibly terrible things to find one, then even more terrible things to force them to fly the flag. She went through a couple people until she learned about my mom and Alistair and their kids.

"I wanted to deal with Everleigh while we were alone in her cabin." I let them imagine what I meant by that. "But I couldn't after I saw that. The club members who took those dares are walking around innocent and unpunished. The people who suffered don't know why or who was truly behind this. Win—" I swallowed hard. "Winter wasn't the first sexual assault."

Katie covered her mouth, eyes huge. She clearly didn't think she could still be surprised by the depths of Everleigh's depravity.

"If all that evidence goes up in smoke, they'll never get justice. I can't take that away from someone in the name of getting mine. We have to figure out a way to break Everleigh's control over the Royal line, destroy the T.O.D., make sure no one can ever revive that disgusting dare club, and get justice for all the people Everleigh has and will hurt to avenge her father.

"If I knew how to do that all on my own, or even with my guys—I wouldn't be here."

"Of course you can't do it by yourself. Who knows why you even thought you could? You're a Dreg."

"Saylor," Katie hissed.

She blinked. "No, I'm not being mean."

"Really?" I shot back. "Because everything you said was mean."

"What I meant is that you didn't grow up here playing the game that Everleigh perfected before preschool." Saylor drained my glass. "Why do you think no one knew what she was doing before she wanted them to know? She's covered herself in so many layers of protection when the shit blows up, it won't even hit her windshield. The only way you're going to hold her responsible for any of it is if she confesses. Do I have to tell you that she won't?"

It cursed me not to argue with her. Rafael, Cato, Wilder, Lucien, and Victor all said the same thing. Without a confession, we had nothing.

"Then we get her to confess. Put the pressure on her until she cracks."

"How?" Katie asked. She typed something in her phone, giving us both half her attention. "We can't come at her the same way. Piper and Gabriella joined the club, but Saylor and I didn't. From what happened this morning, they're on her side, so they won't put in any dares for us. We can't threaten her with removing her from the Royal line. We can't turn the Royals against her. We've got nothing."

"We know where the cabin is," I put in. "What about an anonymous tip to the captain...?" I trailed off as they shook their heads.

"Luna, she didn't do anything when you went into her office and told her that Everleigh tried to kill you," Katie said. "What do you think she'll do when a pile of evidence lands in her lap? She'll destroy it. Crazy as it is, we have a better chance of protecting that evidence if the cops *don't* find it."

I groaned, flinging back. "I know, I know. You're right. It has to be a confession, and it has to be public so that no one can deny, dismiss, or erase it. Okay, let me think."

"No, I'll do the thinking," Saylor said. "You've strained your brain cells enough."

Again, what did this girl think mean was?

The three of us fell quiet. The only interruption was Giselle bringing me another plate of food. That's who Katie texted.

"Secrets."

Katie and Saylor broke out of their musing. "What?"

"Secrets," I repeated. "That's the best leverage. Better than threats or money. We couldn't dig up any on Everleigh, but you've known her your whole lives. There's got to be something you know about her that she'll do anything to protect."

Katie shook her head. "We're talking about her going to prison for the rest of her life."

Actually, we're talking about her death.

"We know a few embarrassing secrets, but nothing that she'd choose prison to protect. I mean, it's obvious she was smart enough to hide any secrets like that. We didn't know anything about the Book Lady."

"You know the truth about her parents and how they treat her," I offered. "You knew about Everton. She told you about meeting him when he was in hiding. Maybe we could use all of that somehow."

Saylor worried her lip, making me stiffen. We shared the same nervous habit.

"She wouldn't care about us ruining her parents' image," Saylor said slowly. "Everyone has always known they were a bunch of toxic assholes from the constant cheating, backstabbing, and naming her Everleigh out of spite. But if she's doing all of this out of love for Everton, then that's her weak spot." She nodded to herself. "We shouldn't be trying to find out everything about Everleigh. We need to find out everything about her bio father."

"I told you everything Alistair told me, little Everleigh told you everything about her hero father, and the court transcripts told everything about his crimes," I said.

"Not everything," Katie said. "We know the crime that got him caught. We don't know the rest. As it is, Everton Starling is just a footnote in Regalia history. What he did—leaking the lawyer's strategy—that was bad, but of course, everyone blames the evil, abusive piece of shit that beat poor Davey Brennan to death.

"We need something that we can tie directly to Everton. Something so awful that it'd still be a scandal years after his death."

I picked up her trail. "Something so bad that associating with anyone named Starling would ruin a Royal's reputation. They'll cut ties with Everleigh all on their own."

"That's good," Saylor said. "That could work. But it only takes care of those traitorous bastards that tricked themselves into believing I can't still hurt them. It doesn't stop the T.O.D. Club."

"Ugh! I could stop the T.O.D. Club if I could figure out what she uses to log in," I cried. "Have you ever seen her with another laptop? Not a rose-gold one. Another one. Or could she be using the computer at her folks' place?"

"Nah," Katie said. "Definitely not at her folks' place. Her room is a museum. Everything there is just for show. How about this? I'll invite her, Gabby, and Piper over for the weekend. They'll bring their laptops because no one can go that long without one. I'll scope it out. See what I can find. If anything, I can get on Piper's or Gabriella's account and continue what you started," she said. "Sabotage from the inside out."

"That could work. Keep me updated," I said. "As for learning more about Everton, I need to talk to William Burkhardt."

Saylor cocked a brow. "Excuse me? Why would you need to talk to my grandfather? He had nothing to do with him."

"Alistair said he and Everton were best friends. They owned the town and acted like it. That means every time the cops picked the two of them up, William got the call to slide some bribe money their way and let them off the hook. Katie said we need to know the crimes they didn't charge him of, and William is the best person to tell us."

"Maybe," Saylor said grudgingly. "But he was a teenager. I assume he didn't start his life of crime with aiding and abetting child murder. Grandfather could only tell you about petty crimes."

"That's why I also want to ask him what he knows about the Rogues."

The expressions froze on their face.

"Alistair also told me that his father spent a fortune trying to hunt down the Rogues and end the organization for good. It didn't work, but I don't believe all his money, influence, and connections turned up nothing. If it didn't, it wouldn't be an open secret that Leon Dumont is on the Burkhardt payroll."

"You have no proof of that," Saylor snapped. "My father and grandfather would never get involved with a known criminal."

"Saylor, relax." I started eating my rapidly cooling food. "I'm not trying to catch anyone out. What I'm thinking is that Everton made a name for himself by selling his clients' information to the highest bidder—some of them Rogues. After my father punished him for it, he tried to have him killed—also by Rogues. One of them tried to kill us days after I was born.

"Whatever evidence your grandfather collected back then about known Rogues could help us now."

"Why even go to William?" Katie asked. "Sounds like Alistair's got all the info we need. Just ask him."

"I... I can't."

"Why not?"

"He's gone," Saylor dropped. "Blew out the door as quickly as he blew in."

"It's for the best," I said firmly. "Killing him is at the top of Everleigh's list. The last place he should be is in Regalia. Besides, I did ask him all this stuff and he refused to answer. He doesn't want me any deeper in Rogue business, and he definitely doesn't want to go to war with a nineteen-year-old girl.

"William is my best bet. Saylor, put me back on the list, so I can speak with him."

"No." She folded her arms. "I won't have you bringing him into this shit. I'm only here because I'm getting my town back, and you two are going to help me do it. But Grandpa? You're not pumping him for information you can use against him later. What kind of idiot would admit to having knowledge of criminals and criminal activity and keeping it to themselves for decades?"

"Why in the hell would I use it against him?" I flashed her a beaming smile. "Burkhardts don't go after Burkhardts."

"You're not a Burkhardt."

"I am a Burkhardt. That's why Grandpa William will admit he has knowledge of criminals and criminal activity. Especially when I play up the long-lost granddaughter bit. He owes me. He owes Winter. And my tears and snot over how his secrets destroyed us will go a lot further with his guilt than yours, Saylor."

"Wow." Her tone was mild. "What a manipulative, diabolical troll you are."

"See? I am a Burkhardt."

She sniffed. "I'll think about it."

"Stop being difficult. William already said he wanted to see me. The sooner, the better. The longer we wait, the longer Everleigh has to engrave her butt cheeks into your throne."

Pushing back from the table, Saylor grabbed her stuff and flounced off. "I said I'll think about it. Keep your phone on and answer every time I call. I'll have further instructions for you soon."

I turned my deadpan expression on Katie. "I'm sure you're not asking why Piper and Gabriella jumped at the first chance to ditch her."

She cracked a smile. "What are you going to do if she doesn't let you in to see William?"

"I don't know, but I'm not giving up. We need to force a confession somehow. If I can't do it by digging up dirt on Everleigh, then I'll come at it through the only person she cares about."

***

I left Katie's house brimming with determination and certainty that I was closer to bringing Everleigh down.

Five days later, I was feeling none of those things.

"I can't believe this. Look at her laughing it up like the smug piece of shit she is."

Victor and I posted up beneath an oak tree, watching the Royals basking in their Royalness.

Gone were the days of them eating by the music hall. The day after Everleigh took over, she declared that the music hall was out and the quad was in. In the time it took them to force all the Dregs out, they laid out their blankets, brought their parasols, snuggled up with their squeezes, and claimed more space than needed for every meal and all the time in between.

The two of us stood on the perimeter next to the quad, watching Everleigh sun herself by the fountain with Piper and Gabriella by her side.

"Her ankle monitor's gone," I said, gazing at Gabriella's bare legs. "Everleigh must've made her charges go away somehow. Explains why Gabriella's on her side."

Everleigh flipped over and kissed Piper full on the mouth. There was nothing friendly about their tongue-tangling.

"Annnd that's how she got Piper." I blew out a breath, biting back my rage. "What are we supposed to do, Victor? She's got everyone wrapped around her finger through sex, blackmail, and bribery while Saylor is still refusing to let me near William. Cato, Rafael, Lucien, and Wilder are basically in hiding, and I'm no closer to taking down Everleigh or the Royal line."

"We could be," Victor mused. "We could burn down her secret cabin with Everleigh inside. She still doesn't know we found it."

I shivered. It was easy to forget that under his smiling all-American persona, Victor had a dark side that rivaled Cato. Whenever he reminded me, it was all I could do to keep my pants on.

"You know why we can't make that move yet. There's evidence in the cabin that we can't use yet. Katie was right that if I turned it over to the captain now, she'd make it disappear. But if it turns up *after* Everleigh confesses to being a psycho murderer, Captain Capaldi would have no reason to hide it. A few extra charges don't make a difference when you're already looking at life in prison."

He stroked my arm. "I know you want to give her other victims justice, but won't killing her do that? She won't be able to hurt them or anyone else ever again."

"She didn't do any of it herself," I said, staring at a monster in pretty wrapping. "She paid and threatened people to do her dirty work, then when she got her claws into the T.O.D. Club, she let the members handle the rest. Levi and those bastards were just as guilty as Everleigh for what they did to Winter. It's the same for the others she tortured. They all have to pay."

"And for that, we have to cut off the head of the queen so all the snakes spill out."

I grimaced. "Why is that description so gross, yet so perfect for her?"

"Is there any way we could get around Saylor to get to William Burkhardt? Could you try her dad?"

"I would, but their guards won't even call up to the house and tell them I'm at the gate. Frank plays dumb when I mention Alistair." I kissed my teeth. "The jerk laughed when I lost it and said I'd kick his ass if he didn't stop playing games with me. I didn't know he could make that sound."

Victor laughed too. "I have a feeling you won't have to resort to violence. Saylor will get her throne back, or she'll die trying. Eventually, she'll stop fighting you if it means beating Everleigh."

While we watched, Dean and Katie crossed the quad and plopped down next to Everleigh and her crew.

Katie threw a sleepover the weekend before like she promised, but only Piper and Gabriella showed up. Everleigh begged off saying she had two essays to write due Monday. She never got a chance to snoop on her computer and find what I couldn't.

Everleigh suddenly looked up and latched on to me. I didn't look away and neither did she.

"I bet it burns her up that you never joined the T.O.D. Club," I told Victor. "If Saylor's the queen, you're the heir to the throne. You'll always be a threat to her rule."

"Not me, babe. You."

I broke off to pull a face at him. "Me?"

"The only reason the throne is Saylor's... is because you didn't know it could be yours." I'd never seen him so serious. "Everything around you is rightfully yours, Luna. No one is loyal to a blackmailer, but they could be loyal to you. It's you who Everleigh's afraid of. That's why she can't come at you either. She has to make sure the next strike takes you down for good."

I literally never considered I could lead the Royal line until that moment. I immediately shook the thought away. "We don't know that for sure. Alistair said I'm a Burkhardt heiress too, but I don't know what I'm supposed to inherit. Could be five dollars."

"It's not five dollars. Mom arranged my marriage to you because she knows what we both don't. Not that she'll admit it," he gritted. "I've confronted her multiple times, but she swears up, down, and sideways that she didn't know you were a Burkhardt and that she only chose you because she knew we'd be perfect together. Then she sprinkles tears and guilt-tripping on top of her bullshit, acting all hurt by my accusations."

I smothered a laugh. "And I get called diabolical."

"You're not pissed at her?"

"I am, but..." I hooked my pinkie through his. "If it wasn't for her plotting, we'd never have gotten together. Knowing that takes the edge off my anger."

"We would've gotten together," he argued. "I was plowing my way through the freshman pussy either way. Once I'd gotten to you, I would've known I was meant to stick with yours for good."

I dropped his hand. "Go away."

Cackling, Victor grabbed me up and smooched my squealing lips. "Not a chance. You're stuck with me. Till forever does us part."

"Guess I have to accept my fate." I kissed him deeply. "Speaking of plowing pussy, should we find an empty classroom and practice for the wedding night?"

"That is happening for sure, but"—he flicked over my shoulder—"it looks like someone wants to talk to you."

I turned around. Sitting on the edge of her fountain—sipping a pink drink that appeared out of nowhere—Everleigh waved me over.

"What could she possibly want with me?"

"Only one way to find out. Want me to go with you?"

I nodded. "Yeah."

Together we crossed the quad, closing the distance between us and a smiling Everleigh. I returned her grin.

"Hey, murderer. What did you want to talk to me about? Could it be when you *shot me and left me to die in a burning building?*" I shouted, drawing the eye of everyone on the quad. "Or should we talk about the *Truth or Dare Club*? The stupid but dangerous club that you've been using to carry out your dirty work.

"You all know about the T.O.D. Club. She's been using the secrets the club collected against you all to turn you against Saylor and make you bow to her."

Everleigh wasn't smiling now.

"Psycho kiillller," I sang. "Murderous bi-bi-bitch. Yeah, she's a psycho killer. Sha-la-la, oooooh." I snapped my fingers. "Sorry, I'm no songwriter, but still pretty catchy, right?"

"Now I see why Saylor spent hours ranting about you," Everleigh forced through snarling lips. "You're a particular pain in the ass, Sinclair. You will tell any *lie* to get attention."

"You know all about things in your ass, Book Lady." I smiled sweetly. "Last I saw, you're super into anal, so you should be loving this."

She shot to her feet. "Careful, bitch. One more word and I'll—"

"Kill me?" I practically screamed. "You're threatening to kill me again! What is wrong with you? Why can't you let me and my family live in peace? What do you get out of torturing random Dregs?"

"Stop it!" Everleigh balled her fists and took a breath.

I took an inordinate amount of pleasure in getting to her.

"This isn't why I called you over here." She got in close, dropping her voice. "There was a boat in the marina and now it's gone. I don't know what you said and did to convince him to leave you behind, but it won't work. I got him here once. I'll make him come back again."

"You're not touching another member of my family, Starling. Your silly little plan is out in the open. No more cards to play. No more tricks. No more traps. It's over."

She smirked. "Oh, Luna. It's so far from over. There are still a few pesky little contracts to be broken with your stepfather's business."

My expression hardened.

"The Burkhardts still own his land, but I'll have everything else. Wonder if Daddy will come back and save his old whore and her new rich fuck toy when they're eating cold soup on an empty mansion floor.

"There's still his niece, who I haven't even begun to screw with yet," she said. "Saylor got her kicks from making everyone dangle on the edge of her strings. Let's see how cocky she is when she's expelled, arrested, and exposed. In a month, everyone will be saying, 'who's she again? Could've sworn I've seen that raggedy trash slut somewhere?'

"And then there's you," she hissed. "After what happened to the last one, I can't believe he left another daughter behind."

"What, Everleigh? What happened to the last one? Admit what you did." I threw my hands out. "You're clearly proud of it. Why keep lying and hiding? Everyone already knows the real you."

She drew back. "I have no idea what you're talking about," she breezed. "Anyway, I called you over here for a reason. I have a proposition for you. I've won, Sinclair. You just haven't seen it yet because you think the guys you're fucking can protect you, but they can't.

"Your Rogue freaks will be arrested the second they pop their heads out of the dirt, and that guy"—she flapped a hand at Victor—"has been neutered. It's bad enough for you, but I'll make it worse unless you get Alistair back here and make him face me."

"Huh, let me think about that— No," I blared. "Now here's a proposition for you. Go fuck yourself."

"Everleigh," Katie spoke up. "Let's leave it, yeah?"

"She's right, Everleigh." Piper popped up and kissed her on the cheek. "Don't waste any more of your time on this trash."

Everleigh held up a hand, silencing her. "I'll make this simple for you. Get Alistair back here, or your stepfather is out of the Royal line. I'll have you and your *fiancé* expelled. Everyone will find out Professor A is fucking a student. Yeah," she said, catching the shock on my face. "I know all about that."

"If you say a fucking word about my brother—!"

I swung out my arm, holding back Victor. "Are you done?"

"Not even close. I've got a hacker on my side too now. From what I hear, he's even better than yours." She winked. "Wilder loves threatening people with putting them on the sex offender registry? Wonder how your mom will like it? After I leave your folks with nothing, the poor old perv won't even get a job cleaning houses. Can't have a handsy housekeeper around the kids."

I blinked lazily. "Really, Starling? You think those bluffs are enough to get me to offer my father up to die? You really are dead inside."

"I'm not bluffing. All of that is just to start." The look in her eyes chilled me. "We haven't even gotten to what people could be dared to do."

I nodded slowly. "All right, I heard your proposal. Now hear mine. You back off, stay away from the people I care about, confess all your psycho-killer crimes... and I'll tell you where your sister is."

Her smirk twitched into a frown. "What? I don't have a sister."

"Don't you? You're telling me Daddy Everton never got around to telling you about that one-night whoopsie he conceived while on the run?"

Everleigh stilled. I couldn't be sure she was breathing.

"That's right," I continued. "You have a little sister. Cute kid too. Looks just like her daddy. The only other piece of him living in this—"

"You're lying." A dangerous ferality darkened her face. "You're a fucking liar."

"I'm not lying." I was lying through my shiny teeth. "Her name is Melanie. She's ten years old, and living a sweet picket-fence life in... Oh, where is it again?" A grin stretched my mouth. "I'm so forgetful when people are threatening my family. I can't remember anything until they confess, turn themselves in, and swear to stop.

"That's all you have to do to see your sister." I inclined my head. "Well, see her in twenty-five to life."

"You're not fooling me." Her laugh couldn't have been more forced. "I know you're full of shit."

"Everything I've said is true. I had a little chat with William Burkhardt." Katie's brows shot up over Everleigh's shoulder. "Back in the day, hunting down Rogues was his favorite pastime. After your dad went on the run, William was afraid Alistair's old troublemaking friend would run back here to Regalia. He had private investigators hunt him down, but they were always a step behind. On one of those steps, they found his daughter."

"No."

I shrugged. "Fine. Don't believe me."

"Of course I don't believe you. Even if I did, why would I confess to fake crimes for this imaginary sister?" She shrugged. "Haven't needed a sister for nineteen years. I'm cool to keep going without one."

"Too bad for her."

That nose she had high in the air came down an inch. "What's that supposed to mean?"

"It means if you come after my family, boyfriends, or fiancé." I looked her dead in the face. "I'll do to your sister everything that you did to mine."

A flicker of something lit in her eyes, then went out too fast for me to recognize. "Ridiculous. Even if she did exist, you wouldn't do that to a ten-year-old girl."

"Before this conversation, I wouldn't have. But you're putting everyone I love in danger so that you can kill my father," I barked, and not quietly. "If it's a choice between your family and mine, I choose mine. What's your choice, Starling?"

Her gaze darted around. I could tell her thoughts were flying a mile a minute. I was lying. I had to be lying. But... what if I wasn't?

"I'm not falling for this." Her voice was an octave higher than usual. They called that doubt. "You think I can't check up on your lies?"

"There's a lot of Melanies out there."

"But I know my dad." She took out her phone and waved it in my face. "I know everywhere he went those years he was hiding from trumped-up charges and your father. I'll find out in two seconds if he fathered some kid along the way."

I zeroed in on her cell. *Of course. Why in the hell didn't I think of this before?*

"—more proof that you're a liar, spewing whatever garbage pops in your head."

Everleigh is accessing the club through her cellphone.

"Better come clean now," she said, unlocking the screen. "Because if I have to call your bluff, it'll be even worse for—"

I snatched the phone and bolted.

"Hey! What the—? Give that back!"

I beat it across the quad, dragging a nonplussed Victor along for the ride.

"Uh, future wife? Want to explain why we're adding petty theft to the rap sheet?"

"Don't just sit on your asses. Stop her," Everleigh screeched. "Get my phone back."

No one moved. Everleigh was barking at a bunch of pampered Royals. They weren't playing linebackers for a cellphone she could replace with one swipe of her credit card.

"Whoever gets it back has their slate wiped clean."

I didn't know what that meant. I just know it worked.

I jumped—leaping over a grabbing hand that went for my ankles. Thunderous foot stomps pounded the ground, charging straight after me. I screamed went a figure came in from my right—a huge, bulky guy running too fast for anything but one hundred and ten pounds of me to slow him down.

Victor flashed out of the corner of my eye. He rammed the guy, dropping him flat and shaking the earth.

I'd never seen Victor in action on the rugby field. After that, I'd attend every game and the practices too. That was damn sexy.

I drew ahead, plowing down the path he was clearing for me. I had no idea where I was going. Half the school was on my back, and whatever building I tried to duck inside or behind, they'd see.

So let them see.

Veering left, I sprinted flat out across the lawn and up the steps. The executive administrator jumped out of her seat when I ran in.

"What the— Excuse me, miss— What are you all doing?" she shouted at my angry mob. "Stop running!"

I dove into the stairwell, running up and up and up. My lungs were liquid fire. I wheezed more than I breathed, but I didn't let go of the phone. No matter what happened, I would never let go of the phone.

"Give it up, Sinclair!" someone shouted. "We've all got our own shit to fight. I'm not lying down for yours."

A sharp grunt, then he was silent. I guessed Victor proved him wrong. He lay flat on his ass.

Almost there, almost—

I burst out onto the floor and didn't pause for a second. Ripping open the door, I skidded into the dean's office—sending the man's coffee cup flying.

"What on earth—? What is the meaning of this?!"

The five guys chasing me ground to a halt, colliding just inches from the threshold. The looks on their faces brought a smile to mine. Victor caught up and threw them back.

"Go on," he barked. "She just saved your asses because if you had laid a finger on her, I'd have broken every last one."

I relaxed as he forced them back. The dean was spouting some nonsense, but I took a minute to catch my breath.

"Excuse me, Dean," I gasped. "Didn't mean to burst in on you like this. There's just something I have to tell you and it couldn't wait."

The dean furiously dabbed the massive coffee stain on his white designer shirt. "What would that be?"

"Last year, you expelled Winter Sinclair for making a supposed false rape allegation."

The dean stilled in the middle of removing his tie.

I squeezed the phone tight. "Start praying for forgiveness now because the truth is coming out."

Chapter Seven

"Should we be doing this here?"

Victor and I huddled in the stairwell outside the dean's office. He chased all my pursuers off, and it didn't look like they were coming back.

The first thing I did when he returned was tell him I finally had Everleigh's access to the T.O.D. Club. He led me into the stairwell to search her history.

"We have to," he replied. "Everleigh knows what's on this phone better than anyone, and she wants it back now. These things have GPS. She knows we're in the administration building, and you can bet she's waiting for the moment we leave."

"You're right," I whispered, who knew why. No one could hear me. "We can't let her stop us now that we have it. We know that she can see who the members are because there's no way she assigned Wesley, Levi, Giovanni, and the other guys their tasks blind."

"She didn't." Victor's expression was grave. "I found it."

I nearly tripped rushing to his side to see. There it was. The website Wolf kicked me off of, but also not. This page was nothing like the one I was on a short time ago. That one was all screen names and anonymous dares.

This one laid it all bare.

"Rachel Price dares someone to hurt Professor Stein and make it look like an accident," I read. "The public dares go into the lottery. There's a list of all the potential names and— There we go. The dare just went to David Maypole. Can we see the private messages too?"

"Right here." Victor tapped the *Private Messages* tab on the screen.

A long, unending scrollable list appeared.

"Becca Savage sent a private message to Natalie Burgess in the amount of one thousand dollars," he read. "It's all here, Luna. Everyone in the club and all the terrible things they've been daring each other to do."

"How far back does it go? Do we have the dares she gave to those monsters who hurt Winter?"

"That was a year ago and..." Victor scrolled down and down. "This is just this week. We'd need time to go through it all."

"We can't stay here forever." I chewed my lip, thinking. This was it. This phone was Everleigh's leverage over the Royals. It was proof the T.O.D. Club was behind Winter's torture and who knew how many other crimes. In our hands was the key to exposing the club and putting things right for a lot of people. The next move we made had to be perfect.

"Everleigh wants to keep her good rep, but if she comes in here, screeching to the dean that we stole her property, we can't defend ourselves." I blew out a breath. "I know what we have to do."

I took out my phone and dialed a number that she refused to give me, so I had to get it from Katie.

"What?"

My brow twitched. I was already annoyed. "Good evening, Saylor. How are you this fine day?"

"I'm hanging up."

"Wait," I snapped. "Fuck's sake, you make it impossible to be nice to you."

"I was about to say the same thing to you, Tambourine."

"Tambourine?"

"Everyone gets a turn banging you."

I dropped the phone and counted to three. I didn't call to trade insults with her. I would not rise to her bait. Putting the phone back to my ear, I said, "Fuck you. The price for solving all of your problems just went up."

"What are you talking about?"

"Everleigh used her all-access, behind-the-scenes pass to the T.O.D. Club to make the Royals turn on you. That pass... is mine now."

Something crashed on her end. "Give it to me."

"Of course. What else would I do?" My smirk was wicked. "But like I said, there's a price."

"What do you want?"

"I'm on my way to the ancestral home right now. You'll put me back on the list and let me talk to William. I'm giving you the key to bringing the Royals back under your control. Now he helps me find something on Everton that I can use against Everleigh."

"You just will not quit, will you? We can find dirt on Everton without you dragging Grandpa into this."

"My other demand," I plowed on, "is that we go through it all together. If we find any more rapes, murders, or any other evil, violent shit like that, we turn in both the darer and the daree. They're sent to jail and removed from the Royal line."

"Obviously. Why would I say no to that?"

"I've read your texts," I replied. "Any time you got dirt on someone, you used it to your advantage. You sure as fuck didn't help them, tell them the truth, or save them from the blowout. You're not doing that again. These victims will get justice."

"You don't know me," she snapped. "I never found out about any rapes or murders and covered them up. I would never do that. I'm not some sociopath."

I scoffed. "Could've fooled me. A guy dares to end your hookups, and you sabotage his relationships and spread around that he has a kid. A girl beats you out for valedictorian, so you destroy her family. Sociopath sounds like the right word to me."

"Course it does because you're clueless. A no-nothing Dreg that got the name Burkhardt without any of the responsibility. You don't know what it's like for me!" The sudden shout pounded my ear. "I have to be perfect all the time. Every day. The slightest weakness is used against me, not just by the Royal line but the whole country now that it's an open secret that my father wants to run for president.

"You're so worried about precious Shane because I told girls he had chlamydia and a kid. Ever think I was trying to help them? That bastard pressured and pressured me into sending him nudes. When I refused, he called me a frigid bitch and dumped me. It turned out his friends were bidding on the pics, and he was pissed I cost him thousands.

"And yeah, I did tip off Lizzie Duke's mom about her cheating husband because I didn't know what else to do. I had to be valedictorian. Second place wasn't an option."

I shook my head. Saylor would burst into flames before she ever admitted responsibility for the pain she caused. "What about Ahmed and Piper? What's your sob story for lying and telling him Piper cheated on him, then throwing it in Katie's face when he hooked up with her out of revenge?"

"Ahmed is a douche. He treated Piper like crap, but she stayed with him to cover up what she was doing with her cousin. She wouldn't end it, so I ended it for her. No one treats my friends like that."

"*You* treat your friends like that! You caused problems between Katie and Piper by spilling her secret about Ahmed."

"I didn't mean to! I was pissed because Katie was blowing us off to hang with your bitch ass. It just came out."

"Ugh!" I threw up my hands, almost sending my phone flying. Victor edged away. "Only you can twist everything to make it not your fault. You came after my bitch ass from day one. You threw my sister's suicide in my face. Said horrible things about her! How do you justify that, Saylor? I dare you to try!"

"I can't," she screamed. "I was wrong. I'm sorry!"

Words clogged in my throat. *What did she say?*

"I'm sorry, okay. I didn't know until a few days ago how wrong I was." She dropped her voice. A gusty sigh crackled through the phone. "The Wilsons didn't start with you. They sniffed around Winter first. I didn't care. I thought she was just some Dreg they were using to lock him down before Victor knocked up another Royal.

"But then Everleigh got in my head. She said the Wilsons were using the marriage as some kind of play against the Burkhardts. Claimed she overheard Martha and John talking in her office the night we all went to their Christmas Eve party.

"When people started going after Winter, I didn't stop it. Figured the Dreg deserved it for plotting with the Wilsons to overthrow me. But if I'd known the truth about Everleigh. If I'd known it was all heading toward... Ashton. I would've, Sinclair. I would have stopped it."

I was quiet for a long time.

"You're saying you just took Everleigh's word that Winter, and then me, was a threat. You didn't bother to find out why? You—" My fist balled. "You didn't discover that we're cousins?"

"She didn't say that we were cousins," Saylor confessed. "She said you were my aunts."

I frowned. "Your aunts?"

"Grandpa William's daughters. I didn't believe her at first. My grandpa siring a bunch of illegitimate brats with the help? I thought it was a lie until I found out I wasn't set to inherit the entire company. The lawyer wouldn't give me names or information. All they'd say is that Grandpa's will gave me a thirty-three percent share," she said. "It didn't make sense. I was his only grandchild. The only person to take over after Daddy stepped down to take office. Unless... I wasn't."

The pieces began falling into place. "You figured it had to be Winter. But Burkhardts don't go after Burkhardts, so you let everyone else get rid of her for you."

"Yes." She spoke so softly I almost didn't catch it. "Then you showed up and had to go too. You definitely couldn't marry Victor and give the Wilsons a third of my company. Everleigh played me. She made me think you two were the enemy when it was her all along."

I swallowed a few times, trying to form a response. "If this is true and you're sorry for what happened to Winter, why are we still fighting, Saylor? Why won't you let me see William?"

"Because Winter might have been decent, but you're a bitch. You turned the whole town against me. Piper and Gabriella wouldn't be with Everleigh if you didn't make it easy for them."

Any soft feelings I might've felt for her imploded. "Family doesn't have to like each other. Thor knows I'll never like you."

"Feeling's mutual," she returned. "But that's not why I won't let you near Grandpa. You can't see what's right in front of your face, Sinclair."

My brows snapped together. "What does that mean?"

"Have you asked yourself where I got my info? Worthless husbands sleeping around. Ava's father raping and impregnating his sister. How would I know any of that stuff?"

"How did you know?" I asked, glancing at Victor. He was scrolling through the club site with his brows all the way to his hairline.

"I was given that information and told I had to use it. Use it to help Daddy's campaign, to keep me on top, to keep the Burkhardts on top."

"Wait. Are you saying your grandfather told you to fuck with people's lives just so you could—"

"No," she sliced in. "My grandpa didn't know about any of this until you told the world. Half of the stuff I'm being villainized for, I did under Grandmother's orders."

"Your grandmother," I said quietly. "You mean Alistair's mother. The coldest, most unforgiving taskmaster that ever wielded a Mastercard."

"That's putting it nicely." A sharp edge crept into her voice. "My dad and grandpa weren't even mad at me when they heard about the texts. They knew I couldn't have done all of that on my own. Now they're furious at her, and she's furious at you."

I started. "Me?"

"She hates you. Everyone is telling me that I can't strike back at you because of the code. Everyone except her. Grandmother doesn't consider the housekeeper's bastards as part of the family. She wants me to put down the Dreg that ruined our reputation."

My stomach twisted, shooting bile up my throat. Her grandmother—*my grandmother*—said such horrible things about me?

Saylor went on. "My grandpa did put a lot of time and money into hunting down the Rogues, but if he found anything on them, he'd have exposed and turned them in. Everyone would know about it already. But the person who would've kept the information to herself until it could be used to her advantage—"

"—is Grandma Burkhardt," I finished. "She's who I'd have to speak to, and she wants nothing to do with me."

"Now you're getting it."

I was quiet while I thought. The idea that there was some deep, unrevealed secret about Everton that I could use in the fight against Everleigh was a long shot.

But I saw her face when I lied about her long-lost sister. Then I saw her face when I threatened to hurt her. Maybe there were no other sisters out there, but her grandmother could be sitting on damning information that she ignored because Everton died years ago. It didn't matter to him anymore, but it could matter to his daughter. If she knows anything, I need to know it too.

"Put me back on the list, Saylor."

"Did you not hear anything I said?"

"You said I'm dealing with Grandma, not Grandpa. That's fine. She can hear what I have to say just as well. From what you're saying, it sounds like she has a few choice things to tell me too."

I sensed her hesitating. "This is my price if you want the keys to your kingdom back. What'll it be?"

"Fine, Sinclair. You want to be a Burkhardt so badly, it's time you learn what it takes. Be here in twenty minutes."

***

Victor drove up to the gate and stopped. I leaned over him and smirked in Frank's eyes.

"How are you, friend? Luna Sinclair to see Saylor."

Frank gave no reaction. "Good evening, Miss Sinclair. You are welcome inside, but your guest must remain out here."

Victor shut off the car and handed me the keys. "Do what you need to do, babe. My folks' place is down the hill. Pick me up there when you're done."

I kissed him goodbye, then took his place. The gates screeched open, beckoning me inside the Burkhardts' paradise. Frank must've called ahead to tell Saylor I was here because she stood before the grand double doors, waiting for me to pull up.

"Where is it?"

"Hello to you too, Saylor. That's a nice beret. Where did you—?"

"Cut the shit!"

I laughed out loud. At this point, I was being pleasant to piss her off. Weird that kindness was a trigger for Saylor Burkhardt.

"Where is it?"

"By it, I assume you mean this." I wiggled the phone above my head. "Let's toddle up to your room. This is going to take a while."

A frustrated breath flared her nostrils. Opening up to me on the phone hadn't softened her a fraction. Saylor did not wish to spend more time with me than was necessary, but this was. I was ending T.O.D. for good. Everyone who was hurt by them would receive justice.

The justice that Winter deserved.

"Follow me," she barked, marching up the steps. "Don't loiter, don't gawk, and don't pretend like you belong."

"Whatever you say, cuz."

The tense line of her shoulders showed me what she thought of that.

Saylor took me down the same hallway from that night I spent with Alistair—eating, joking, and talking of the days we didn't get to spend together.

Stepping inside Saylor's room, the pang of hurt fled under awe. Think of a luxury department store with high-priced items everywhere and all displayed in the perfect arrangement to make you want, want, want. Think of it, and you still wouldn't be close to what it was like walking into the fever dream of towering ceilings, a revolving bed, purple chandeliers, and a wall of windows that overlooked a garden even more magnificent than the Wilsons'. I could throw my shoe and hit something I could sell and feed a family of five for a year.

"Wait there," Saylor said, "and don't touch anything."

Saylor disappeared through double doors, then came back out carrying a magazine. She ripped out a couple pages and laid them on the desk chair. "Okay, now sit."

"What the hell is wrong with you?" I slapped the pages off. "I'm not a dog."

"My mistake," she shot back, smirking. "How am I supposed to know if Dregs are house-trained?"

"Okay, just for that, the price went up." I stuffed Everleigh's phone back in my pocket. "I know to you, empathy is just something you read in a book once, but now you've lived it. You know what it's like to not be a Royal. You know what Dregs go through. The difference is *your ass deserves it*!"

Her jaw clenched.

"You attacked, mocked, betrayed, and deceived the Royals. You gave them a reason to ice you out, so imagine what it's like to go through it every day for no damn reason. Treating people like this just because they don't have as much money or connections as the Royals? Do I really need to tell you how stupid that is?

"So, if you want to be queen again, you'll do it right this time. The current system has to go. The Royal line as you've known it is done."

She flashed me big eyes. "Want to elaborate on what the hell that is supposed to mean?"

"Everyone is so obsessed with climbing up the ladder. Five guys tortured and drove my sister to suicide to leapfrog a few rungs. You say you wouldn't have let that all happen if you'd known the truth, but I read through a few of these dares on the ride over. Winter isn't the only one. Royals are using the club to bully everyone on the outside to their lowest point. Prove that you care, Saylor. Put a stop to it."

Saylor dropped on her ridiculously large bed. "What am I supposed to do? This nasty club is finished. Gone today. But afterward, I can order Royals to be nice to Dregs all I want. It won't make a difference."

"It will if there's no longer Dregs and Royals. We're all the same."

Saylor tossed her head. "The Royal line is more than a bunch of rich kids ranking themselves. It's a connection of families ranging from those most threatening to the Burkhardts to the least."

"That's how they're ranked?" My head spun. "And that's why the Wilsons are right below you. You don't control any of the business sectors they dominate, and they've got a boatload of blackmail to sink you."

Rolling her eyes, she nodded. "Royals climb the ladder by making more money, building stronger alliances, and taking more and more pieces of our pie. Dregs are Dregs because they don't matter to the Burkhardts. It can't be that way for the Royals. Their companies, strategic marriages, and the rest don't just disappear."

I smiled. "Don't worry. I've given this a lot of thought."

An hour later, we were neck-deep in the garbage from the site and arguing over what to do about it.

"It's the same problem," Saylor said. "We can't turn this over to the captain. I might as well finance her yacht and third vacation home myself. The first thing she'll do is auction off the chance to make their evidence disappear."

"What if we went to the media?" I offered up. "Put it all out there."

"These are just names on a screen. With the army of lawyers a Royal can afford, they'll have even you and me convinced this site is fake." Saylor flung back on her pillows, chewing her lip while she stared up at the bed's canopy. "I can't believe the things people did for this club. I've done some fucked-up stuff, but framing people? Assaulting them? Stalking them? *Killing* them? All so their secrets wouldn't get outed."

"Or for money," I reminded. "Some of these secrets aren't a big deal. The only thing the club had on Gabriella was that she was dating Giovanni. Raven Jennings too. The worst thing they had on her was that she shoplifted a purse once, then felt so bad she took it back. Yet, she took a dare to plant drugs in Natalie Rivers's car for three grand. She could've turned that down without it costing her anything at all. But she wanted the money."

Saylor inclined her head. This was a record. The longest amount of time we'd gone without insulting each other. I was even sitting on her bed without any cracks about house-training or soiling her sheets.

"Some of these secrets are minor," Saylor said, "but the majority are life-wrecking scandals. If Everleigh gave the Royals a choice between pledging loyalty to her or spilling this stuff to everyone, it's no wonder they gave in. They know I can't expel them all from the Royal line."

"You having this information can force them to break from Everleigh, which is a start. We have to peel away her layers of protection so she has no choice left but to confess."

"Then that's what we'll do."

I wasn't sure when we started saying *we*. It was probably when we nearly vomited at the third revenge rape dare that we realized we were in this together. We both wanted to burn down the system that created these monsters.

"One at a time," Saylor continued. "We bring it all crashing down around her."

I slid the phone away from me, shaking with the violation of holding that thing. "What about the second part of our deal? I get to meet my grandparents."

Saylor made a derisive noise in her throat. The real her was coming back. "They're not here. Daddy's getting ready for the campaign, and Grandpa and Grandmother flew to New York to meet with potential donors personally. Grandpa always said the least you can do when asking for money is to ask face-to-face."

"When will they be back?"

She shrugged. "Tomorrow or the next day. Depends on if they decide to catch a show or visit friends. I'll tell Grandmother you want to talk to her, but I can't guarantee anything. If she refuses, don't think you can come for me and say I didn't hold up my end."

"As long as the refusal comes from her. I don't trust you not to lie."

"Like I trust you either." Saylor slid off the bed. "Get out. The phone stays with me."

She didn't have to tell me twice. There was no risk in leaving the phone with her since I called Wilder from the car and he walked me through how to give him remote access. He knew everything about the members that Saylor and I now did. If she didn't keep up her end to bring the bastards to justice, we'd do it for her.

Victor was waiting for me at his parents' house as promised. Together we took a long, twisty route back to Wilder's hideout. I walked through the door and fell into Rafael's arms. Victor filled them in for me.

"Leave you alone for one day and you get chased by an angry mob." Rafael's touch was soothing on my temples. "I hate that we're stuck in this fucking place when you need us. Meanwhile, Wilder's brother has struck again."

My head shot up. "What? How?"

Rafael led us into the living room. Wilder was hunched over the coffee table, furiously typing on his laptop. "He's locked me out of everything," he hissed. "I can't access the Royals' HapApp messages. I can't get into the school database. I can't even send an email to a Royal. They're all coming back undelivered. Wolf is protecting Everleigh and all her allies from my cyberattacks."

I bent over his shoulder, glancing at strings of code I did not understand. "Does that matter now that we have Everleigh's cellphone? She's about to lose all of her allies."

"They switch their loyalty from Everleigh back to Saylor, but in neither situation are they loyal to us," Lucien said. "Wolf trapped us in this place. Now, he's taking away our eyes. We're planning moves, but he and Everleigh are too. He's making sure we don't see them."

I shivered. "If only he'd been this thorough about securing the site. All the protections he added to stop the horrific bullying and worse have come far too late."

"But he did do it," Wilder said. "I thought it was a clever manipulation to make you think there was a shred of decency in him before you turned over the laptop. Turns out, there is that shred. The past dares and truths are horrific, but the recent ones have no mention of murder, rape, bullying, etcetera."

I nodded. I did notice that. Wolfgang held up his end and blocked those dares from going live on the site. This did not make him a good person. A serial killer can abhor rape. A sex trafficker could draw the line at children. Just because Wolf had limits did not make him a good person.

That night, I snuggled between Rafael and Cato—the sweat cooling on our bodies. The sex had been softer lately, the only way I could describe it. As though they sensed the anger and frustration in me and chose to tease it out with gentle fingers and lingering kisses.

This tenderness was a wonder I did not know Cato was capable of. Don't get me wrong, Cato never pushed me past my limits. He took me to the edge. Danced on the line. Reimagined my body's possibilities. Took what he wanted without hesitation. There were things I didn't know I liked until Cato told me I liked them.

His barking, snarling domination was hot in every way, and then there were his stroking fingers, featherlight on my skin. His barely there kisses under my ear. His slow, mind-scrambling tasting of my pussy. None of these were things I was prepared for, and that night, it undid me in every way.

I couldn't sleep after the Dumont brothers were done with me. I just drifted between wakefulness and peace for hours until sunlight peered through the blinds.

Buzzing drew my attention to the nightstand. I reached over Rafael and grabbed my phone.

Hell Beast: My grandmother has agreed to speak with you, but not at the manor. You're to meet her at La Perla's in three hours. If you're a minute late, she'll leave and you lose your only chance.

My fingers were a blur typing back.

Me: I'll be there. Is William coming too?

Hell Beast: No. You've probably guessed by now, but she doesn't want you anywhere near him. He has a soft spot for you, and Grandmother won't have you take advantage of it.

My brows shot up. William had a soft spot for me? Did she assume that because he didn't cut me out of the will? That was my only guess because ignoring me my whole life didn't seem soft.

Me: Fine. I'll be there in three hours. Do I have to come alone?

Hell Beast: If you want her to say a word worth hearing, yes.

I left the conversation at that. Two hours and forty-five minutes later, I shut the car off in the parking lot of La Perla's.

I don't know why I thought it was a restaurant. Or why I thought a restaurant would be open at eight in the morning. La Perla's was a dress shop. A midsized boutique that was just beginning to open its doors and get ready for the day's patrons.

I climbed out, looking around. There were other cars in the parking lot, but it was impossible to know if one was, Say— *my* grandmother's car or if they all belonged to the employees.

Cautiously, I grasped the door handle—wondering if I should go in or wait until time.

The woman standing behind the register glanced up and smiled at me. She waved for me to come in.

"Good morning. You must be Miss Sinclair."

"Uhh, yes."

Bowing, she swept out a hand. "Right this way, ma'am. Everything is ready for your appointment."

I didn't know what to say, so I said nothing—simply following her from the main room and down a hallway lined with adorned mannequins.

La Perla's was as elegant as its name and twice as beautiful as any shop in Regalia. Which was saying something. Plush, cream carpet tickled my sandals. Bold of a place with high foot traffic to choose a color that captured every stain and trace of grime. The carpets should be filthy, yet they looked like they were put in that morning.

Walking behind, my shoulders brushed dusky-pink wallpaper with golden swirls. Wilder's lips were the same dusky pink. The thought brought an unbidden smile to my lips. When had I gotten so lovesick and smitten that I was seeing my guys everywhere? Even in the walls.

The attendant moved aside as we entered another space. A woman sat on a circular sofa, accepting a glass of champagne offered on a silver tray.

I studied the side of her face without moving. This was Alistair's mother. I didn't need her confirmation to prove it.

Silver had all but overcome the auburn locks she passed on to her son. Small wrinkles appeared at the corner of her eye and mouth—the lightest dusting as though they were hesitant to age her without permission.

She was beautiful because, of course, she was. I didn't need to see her full face to know she was, but she turned and smiled at me. Confirming it.

Astoria Burkhardt. The first and only shadow queen of Regalia.

"Good morning, Luna."

"Good morning, Mrs. Burkhardt."

She laughed—a tinkling sound. "So polite. No need for formality, dear. You may call me Grandmother."

I blinked—not expecting that in the slightest. The woman went out of her way to ignore my existence, then wouldn't allow me to enter her home to speak to her, but now she was Grandmother?

"I'd like to stick to Mrs. Burkhardt if that's all right."

Her smile didn't waver. "Of course. Whatever makes you comfortable."

I looked around, half expecting to spot Saylor hiding behind a rack of clothes, laughing herself sick because she fooled me with this paid actor.

"Do... you know why I'm here?" I asked.

"We'll get to that." She flapped a hand, sending the attendant away. "This is my first time meeting my youngest grandchild in person. I hope you don't mind, I asked you here so I could spoil you."

"Spoil me?" What the hell was happening?

"Of course." She snapped her fingers and another attendant appeared at my side, startling me so bad I tripped out of my sandal. "On Saylor's sixteenth birthday, I brought her here for her first bespoke gown. I'm a few years late, but I hope you'll allow me to do the same for you. Every bright, beautiful young lady deserves a dress that changes their mood just to look at it."

I was helpless to stop the attendant guiding me to the small raised platform and beginning her measurements.

I knew what Astoria was doing. Everything—the dress shop, the sweet smile, compliments, pleasant tone. All of it was meant to throw me off-balance.

I blew in there expecting a fight. Thinking I was going to face sneers and insults for being the maid's daughter. Expecting her to sniff and tip her chin at my questions. Preparing to fight for every inch in a battle with the Burkhardt matriarch.

I was ready for it. I had my responses and rebuttals ready to go. So she did the opposite.

I doubted very much that she saw me as bright or beautiful, and I'd eat my shorts if the lady actually gave a crap about meeting her youngest grandchild for the first time. All of this was a carefully choreographed dance intended to give her the upper hand.

I knew what she was doing, but that didn't mean I knew how to stop it.

I dithered on the platform, opening and closing my mouth a few times while the attendant whipped her tape measure up and down my body. How did I start this conversation? If I was accusatory, it'd be my rudeness that was to blame for this meeting going sour.

"Thank you," I said when I found my voice. "My mom's parents died before I was born. I never got to do anything like this with a grandparent."

Her smile was soft. You could even fool yourself into thinking it was genuine. "That breaks my heart, dear."

I waited for more, but none came. No acknowledgment that not ignoring me my whole life could've saved her a broken heart.

"You look like Winter," I blurted. I didn't want to say it. I just couldn't help it. The auburn hair; cupid's-bow lips; oval face; and the teasing light in her eyes when she smiled made her look like she was up to something at all times. Everything about her was so heartbreakingly Winter I was certain I would've known instantly that we were related had we met before Alistair dropped this bomb. "Just like her."

Astoria said nothing. No change in expression gave her thoughts away.

"You're an autumn," she said. "I can tell by looking at you. You'd look lovely in a peach A-line gown. Nimia." She tipped her chin to my tailor. "See to it."

"Yes, madam."

"How long do we do this?" I asked. "Pretend like we're grandmother and granddaughter out for an early morning bonding session."

Still no change in expression. "Are we pretending?"

"I know you don't see me as a part of your family, Mrs. Burkhardt, and that's fine. Honestly, I never bought into the 'blood is thicker than water' idea. Love is a choice, not a lineage."

She sipped her champagne—unblinking. She seemed content to let me fill the awkward silence.

"Even so, I was hoping you'd have information that could help me and your son."

"Information," she drew out. "What information would that be?"

"Everleigh Starling wants Alistair dead and she killed Winter to make it happen." I dropped that with the same mild look she was giving me. I didn't come here to play her games. "She's spun a web of lies, betrayals, secrets, and murder in the name of avenging her father, Everton, and the only way to untangle it is for her to confess her crimes.

"I thought you might know something that'd help her along. Something about the only person she cares about—Everton."

Astoria nodded, humming. "I see. If what you say about Everleigh is true, it's quite concerning. But, forgive me, I don't understand why you believe I can help you? Everton was an old school friend of my son's, but our interactions were limited."

"Yes, but then he became a member of the Regalia-born criminal organization called the Rogues"—I matched her smile—"and got a lot more interesting than the troublemaking teenager. You kept tabs on him. I simply want to know if there's anything he did—besides his partial responsibility in the death of a child—that would hurt his daughter all these years later. Something she'd do anything to know or anything to stop others from finding out."

Another sip. "Why do you believe I kept tabs on him?"

"Because I've seen—and burned—your scroll detailing all the ties connecting the families of Regalia. I wondered how you could know the secrets that connected the families until I got a peek into the Truth or Dare Club. People around here make a habit of digging into each other's lives until they find a gem that'll ruin them.

"If you'd do that for the law-abiding citizens, why wouldn't you do the same for anyone you found out was a Rogue? Having someone like that under your thumb is infinitely more valuable."

"Under my thumb? My dear, if I had knowledge of a member of a criminal organization, I would turn that information over to the authorities."

Nimia turned my cheek and held different swatches of shades of pink up to my cheek.

"Maybe if we spoke in private—"

"My answer will not change in private," Astoria sliced in. "I know nothing about the late Everton Starling that can help you. It wasn't until this moment that I learned he was one of these... Rogues?"

She actually said it like a question. As if she didn't know exactly who the Rogues were and knew them better than me.

"Now, how about we stop all this unpleasant talk, and you tell me more about yourself? I'm told you completed your high school education in France. How did you enjoy your time? I've always loved France."

"I didn't enjoy my time. While I was there, my sister was bullied so badly she committed suicide, and there was nothing I could do to help her," I replied. "The person responsible is running around free, and with what you know, I can do something about that. I know you don't care about me or Winter but—"

"Stop saying that."

The sharp bark trapped my tongue.

"I never said I was indifferent toward you. I never felt it either." She rose from her seat. "The decision to not be a part of your life was one that was made for me. After I lost my son and your mother was left to raise the two of you alone, I offered to adopt you and your sister. It was my desire to raise you in your home, with your family."

I rocked back. She what?

"Your mother said no *heatedly* and *colorfully*. She said she wouldn't allow me to raise her children to be ashamed of her. Strangers to her. She resisted all my attempts to help her rear and educate you both in the right ways. Instead, choosing poverty and struggle as though her spitefulness was hurting me more than the two of you."

Astoria's sweet tone was gone. Finally, I was meeting the real her.

"In the end, she married your stepfather. Proving she wasn't opposed to privilege and money. Just mine."

"You wanted to take her children away. How else was she supposed to react?"

"I wanted to raise you both as Burkhardts. To give you everything my son rejected. To keep you *safe*." She sniffed. "But Eloise wanted me to stay away, so that's what I did. She does not get to make me the villain all these years later, claiming abandonment. All I've done is honor the wishes of your parents. I stayed away."

I clenched my teeth, penning in a hasty response. From her point of view, I could see why she believed she was wronged. There was a difference between ignoring your granddaughters and being told to stay away from them. Hurt like that easily turned into resentment.

All the same, what happened eighteen years ago couldn't be changed. It was done.

"Seems like all of this was out of both our control," I said, keeping my tone even. "It can be different now. We can get to know each other now, but only if you mean it. Saylor said you hated me for what I did to her—selling her texts to the town."

"Hmm. Hate is a strong word, dear." She returned to her seat. Ever the placid billionaire, her mask slid back into place. "I can't say that I was pleased that you broke the one and only rule of our family and thus exposed the Burkhardts to embarrassment and repercussions that resound longer and deeper than your rivalry with Saylor.

"You've left me with quite a mess, Luna. I won't deny it. But"—an echo of a smile changed her features—"had your target been anyone else, I'd be impressed. You are your father's daughter through and through. Who raised you couldn't change that."

Discomfort shuffled my feet. Astoria was complimenting me. The part of me that couldn't help seeking her approval preened. The other part started to see myself in a new light.

Astoria also approved of Saylor and all the things she did. It was hard not to think that Astoria's happy... that I'm a bully.

I shook the thought away. *Not going there.*

"If you don't hate me, why wasn't I allowed back in the manor after Alistair left? Why can't I see William?"

"A sweetheart neckline is just the thing, Nimia," Astoria called. "Or would you prefer a V-neck, Luna?"

I stared at her. She nodded.

"Sweetheart it is."

She wasn't going to make me repeat the question, so I waited. Astoria took her time sipping her drink, pulling her compact from her bag, and reapplying her lipstick.

"You asked about your grandfather," she finally said. "He's been under a lot of stress lately. The company is losing contracts. My son is losing campaign contributors. Saylor's distressed. Alistair disappeared as quickly as he reappeared. Forgive me if I needed peace to return to our home and to allow my husband time to relax. I very much hope that you two will meet. When the time is right."

In other words, when I can't use William to get around her.

"I know you're holding something back." Nimia came at me with more swatches and I ducked her. "Everyone is! If I even say the name Rogue, it's all tight lips and pinched faces. Please, just tell me if you know something that could stop Everleigh. If you really cared about Winter and what she did to her, I wouldn't have to ask more than once."

Astoria lifted her chin, staring down her nose at me. I couldn't begin to guess what she was thinking.

"Let me see." She turned away, drumming her fingers on the chair. "You know that Everleigh Starling is behind the horrible bullying done to Winter, as well as other awful acts. The issue is you can't prove it, so you're hoping to push her into confessing with some life-altering secret about her dead biological father. More so, you assume I'm aware of this life-altering secret based on nothing other than an alleged scroll that you burned."

My face heated. Laid out like that, I sounded ridiculous to me too. "I know it's a long shot. Let's be honest, getting rid of Everleigh is easy, but it wasn't only her that killed Winter. It was the club she used as her weapon. It was the soulless members that tortured her for money, status, and self-preservation. It was the dozens upon hundreds of students that weren't even in the club, but when they saw what was happening to her, they either joined in or ignored it.

"If the strike that takes down Everleigh doesn't bring everyone else down with her, there's no point. Everleigh has to admit she was behind Winter's rape and murder, as well as the rapes and murders of too many other people.

"She has to say that she used the T.O.D. Club to wield her revenge so that all those privileged little rich kids can't hide behind lawyers who say the club is just a joke and no one can prove they carried out those dares. She has to turn on her new hacker buddy and tell the world that she burned down the Gallery and had my boyfriends framed as terrorists.

"Do I know that it'll be next to impossible to get her to do any of that? Yes," I snapped. "Of course I do. But I'm desperate and out of options. All I know is that Everton was the only person in this world that she cared about, and love like that doesn't go away just because they do. If it did, I wouldn't be here right now fighting for Winter."

Something flickered in her eyes too fast for me to identify.

"You've done a lot of dodging, deflecting, and answering a question with a question, but now I'm asking you flat out. If you don't give me a straight answer, I'm leaving now. Among all the dirt you've collected on the people of Regalia, do you know something that can take Everleigh down?"

Astoria watched for a long, silent spell. Long enough, the hairs prickled on the back of my neck.

I imagined growing up in the Burkhardt mansion, enduring her penetrating gaze and all-knowing air of superiority. *Thank you, Mom, for turning down her offer. Growing up with you beats growing up a Burkhardt any day.*

"All right, Luna," she said. "Let's say I do know something that can help you. Let's say I'm willing to help you dig yourself further into this ugly mess and put yourself more at risk by continuing to engage with someone you've named a murderer. It's a high price you ask of me—putting my youngest granddaughter in danger. It's a high price I expect in turn."

It took me a minute to pick through her reply. "Did you just give me the proper version of 'it'll cost ya'?"

She laughed. "I guess I have."

"Why would I give you anything? You should want to help me."

"I do want to help you, dear. I desire the same outcome as you, but there is an opportunity for both of us that isn't likely to come around again. I must seize this chance for your own good."

I frowned. "Riddles and more riddles."

"Fine, then I'll be plain. I do have information that can help you, but in exchange, I'll need you to sign this." Astoria took a folder out of her bag and handed it over.

I read the line at the top and froze—reading it again and again. Disbelief brought my gaze lower, forcing me to read the rest. "But this is... This says that I revoke any claim to the Burkhardt companies, monies, or property. You want me to sign away my inheritance."

Her smile was pleasant. "I do."

"But why? What about that tale of victimhood you spun five minutes ago about being forced out of my life? Now you're the one forcing me out of the family."

"Don't be so dramatic, dear. It's not you I'm keeping out of the family, it's Martha Wilson."

"Martha?"

"Oh, yes." She looked down at her nails, almost too fast for me to catch that look again. Something about it unsettled me, but I couldn't place why. "I had a bad feeling when she announced you and Victor were getting married, but I dismissed it because it wasn't possible for her to know your true parentage. Then, Alistair informed me she knows everything.

"Martha cannot be allowed to sink her claws into your shares of the Burkhardt holdings. Your other option is to dissolve the engagement between you and Victor—"

"No!"

"Now, now. Don't be too hasty," she said, clicking her tongue. "You both are young. Still teenagers. As it is, I'm told you have many paramours."

"I wouldn't say many," I gruffed.

She looked at me knowingly. "Why bother with the relationship imbalance that comes from marrying one of them when they can all equally be your lovers?"

I had no idea how to respond. How was I getting relationship advice from my grandmother on how to date six men?

"I won't pressure you to end the engagement—even though if I had my way, no grandchild of mine would bear the name Wilson."

There it was again. That look. *Predatory.*

"But knowing Martha," she continued, expertly tucking away her anger. "She'll have threatened to disown him like she did her eldest. I will say that what you'll receive from your inheritance will more than replace what Victor will lose, but I'm kind enough to not ask you to make him choose between you and his family."

"This is kindness?"

"Yes," she said firmly. "I will tell you everything I know about Everton and Everleigh Starling. All you have to do is renounce an inheritance you didn't know you were receiving until recently. Do we have a deal?"

I flicked from the folder to her. Holding her gaze, I plucked out the agreement and ripped it into confetti.

"I don't need your information. By the way, I don't need your money either, but I'll have it and my revenge no matter what you do or say. You're so worried about Martha fucking Wilson that you're betraying your granddaughter. And she's so worried about you that she cast out her son. You're both ridiculous!"

Astoria leaned back slowly, brow arching. I knew that look just fine.

"The most fucked-up priorities I've ever seen. Just for this mess"—I gestured at the shredded contract—"when I get my inheritance, I'm liquidating the whole thing and donating it to the Center for Suicide Prevention. Hope that doesn't break your wooden heart, Gam-Gam."

I stomped off, so steamed I couldn't see straight and nearly walked into a mannequin.

Astoria's voice drifted to my ear as I threw open the door, but I couldn't have heard her correctly. It sounded like she said, "Definitely a Burkhardt."

***

"—then I stormed out."

Silence followed my story.

Cato, Wilder, Rafael, Lucien, and Victor stared at me open-mouthed.

"Sinclair," Wilder began. "Remember when I asked if you have a death wish? Do you want to amend your answer?"

I threw my pillow at him. We were in my bedroom with me stretched out on the bed with the six of them sitting or standing around me. Cato liked to give me orgasms when I was upset. I was eagerly awaiting him to continue that tradition, but even he was looking at me in disbelief.

I waggled my legs to give him the hint.

Nothing.

I sighed. "What was I supposed to do? I was asking for help to stop Winter's murderer, and she's worried about Martha getting her hands on a piece of the Burkhardt fortune. It's so asinine and selfish I almost wonder if she did it on purpose to piss me off and stop me ever coming near her again."

The sentence popped out of my mouth and my eyes bugged. "Fucking hell. Do you think that's why she did it? Made an offer she knew I would refuse so I'd burn the bridge all by myself."

Lucien twirled his cane, looking thoughtful. "If that was her plan, don't let it work. It never occurred to us to use the Burkhardts' network of spies to our advantage, like Everleigh has been using Wolfgang and the T.O.D. Club to hers, but if there is something to know about Everton Starling, she'd be the one to ask."

"Or William, right? Maybe I can skip her and go straight to him. There has to be a reason she doesn't want me to. Does he ever leave the manor?"

"Not as often as he used to," Rafael admitted. "He's getting up there in age. When he does leave, he doesn't announce his itinerary. You'd have to arrange to meet him on neutral territory. Saylor's got the phone. You might have enough goodwill with her that she'll slip you Grandpa William's direct number."

"You were right about one thing," Victor said. "We don't have a secret to use against Everleigh, but we're not out of the game. Forget our families and their competitive, toxic bullshit. You'll get your revenge, Luna. We will finish it." He shared a look with the guys. "For you."

I smiled soft, feeling so loved my chest ached. That was just as good as an orgasm. "Thank you, guys. I love you."

"We love you back," Rafael said. "Speaking of getting your revenge. Saylor's got the leverage to force the Royals under her rule. We've got the site's archives. Know what this means?"

I didn't know what it meant until Cato linked his fingers through mine with one hand and lit a lighter with the other. A slow grin spread across my face.

"I love you, Cato, but this time, I want to do the honors."

***

The six of us crept through the trees, each of us carrying a container of gasoline. It was a big cabin. It needed a lot to burn.

"Are we sure she's not inside?" Victor asked.

"I texted Katie before we left. Everleigh's at her place, drinking wine and painting her toenails. We're good."

"Remind me again why we need a confession so badly? We can wait a few hours and end this tonight."

I shook my head, though he couldn't see in the dark. "Without a confession, it'll be ten thousand times harder to prove the guys aren't terrorists. Not to mention we've got to get that fool Connor Langston out of prison. I looked him up on the site—just to make sure he didn't belong in that cell.

"Connor's big secret is that whatever money his family did have, all went to countless doctors and specialists for his sick little sister. He's consistently refused dares that hurt people, even though he's only allowed to refuse one. I bet anything that he took this dare because it came with a seven-figure reward, and the only one who suffered is himself."

I found Victor's hand in the dark. "Trust me, I want to end this tonight, but the wounds Everleigh left behind will keep bleeding. We have to force her to set it right... and then we can force her to hell."

He sloshed his container. "Just tell me where to—"

A flash of light brightened the forest.

"Looks like Cato already started," he said drily.

Giggling, I shot through the trees and ran straight for the front porch.

Spinning, twisting, sloshing the can—I wrote a single name on the wooden slats, then lit the letters on fire.

Winter.

"She took away our home," I shouted over the rushing flames. "She made Winter feel so unsafe and hostile she didn't know another way out. Let's see how she likes it."

I stumbled off the grass, laughing as the fires grew. Consuming the house. Sending black tendrils into the night sky.

I hoped Everleigh looked out Katie's window, saw the smoke, and dismissed it as some poor sucker's bad luck. Not knowing the poor sucker was her.

"Guys?" I called.

We split up—each of us surrounding the massive cabin and taking a side to burn.

"Cato, my love. Get over here and drop your pants. I want to fuck while it burns."

Victor whipped around the corner, running full speed. "Luna!"

"Victor, this is amazing. Feels even better than—"

"Run!" Victor sprinted faster. Two shadowy figures were on his heels. "Luna, run! It's a trap. She knew we were coming. It's a trap!"

Pain burst in the back of my head. I dropped—darkness taking me before I hit the ground.

Chapter Eight

"Wake up."

My head snapped around, jarring my eyes open with the fierce pain in my cheek.

"I said wake up!"

Another slap bounced my head off something hard.

I glared at the blurry figure before me. "I was up," I croaked. "That second slap... was for fun."

"Why shouldn't I have fun smacking you around, bitch? You burned down my house! Those idiots were supposed to grab you up the next time you came back. They weren't supposed to stand around with their thumbs up their asses while you danced around my burning home."

My lids fluttered, eyes straining to make sense of her. It took me a long, scrambled minute to realize there wasn't something wrong with my eyes. It was dark. Moonlight filtered through the leaves and dissipated before it touched the ground. I was still outside.

I forced myself to focus—forming the moving edges of the figure in front of me into something solid and clear.

Everleigh glared down at me—more enraged than I'd ever seen her. Angrier than when I cornered her in Toussaint's and announced that she was an arsonist and attempted murderer.

I smirked.

"Wipe that fucking smile off your face!"

I saw the punch coming and tried to block it. My hands snagged, bound with something rough and unforgiving. Her fist smashed into my face, and blood spurted on her knuckles.

"You think you're so clever, Sinclair? You actually fooled yourself into thinking you were getting the upper hand."

Head lolling, I swayed from side to side, looking for—

"Where are the guys?" I interrupted. "Rafael? Wilder? Cato!"

"You can screech all you want. They're not here."

Here was the woods not far from Everleigh's cabin. I knew because acrid smoke tickled my nose and throat—turning my speech raspy and making it harder to see through the thin haze. Rushing water sounded behind me.

We were by the river... and nowhere near help.

"What do you think I did with them? Like any responsible citizen, I turned the terrorists over to the police."

Horror leadened my bones. I couldn't think. I didn't speak. *Cato... Rafael... Wilder... Lucien... She couldn't have. She didn't...*

"A few of my T.O.D. friends were kind enough to cart those shits off to prison for me. They're on their way right now. Captain Capaldi will be sure to add arson to the charges after what they did to my home tonight." She slapped me again for good measure. "Although, I did keep one of your sex toys for myself because we're ending this. Tonight."

I didn't know what she meant until Everleigh hauled me around.

Victor knelt on the riverbank, shouting through his gag. Standing next to him was someone I was coming to know all too well.

"Evening, Sinclair," Wolf chirped. "Lovely to see you again. May I say I'm loving you in ropes? Very sexy."

Wolf apparently had a thing for Victor in ropes too. My love was tied and bound like me, but Wolf looped another length of rope around his wrists and held the end like a leash.

"What are you doing? Let him go!"

"That's exactly what he'll do," Everleigh said. "You're so off-the-charts stupid, Luna, that I almost feel bad for you. Did you really think you could sneak into my place and I wouldn't know? I have hidden cameras all over the property, dumbass. I knew you broke in, but when you didn't take or do anything, I figured you had something else planned. All I had to do was wait until you came back."

I barely heard her. My gaze fixed on my Victor. "Just let Victor go, Everleigh. This is between me and you."

"If it was, you wouldn't have involved Wilson or the Rogues. We're playing by new rules now, and you set the terms." Everleigh shoved in my pocket and took my phone. "I'll make this simple for you. You're going to call Daddy, tell him I have you, and that if he doesn't come back and face me, he'll bury another daughter."

I spat in her face. "Fuck you!"

Everleigh punched my broken nose, ringing agony through my skull. I choked on a sob.

"You didn't let me finish." Everleigh towered over me in a pink jumpsuit—ever the psychotic princess. "You call him now... or Wolf tosses your little fiancé into the river. We'll see how long he lasts with his arms and legs tied."

My jaw slackened. "Y-you— You wouldn't!"

Everleigh laughed her ass off. "I wouldn't? Are you serious? I tied you up in a burning building and left you for dead. All to make that coward face me. Do you really think I wouldn't drown him to get what I want?" She got in my face. "He's the only one you've got left. Your other boyfriends are looking forward to a life sentence because you dragged them into this. Don't get Victor killed on top of it."

She opened my phone and found Alistair's number. I never deleted it. Deep down, I was looking forward to the day I called and asked him to come back home.

That day was not supposed to happen like this.

I panted—chest heaving as I strained against my bonds. *What do I do? What do I do?!*

"Everleigh, listen—"

"Listen to what? More bullshit about me having a little sister?" She snorted. "Yeah, I know you made all that up. Good job on distracting me to get to my phone, though. I bet you had loads of fun trolling the T.O.D. site again."

Everleigh smirked at my look. "Don't know what good you thought that would do you. So what, you got admin access to the site? Wolf shut that down the minute I realized why you took my phone. All that, and you didn't know you were walking into a trap tonight. You had no idea this was the Rogues' last day of freedom.

"You tried fighting back against me, and you lost. Now you have one chance and one chance only. Tell him to come here, or Victor dies." Mania lit in her eyes, made scarier by the shadows. "I will not ask again."

She hit *call.* The dial tone rang through the night.

"You can hang that up. I won't let you hurt him. I won't—"

"Wolfie, baby," Everleigh sang.

Without a pause to breathe, Wolfgang kicked Victor in the chest.

"Hphhm!" Victor rolled down the bank and plunged into the water. His dense, muscled body sank like a stone.

"Nooo!" I thrashed harder, flinging my body to break free. *Run to him. Save him.*

"Want to try that again?" The call rang out, and she dialed again. "Better hope he picks up. Victor stays under until I get what I want."

I sobbed, unhinged and messy. Wolf whistled, his whole vibe calm and collected, while on the other end of the rope, my love was thrown into his worst, most traumatic nightmare.

The call picked up. "Hello? Luna?"

"D-D—" I couldn't speak for the stone in my throat. How could I do this? Trade the father I was beginning to know for the man I loved. "You're a monster," I shrieked. "You deserve everything that's coming to you. I wish I could bring your fucking father back and kill him all over again!"

"Luna?" Alistair cried. "What's going on?"

Everleigh smiled over my head. "Go ahead. Keep wasting time yelling at me. It's not like Victor's life depends on it or anything."

I have no choice. Victor can't die. He just can't.

"Dad," I sobbed. "Everleigh caught me. She has... me tied up in the woods and she's going to kill Victor if you don't face her. I'm sorry, Dad." It'd be a miracle if he understood anything I said. I was crying so hard, every word was a racking wheeze. "I'm so sorry."

"What the—? Luna? Luna, I'm coming! Everleigh," he shouted. "Are you there? I know you're there."

"Present," she sang.

"Don't you dare hurt her! I'm on my way. Keep your fucking hands off my daughter!"

"That's entirely up to you."

I thrashed in my bonds. Victor! He'd been under for too long. "Let him up! Please, let him breathe!"

"I don't care where in the world you are. You have until sunrise to face me or Luna's dead. Oh, and bring the laptop. You know the one I want."

She ended the call, typed something, and then tossed my phone in the water. "All right," she said, sounding like it was pulled out of her. "Let him up."

Wolf dragged Victor out of the water. He slid along the bank—not moving, not gasping, not breathing.

He was still.

Wolfgang hummed. "I think he's dead."

"Oh well," Everleigh said over my cries. "Not my fault Sinclair made it difficult."

Kneeling down, Wolfgang untied Victor's ropes. My eyes widened as he flipped him and started CPR.

"What are you doing?" Everleigh snapped. "Leave him. Who cares if he dies?"

"Are you kidding?" Wolf bounced on his rib cage—each pump pounding my own chest. "Do you know how much the sole heir to the Wilson fortune is worth? Just because he's not useful to you anymore doesn't mean he can't be useful to me. The Wilsons will give me billions to get him back in one piece."

"Fine. Whatever. How greedy are you? It's not enough for you to take over the Rogue empire? Have to drain the Wilsons' bank account too?"

Victor shot up, spewing river water. My body gave out. I slumped against the tree, cycling through bawling and thanking every deity there was that he was alive. What was wrong with this monster? Why was she determined to take everyone I loved away from me?

"You think this means you won?" I kicked out, catching Everleigh's shin. "My father's going to show up here and take your fucking ass down. It's over, Starling. It was over the second you made that call."

"Blah, blah, blah." The dark did nothing to hide her eye roll. "You're cute to warn me, but Daddy isn't getting away from me this time. Trust me. As long as I've got you, he'll do whatever I say. By now, he knows I don't bluff."

"By now, he knows you're crazy! He knows that no matter what he does, you'll kill us all anyway."

She giggled. "Yeah. I will."

My rant lodged in my throat. I wasn't expecting her to admit it that easily.

"What choice will you give me? After he's dead, I can't let you run around shouting about what I've done and getting in my way. I've paid Captain Capaldi a lot of money to throw any complaint with my name on it in the trash. Trouble is," she sighed. "You, your boyfriends, and your fucking fiancé have money too. Way more than me put together. That's why I had to take them out and why I'll have to take you out when all this is done."

"But you—"

"Shut up, or I'll gag you. We're done chatting." Everleigh spun away. "Wolfie, get him on his feet. I told her bastard father to meet me at your place."

"What? Why?" He did not sound pleased.

"Duh. I'm not going to kill him anywhere that's connected to me. We also can't do this in the woods in the middle of the night. He and a dozen Rogues could surround us before we know what's happening. Your place has security and cameras everywhere. He'll have no choice but to come alone."

"Luna," Victor rasped. "Luna... are you okay?"

"I'm okay, baby. I'm right here. Everything's going to be okay."

"It really won't be." Everleigh snatched my collar and forced me up. She sent me flying. I crashed to the ground, skidding through dirt and leaves. "Get up and walk. We're going to the car. If you try anything, you'll regret it."

"My car is the other way," Wolfgang said. "I'll take him and meet you there."

"No!"

"Fine," Everleigh replied over me. "Give me the code in case I get there first."

Wolf snorted. "Nice try."

He forced Victor to his feet, practically dragging him across the bank and away from me.

"No, let me go with him!"

"Like hell." Everleigh shoved my back. "Get moving."

I didn't know what else to do but put one foot in front of the other, trudging away from the river Everleigh used to fish with her dad. Long after their father-daughter duo was torn apart, they were still spreading misery everywhere they went.

The sooner we get to wherever we're going, the sooner I'll be with Victor. And the sooner I figure a way out for all of us.

Alistair took off on his boat. He could be anywhere in the world by now, which gave me hours to make it right, get free and stop Everleigh, then do what I should have done that night she walked around clueless in the kitchen—having no idea I was right there watching her.

Everleigh was right about one thing. *Tonight, this ends.*

"Why are you doing this?" I spoke up, stumbling over tree roots. "I mean, what is the damn point? I get you loved your dad, but look at how far you've gone, Everleigh. Look at what you've become. You've lied, and deceived, and killed all to avenge a man who deserved what he got."

"Shut up!"

"No! I won't shut up. My father didn't want to kill him. He gave Everton every chance, and he didn't take it. He kept coming after him, his family, his business. He kept putting innocent people in danger until Alistair had no choice but to take him out." I tripped and dropped to my knees. Everleigh kicked me on the back, pitching me forward face-first on the ground.

But I didn't stop.

"If you... should be mad at anyone, it's Everton. He could've lived in peace, in secret, with you. He had the money and contacts to live it up in high style—exiled or not. He could've taken you away and would've been happy. But no," I snarled. "He chose revenge. He chose power. And he didn't choose you."

Everleigh stepped on my head, grinding my face in the mud. "If you say another word—"

"You'll what!" I wrenched away, getting free of her. I leaned against a tree to get on my feet. "What will you do that you're not going to do already, psycho? If I'm dying tonight, you're going to hear what I have to say. I'll make sure the words ring in your head long after your hollow victory until you discover none of this shit was worth it... because none of it brings him back."

She barked a laugh. "That's rich coming from you. Revenge is pointless because it won't bring him back? If that's true, why did you go through all of that to avenge your sister?"

The question stuck me through—pinning me to the tree.

"Huh?" she asked. "Nothing to say? That's what I thought. Nothing stopped you from making it right, seeing the people who hurt her pay. And nothing's going to stop me."

"The difference is Winter didn't deserve what you did to her! Ashton raped her, you evil freak!"

"I didn't tell him to do that! I said she wasn't learning her lesson, so he had to top Wesley, Levi, Giovanni, and Owen. He's the sick freak for jumping to rape," she shot back. "I told you, I didn't want Winter dead. I just wanted her to hang the flag.

"You're mad at me when you should be mad at that coward who spawned you. If he hadn't hidden away, floating off from all the pain and destruction he caused, none of this would've happened." She clicked her tongue, shaking her head. "My father is the monster for choosing revenge and power over me? So what does that make yours, Sinclair?"

I pressed my mouth together, lips trembling. Her digs were a physical ache in my chest. On my worst day—deep down inside—I resented Alistair for leaving us.

Why couldn't he give Everton the Rogues if the jerk wanted them so much? Weren't we—Mom, me, and Winter—the true gift worth fighting for?

"You know I'm right." Everleigh dug the knife in deeper. "Alistair didn't have to be such a hypocrite, punishing my father for what happened to that kid when other Rogues have done worse. Hello! Leon Dumont is a fucking assassin. He murders people for money, but it's my dad who crossed the line? Broke the rules? Oh, please." Her hatred and derision were a living thing crawling up the back of my neck. "You've got half a brain, so use it. What's the real reason Alistair drove him out?"

Everleigh forced me up and pushed me to keep going.

"He wanted rid of anyone who threatened his throne. Alistair ruined his best friend so he could never take what was his. He started this war out of greed and paranoia. Don't blame me for finishing it."

I said nothing as we tromped through the forest. The inferno that used to be a multimillion-dollar cabin blazed—lighting our path.

Everleigh forced me to her car and shoved me against the door. "Now, I'll stash you inside Wolf's OCD fortress, and we'll wait for Alistair to show up. Between you and me"—she pressed her lips to my ear—"I'm doing this at Wolf's place because he's going down for it. It'll look like he attacked Alistair for the laptop, it all went wrong, and they took each other out."

My eyes widened.

"I was never going to let him take over the Rogues. He knows too much about me and what I've done. Why would I let someone who can, and would, blackmail me become more powerful?" She laughed. "I swear, it's some kind of male arrogance that makes them think they're always the smartest person in the room. It never occurs to them that a woman is telling them what they want to hear until their back is turned and they shut them up for good."

My chest heaved, practically bouncing me on the car. I had to do something. Think of a way out. If Wolf was anything like Wilder, then fortress was putting it lightly. I had no doubt that there was one way into his place and no way out. I couldn't let Everleigh lure Alistair into that trap.

"Must be some kind of psychopath's arrogance that makes you monologue your entire plan," I blurted. "In a world full of locks, the man with the key knows everything. How hasn't it occurred to you that Wolf has a backup plan for his backup plan in case you try to betray him? He rips through people's dirty secrets for fun. He knows no one can be trusted."

"Eh," she breezed. "I'm sure it has occurred to him. Doesn't mean he can save himself. Get inside." Everleigh shoved me in the passenger seat. She shut the door and leaned through the window. "I've got backup plans for my backup plans too. When this night is over, I'll achieve everything my father died for. That shit-stain Burkhardt dead, the Rogues mine, and as a bonus, the Royals begging and nipping at my heels."

"Saylor will get the Royals back."

"How?" She laughed. "Because she's got my phone and can blackmail them now too? The difference is they've all read her text messages. Nice job, Baby Burkhardt. You've turned everyone off your family for good. There's nothing they can do, say, or threaten that'll make anyone go back to them."

I turned away, gazing out into the dark. "This isn't going to turn out the way you want, Everleigh. People like you, you're destined to fail. It's just how it works."

I saw her jaw clench from the corner of my eye. "We'll see about that, bit—"

Everleigh seized up—mouth ripping open in a silent scream. She jerked and flopped against the car, the only thing holding her up... until she wasn't. I couldn't stop a smile as she tipped and collapsed in the dirt.

Alistair flipped the stun gun on his palm, looking down at her with vague interest. "So much hate in one small young woman."

"Alistair!" I burst into tears—pain and stress bowling me over in an instant.

"Luna, sweetheart. It's okay." He reached in and lifted me out of the car. "It's okay, I'm here."

"H-how are you here?" I buried my face in his chest. It was likely he couldn't understand my muffled moaning. "You were gone. The boat—"

"The boat left without me. I never left, Luna. I'll never leave you again." He started walking, carrying me—I didn't know where. All I could do was cry.

We thought we were so clever. Getting the one up on Everleigh little by little, but she was always a step ahead of us.

"We have to get away from here. I called the fire department. They'll show up any minute."

"We have to get away and save my guys," I cried. "Wolfgang separated from us. He took Victor while Everleigh had Wilder, Rafael, Cato, and Lucien turned over to the police."

"One thing at a time, Luna. But I can tell you right now, those terrorist charges won't stick." I bobbed in his arms—warm. Safe. "Captain Capaldi learned not to cross me a long time ago. A private chat with her will clear this whole mess up."

"And Victor?"

Alistair carried me through the trees into a small clearing. A black, shiny Porsche waited for us.

"Wolf wants to ransom him," I said. "He won't accept less than millions and... your laptop."

He paused for a second. "He wants the laptop? It shouldn't surprise me that word leaked of how valuable my laptop is. But if I must, I will give Wolfgang O'Rourke what he wants. I'd never choose the Rogues over your happiness, Luna."

That hard, painful ball of resentment ignited.

"Never, baby girl. I love you."

Tears streaming, it turned to ash. My dad was here. He picked me.

"I love you too."

Alistair set me on my feet. I shook my head clear while he worked on the thick band of ropes binding my wrists.

"You didn't leave Regalia, but how did you get to me so fast?"

"Put a tracker in your phone obviously."

"You— I—" Shock closed my mouth. Not only did he see through my desperate attempt to chase him off, but he made sure to keep an eye on me while I tangled with an opponent I continued to underestimate. "I guess I can't be mad at you, huh?"

"You can," he said, amused, "but I feel no remorse."

I laughed—a short, faint sound that ended as soon as it started. "I'm just happy you're here. Everleigh's plan was to lead you to Wolf's place, kill you both, frame him for it, and then take the laptop. You're right about that hatred. It washed away any trace of humanity in her a long time ago."

"Not a bad plan, but— Shit." He snatched his hand from the ropes. "What the hell is this stuff made of?"

I twisted. Alistair nursed a wicked gash on his index finger. "Do you have a penknife or something?"

"Hold on." He popped open the trunk and pulled out a knife much bigger than a pen. Carefully, he sliced me free. I didn't waste a second throwing myself in the car.

"We have to go. Everleigh sent you the address. Victor's waiting for us. We have to save him."

"On our way."

He hopped in and I breathed for the first time that night. Everything would be all right. Everleigh lay in the piss-soaked dirt next to the burning remnants of her father. And Wolf didn't know he was driving straight to his punishment. We'd save Victor, then I was coming for the rest of my guys.

Why did I think I could save Alistair by sending him away? Why did I think he needed me to save him? He refused to kill or be killed by his former friend's daughter, but he wasn't helpless. We were stronger together.

That's what family is.

Alistair took off, speeding out of the forest. "I've kept an eye on Wolfgang." He covered his mouth, coughing. "A close eye on him and the entire O'Rourke clan. There's no one more paranoid than"—*cough*—"a spy. Whether we beat him there or not, we're not waltzing into the place easy." *Cough, cough, cough.* "I wouldn't be surprised if he's got cameras all over the block that a-alert him when—"

Alistair gripped the wheel, exploding into a coughing fit.

"Are you okay? Do you need water?"

"Yea— Yeah," he wheezed. "Under the passenger seat."

I squeezed through the seat, reaching to grab the water bottle. I was thrown to the side when the car jerked—swerving off the road and coming to a sudden stop. "Alistair!"

"I'm sor-ry," he hacked, bursting into another coughing fit. "Are you okay?"

"I'm fine." I righted myself and grasped his shoulders, trying to straighten him up. "What's wrong with you?"

"I—I don't know—" Sweat beaded on his forehead. "Black spots... in my vision... Couldn't see."

Gasping, he clapped his hand over his throat.

"Dad! Your finger!"

Within minutes, the weeping appendage turned a putrid, mottled purple. Alistair reached for me—eyes red and bugging as he tried to speak.

"I've got backup plans for my backup plans too. When this night is over, I'll achieve everything my father died for."

"The ropes," I whispered. "She booby-trapped the ropes."

I launched forward—pulling at his collar, tilting his head back, trying to think of something. *Anything*! "Please, Dad, breathe. Breathe!"

Sirens broke the peace, blaring through the night.

"Listen, it's the firefighters. They're coming. They'll help you!" I threw open the door. A firm hand pulled me back in. "What are you doing? I have to stop them. I have to—"

Looking into my eyes, Alistair cupped my cheek—soft and gentle as his blood mixed with my tears. "I—I..." He slumped over, head falling onto my lap.

My scream ripped through the night.

Chapter Nine

"Luna?"

A knock sounded at the door. I burrowed deeper under the covers, wishing her away.

"Luna, baby." Mom stepped inside. I felt the bed dip. "Sweetie, what do you think about coming downstairs with me? We'll weed Winter's garden together."

"No." I barely recognized that nasally, raspy grunt as coming from me.

"You've been locked in this room for two weeks. Ever since we came back from the funeral. I know it's hard right now—"

"Hard?" I didn't bother lifting my head from under the covers. "My boyfriends are in jail. Victor's missing. My sister committed suicide. And my dad's dead! Yeah, I'd say it's been pretty fucking hard."

"Baby." Mom rubbed my leg through the covers. "I'm so sorry for everything that's happened. If I had one wish, it'd be to take your pain away. Please, just come out for a little bit. We'll have chocolate chip pancakes on the veranda. Maybe talk if you feel up for it. Or sit in silence if you don't. But you have to leave this room," she said. "It isn't healthy to lock yourself away like this."

I kicked away. "That's rich coming from you."

Quiet smothered the room.

"You're right," she whispered. "I did the same thing. Shutting myself in a room alone with my grief. That's why I know it doesn't help, Luna. Isolation and loneliness never helped anyone deal with trauma. Love and support do. The people who love you are here for you." Tugging down the duvet, she placed a soft kiss on my forehead. "We're here when you're ready."

I buried my face in the pillow, smothering a sob as she left. Yes, my mom and stepdad were here. But Winter wasn't. Alistair wasn't. Rafael wasn't. Cato wasn't. Wilder wasn't. Lucien wasn't. Victor wasn't.

Everleigh went to war with my father, but it was me who lost everyone I loved.

"—not now."

"I will speak to her."

I raised my head, crust-covered eyes blinking at the door.

"I told you—" Mom made an effort to keep her voice down. "—she's ready."

"Nonsense. She's a Burkhardt." My door flew open. "She's too strong to let anyone or anything defeat her."

Astoria Burkhardt walked inside my room and, without so much as a glance behind, shut the door in my mother's face and locked it.

"How dare—? Open this door, Astoria!" *Bang! Bang!* "I said open the door."

I goggled at her as she ripped the curtains open, stinging my eyes with blinding lights. She tsked. "Look at the state of you, child. What is all this misery and woe in aid of?"

"Excuse me?" Something akin to rage crushed my chest. It was hard to tell amid my never-ending sorrow. "What the hell are you talking about? My father just died. Your son!"

The corner of her mouth twitched. "I'm well aware of who died. I'm the one who, after having harsh words with him, faced my child again on a cold mortuary slab. I buried him. My youngest boy. My baby." She pulled up a chair, resplendent in a cream pantsuit and large Chanel tote bag. She looked like she stepped off the runway. I looked like a gargoyle. "So, I am here, asking you why you are in this bed... when you should be making that little monster pay?"

My lips parted, but nothing came out.

"It was Everleigh Starling, yes? She did this? She killed my Alistair?" The mask slipped—revealing the first true, honest emotion I'd seen on her face. Any thought I had of accusing her of coldness fled. "Well?"

"Yes," I croaked. "She killed him by using his weakness. Me."

Astoria turned away, lips pressed tight. It was a minute before she spoke. "I've tried for a week to speak to you. Your mother said you weren't ready for visitors, but this can't wait. I hear the Wilson boy is still missing, and everyone knows those four Rogue boys are locked up, waiting for the FBI to transfer them heaven knows where. If you're to do something to save them, you must do it now."

"Me?" I barked a sharp, short laugh. "What can I do? How can I help? All I do is get people killed."

She kissed her teeth, shaking her head. "Now, stop all that self-pity. You don't have time for it."

"Why are you even here?" I screeched, shooting up. "You're Astoria Burkhardt. One of the most powerful, richest women in the country. Mother of the future president. You could make the charges disappear and pay any ransom ten times over. More than that, you could've helped me when I asked for it! Now you're here wondering why I don't get off my ass? Look in the mirror, you hypocritical old witch!"

Astoria arched a brow. "My dear, I appreciate a young woman with fire, but I am your grandmother. You will speak to me with courtesy and respect. Apologize."

"Are you seri—?"

"Apologize," she said, tone sharp. "Now."

"I..." My jaw worked. My life falls apart, and she scolds me like a little kid. How... normal. "I'm sorry."

She bobbed a nod. "Better. Back to your point, yes. I could make the charges disappear, and I could offer to pay a ransom—though I doubt the Wilsons need our money. But the kinds of deals, brides, and people I'd have to mix with to make that happen, are not suitable for a Burkhardt. If discovered, my son's political career is ruined. Our business image destroyed."

"And that means more to you than helping Victor, Rafael, Cato, Lucien, and Wilder?"

Astoria looked me dead in the eye. "Why wouldn't it? I hardly know them."

I blew back—stunned. Did this woman have to be so blunt?

"Fine," I said softly. "Then I'll ask you this. Does it mean more than Alistair?"

"No."

I searched her face. Once more, I saw no trace of a lie. "Then why didn't you help me when I came to you?"

"Because I exercised poor judgment. I saw an opportunity to save my granddaughter from making a mistake and I took it."

"Marrying Victor isn't a mistake," I said hotly.

"Marrying into a family that uses and tricks you is."

I wanted to snap back. Nothing came out. Damn it, if I wasn't finding it hard to argue with her. Thor knew I already had a low opinion of Martha and John for what they did to Adonis. Discovering why they were so eager to marry off their eighteen-year-old son and snap me up certainly didn't help.

"It wasn't the way to go about it," she continued. "I see that now. I'm afraid I've gotten so used to tricks, deals, and doublespeak it didn't occur to me to simply talk to you. Getting justice for Alistair is worth draining my bank account. It's worth blowing up the business and burning down the shining Burkhardt reputation.

"If it was just me, I'd do just that. But it's not," Astoria said, looking away. "I have another son. Another granddaughter. And a husband who is hurting. I can't carry out the thoughts I have running through my head against a nineteen-year-old girl.

"But you can."

"Me?"

"Yes." Astoria drew something out of her tote and laid it on the bed. I recognized it instantly. "You."

"Mrs. Burkhardt. Do you... know what that is?"

"I do," she said, pushing Alistair's laptop closer. "His man, Ronin, gave it to me after the funeral. He said your father would've wanted you to have it, and I agree. I have everything to lose, Luna, but you have nothing left to lose. That's what makes the perfect Rogue."

I laid my hand on the laptop, imagining all those mornings sharing a reluctant breakfast with Alistair while he tip-tapped away.

I shoved it away. "That does nothing for me. Wolf said it's the names, locations, and rackets of every Rogue. What good does that do me? How does knowing any of that help me take down Everleigh, rescue Victor, or get my guys out of jail?"

"You're a resourceful young woman. I'm sure you'll figure it out. But before you give up, I need to tell you what I should've told you in the dress shop. I do know something about Everton Starling that may help you."

Astoria did. She laid out everything she knew.

My expression didn't change a twitch during her speech. "None of that helps me now. What does any of it matter now that Alistair is gone?"

"It's up to you what you do now," she said, getting to her feet. "But I hope you remember who you are, Luna."

I snorted. "Who am I? A Burkhardt?"

"You're Alistair's daughter."

I didn't speak as she left, meeting my irate mother over the threshold. I stared at the laptop for a long time—considering the implications of it being in my possession. Thinking about what Astoria told me.

I flipped over and kicked the stupid thing off. Snapping the covers over my head, I fell back into a fitful sleep.

***

"—so much, Mrs. Sinclair-Bowden."

I cracked an eyelid open. Judging from the light streaming through the curtains I hadn't bothered to close, it was already the next day.

The two cold trays of food on the nightstand proved it.

"Didn't know you and my Luna were friends. I'm sure she'll be happy to see you. Bring this in for me," Mom said. "Make sure she eats."

"Of course. Looks delicious."

Once again, my door banged open. Once again, the last person I wanted to see strolled in.

"Get your ass up."

Groaning, I pulled the covers up higher. "What is with you Burkhardts? Does your internal mechanical matrix only allow you to fake grieving for a week before the machine runs out of false tears? Why can't you leave me alone?"

"Because you're sitting around, feeling sorry for yourself when there's still work to do." Saylor plopped herself in my desk chair, helping herself to my pancakes. "Grandmother told me she came and spoke to you yesterday. What are you still doing in bed?"

"Well, I don't know if you've heard, but my *father just died in my arms*!"

She clicked her tongue. "Still a sarcastic cow."

"And you're still a raging bitch."

"And you're still moping around while your boyfriends sit in jail, Victor is missing, and Everleigh is doing a victory lap. Did you know she's throwing a party this weekend? Invited pretty much the entire school except me," she said. "Guess what her theme is."

"I don't give a shit."

Saylor plowed on. "It's slumber party themed."

I tensed.

"Yeah, that's right. After she fucking murdered someone at the last slumber party. She's throwing another one that she says will be even bigger and better. She's laughing at us, Sinclair. She's laughing at you. Are you really going to lie there and take it?"

I clenched my jaw. I wasn't sure who I was angrier at in that moment. "When do you do something, Saylor? I handed you the T.O.D. Club on a platter. What happened with that?"

"I was blocked from the site that night. I've got the information to make them break from Everleigh, but I can't use it. For some reason, every email or text I send to a Royal is blocked or bounces back unopened." Her grip tightened on the fork. "I can't go up to every one of them in person and say I've got dirt on them that'll spill if they don't ditch Everleigh."

"That's how you get punched in the face."

"It's Wolfgang," I spat. "Fucking hell, that man is smart."

"Now you see why you need to load that mess in the shower and help me figure out a new plan." She gestured to all of me. I was "that mess."

"I can't help you, Saylor." I flipped over, giving her my back. "She beat me, okay? Everleigh's too good. She's been planning this too long. Every time I think I've one-upped her, she destroys my life in a new way. I can't do it anymore."

"Wow."

A hard, vicious pain cracked my skull. "Ow!"

"Shut up, or I'll throw something else! What is wrong with you, Sinclair? I thought you loved those freaks!"

"I do!"

"Then why are you giving up on them? You know they wouldn't give up on you."

My lips trembled. I squeezed my eyes shut. "Of course they wouldn't. They'd never stop fighting to get me back, and they'd win. My guys are smart,

Saylor. They're twisted, resourceful, clever, and always a step ahead. The reason they've failed... is because of me.

"I hung the stupid flag, lured Everleigh out, and got myself trapped in a burning building. I'm the reason they found the weapons stash. It was my blundering around on the T.O.D. site that turned Wolfgang's attention on us.

"I didn't burn that bitch alive the first chance I got, and she was able to strike back hard—getting Victor taken and my father killed. Me, me, me!" There was a clang behind me. I guessed my scream made her drop the fork. "I'm no badass. I played at being one, and the result got everyone I love hurt.

"If I go after Everleigh again and fail, it'll be my guys that she kills next. I can't go through that again. I won't."

"I, I, I. Me, me, me." Her mocking tone grated on my ears. "You talk a lot of selfish, pitying bullshit, Sinclair. Okay, fine. Everleigh's smart. She fooled you. But the only way she'll truly win is if you and I give up.

"The Rogues and Victor didn't become twisted and cunning overnight. They learned to start thinking like their enemies," she said. "They mastered the art of turning the tables. You have too, Luna."

I turned my bleary gaze on her. "I did?"

"Yes. That whole thing with selling my texts. I hate to say it, but it was genius. Dozens upon dozens of people have tried to take me down, humiliate me, or dent the Burkhardt name. And you did it so simply and easily. I'll always hate you deep down inside for it.

"If you can do that to me, you can do it to Everleigh. She's half the target I am." Saylor handed me my plate. The last pancake—for me. "You're smart enough to win, Luna.

"Better than that, you're strong."

Gently, I took the plate, looking back at the smiley face Mom made out of chocolate chips.

It was true. Every plan I made against Everleigh failed. She was off celebrating her nine-year-long victory while I mourned the loss of almost everyone I loved in a stale room.

I flicked to the laptop that lay on the carpet. Giving it to me didn't make my life easier. I was ninety-nine point nine percent sure that there was now a huge target on my back. Plus, knowing where the Rogues lived didn't give me crap.

It wasn't like I was about to show up on an assassin's doorstep and say, *you work for me now.* Why in the hell would experienced, dangerous criminals fall in line behind a teenage girl? Even one who could expose them and what they do.

Alistair trusted me with this, but I didn't have a clue what to do next, with the laptop or with the information Astoria gave me. I could hop out of bed right then, plaster on some determination, then set off to provoke Everleigh into killing me for good. A lot of help I'd be to my guys then.

"You really think I can do this?" I whispered.

"I think you don't have a choice. So go do it."

I was quiet for a long time. So long, Saylor had time to snoop through my room, use the bathroom, go downstairs for more pancakes, then eat them in front of me while my single one went cold.

"About this party Everleigh's throwing..."

Saylor jumped at my sudden speech. "Yeah, it's at her folks' place. They're out of town and she never misses a chance to trash it when they're not around."

I nodded slowly, grasping the finer details of my plan and piecing it together. *It could work— No, it has to work. This is our last chance.*

"You said everyone is going?" I asked.

"Everyone, Dreg and Royal. The only people not invited are you and me. And yes, the guards will use force to keep us out."

"That's okay. I've got another idea."

***

We sat on the beach together, holding hands in the sand.

"Still nothing from Wolfgang?" The crashing almost took the soft words away.

"No."

I couldn't look at Adonis's face, despite needing to be near him. It was my fault his brother was taken by a psychopath. My fault he'd been questioned three times on why he allowed the terrorist Rogues to live at his place.

The Wilson brothers would've been better off if they never met me, and seeing that truth in his eyes would crush me.

"Mom and Dad are going out of their minds," he said. "They've gone to the press twice, swearing that they'll pay whatever the kidnapper wants to bring him home. The fact that he still hasn't sent a ransom demand has them thinking— They don't know if Victor is—" Adonis cut off, squeezing my hand.

"He's not." My voice was firm. "If Wolf wanted him dead, he wouldn't have given him CPR and saved him that night. He's looking forward to the millions he can collect on the last Wilson heir. I don't know why he hasn't made his move yet. Maybe he's waiting until the heat dies down." I dropped my head on my knees. "I don't understand how we got here, Adonis. Everything went so wrong, so fast."

"It did, and it's awful that it took everything going wrong for my folks to set one thing right. Victor isn't the sole heir anymore," he said, tipping my chin to face him. "They've accepted me back into the family. Restored my trust fund and inheritance. They also... apologized.

"Said they didn't know what possessed them to do something so horrible to me. They love me and my choice to get married or not. Have children or not. Is my choice," he said. "They'll support and be there for me like they should've done when I got the genetic test results back."

"That's great, baby." I wanted so badly to kiss him. "You deserved to hear that and more for so long. I'm happy you finally did."

"No." Adonis sucked in a ragged breath. "I hate that they're saying all of this to me. It's the kind of thing you do when you believe you've lost one child, so you're holding tighter to the other one. I said to you once that humans learn their lessons too late.

"Tragedy shouldn't be what brings us together. I'd just as well stay exiled and my parents remain arrogant and status-obsessed if it meant they still had hope Victor was coming home."

"He is coming home."

A car horn honked, turning my attention to the top of the beach, where a figure appeared on the horizon.

"He's coming home, and when he does, his family will be together again. It's the best gift you guys can give him."

Adonis flicked to where I was looking. "It's time. I'll leave you alone."

"I love you," I said softly. "I'm sorry I gave up, even if it was for a short time."

"You never have to apologize to me. It's not right that this was all on your shoulders. But you have help now. You'll have them," he said, "and you have me because I love you too."

I rose as Adonis left, leaving me the one, two— six people who trudged down the bank, arriving to line up before me. I said nothing since more were coming behind them—parking a range of Lexus and Ferraris to Fords and Toyotas, where concrete began to give way to beach.

I counted as they arrived. "Forty-one... Forty-two... Forty-three..." I breathed. "Forty-four."

Forty-four. Forty-four people received my summons and all of them showed up. Who could blame them? Who wouldn't be intrigued if they read the email I sent?

"Hello, everyone," I called.

They just looked at me. No one spoke.

"I won't waste any time," I began. "If you've been following the news, you know there's no time to waste. If you've been listening to the whispers in the underground, you know why." I dropped it with no more preamble. "The leader of the Rogues, Alistair Burkhardt, is dead. He was killed by Everleigh Starling.

"Alistair kept a laptop with the names, locations, and rackets of every Rogue everywhere—in the country and out. He also," I said, scanning the crowd, "kept a file on future Rogues. The children being groomed to take over the family legacy.

"He kept a file on all of you."

Iris rolled her eyes. "Yeah, so what? Think you're going to use that to put us under your thumb like Daddy did to our folks? That why you brought us out here?"

"No. I brought you out here to tell you the good news. Your folks are free. I wiped every trace of them from the laptop. I'm dissolving whatever stake Alistair has in their business. I'm closing and refunding the accounts they had to deposit money into. I'm shutting down the Rogues."

Disbelief rippled through the crowd and bitter faces disappeared in their wake. They weren't expecting that.

Dean stepped forward out of the pack. Looking at him was night and day to the guy I met before. A bold, confident swagger slowed his steps, as slow as the rugged smirk that spread across his lips, and brought a sudden blush to my cheeks. The air around him bent with a dark energy that I was clearly helpless to—if all the men I loved were anything to go by.

"Why would you do that, Luna?" His tongue caressed my name, staining my face with heat. "Free us from your leash." He licked his lips, winking. "Put down your whip."

"I don't have whips or leashes." *How the hell did the conversation take this turn?* "I don't want them either. An organization filled with people who can't choose between loving or hating me is how I'd become a billionaire recluse, living on a floating bunker in the middle of the ocean.

"The only people I want in the Rogues are those who choose to be in it. Those that accept my rule and want to follow me."

"Oh, well, that's everyone here," Dean said, looking around. My heart shot in my throat when he grasped my fingers and kissed them. "We'll follow you anywhere."

"Stop that," I snapped, cheeks flaming. "Stop all of that. It won't work."

Dean slinked back, grinning away. "I'm sure I don't know what you mean."

The fuck he didn't. Damn, the guy was good, but that didn't surprise me. On the surface, Dean's family money came from washing machines. In the dozens of secret, offshore bank accounts, they filled their coffers from his mother's true business—employing and training an army of grifters.

Men and women who charmed, seduced, fucked, and married some of the most powerful, richest people on the planet. They learned their secrets, helped themselves to their money, then faked their deaths and moved on to the next target.

From Alistair's notes, Dean was planning to take over the family business but not be a part of it. He'd train the next wave of grifters but wasn't going to be one himself. That was the only reason I didn't send everything Alistair had on him to Katie. One second in the presence of the real him, and he had me thinking about falling in love with one more Rogue. If he turned his charm toward marrying Katie for her money, she was toast.

"Fuck what he says," Iris snapped, propping her hand on her hip. "I will not follow you, thank you very much. I doubt anyone here other than that pussy hound will. Thanks for dragging me out of bed at seven in the morning, but I'll be going now."

She turned to leave. Most of them did.

"By all means, go," I called. "If you don't want to make a shitload of money, that's on you."

Iris halted, though she didn't turn around. "I already have a shitload of money. Try again."

"The Royals all have a shitload of money too, and yet they saw the benefit of joining the Royal line. They knew the connections they made from family to family would push their businesses and legacies to new heights.

"Years ago, the Rogues formed with the same idea. Those on the darker side of the street would band together. Protect each other. I don't have to tell you that the Rogues haven't lived up to that idea.

"Everyone is so separated and secretive. I bet this is the first time you've all met each other." I weaved between them, moving in front of Iris and the others, making them look me in the eyes. "My dad tried to change that. He instituted the flag system so that we could help each other, but even that no one wants to use unless the situation is desperate and they've lost all hope.

"While we're fractured and not speaking to each other, our enemies grow stronger. They pick us off one by one like Everleigh did"—I flicked to Iris—"to your older sister. When she had her stalked and beaten to force her to hang the flag.

"And you, Dominic," I said, turning to a short, freckled guy standing near Dean. "When she had your mother kidnapped and held in a dirty, rat-infested cellar, hoping that when your family gave up on the cops finding her, you'd hang the flag and bring Alistair here."

Dominic shot forward. "Everleigh was behind that? How do you know?"

I held up my phone. Yes, Wolfgang blocked me and Saylor from the site again, but not before we downloaded and screenshotted everything. "It's all right here. The T.O.D. Club came back six years ago, and Everleigh's been using it as her own personal hit squad for the last three.

"I have every reprehensible dare and truth she used to mow down innocent people and destroy their lives in the name of revenge. But why didn't the Rogues know any of this? Some knew about the club, but they didn't tell the others. Some knew about the false flags, but not the rest.

"It was so scarily easy for her to come in and play us against each other because we didn't know we were being played.

"No more," I stated, rising higher on the bank. "We'll turn the Rogues into what the Royals should be. The hierarchies and people stepping on each other to get to the top are gone, but the retribution when someone comes after one of us is not. We'll all have each other's backs. We'll all make them pay."

Iris stared at me long and hard. "Everleigh was behind the attack on my sister? You can prove this?"

I tossed her my phone. Why not? I wasn't there to hide Everleigh's secrets.

Iris's eyes widened as she read the anonymous messages that went back and forth between Everleigh and Mitchell Zedra. He carried out the beating, but she told him where she'd be... and how many bones to break.

"And before you think this is just about Everleigh," I said, "I have to tell you that there's a reason I emailed only you guys. Everyone here was made a victim of the T.O.D. Club in ways you didn't even know."

Ripples of shock and surprise went through the crowd. They didn't know.

"Long ago, the Rogues were formed to protect themselves from the Royals. They banded together because no one person—not even a rich, privileged person—was strong enough to take on all of them. For years, that was true until suspicion and secrets drove us all apart.

"I propose we go back to the way things were. The choice is yours." I raised my chin. "Will you follow me?"

The silence was broken only by the crashing waves.

"I told you," Dean said, snapping my head up. "We'll follow you anywhere."

Chapter Ten

I blinked through the dark, mind oddly still as I thought over the plan.

A hard kick caught my shin.

"Move over!"

I gritted my teeth. "For the hundredth time, Saylor. I can't move over. There's nowhere to go!"

"This was such a stupid idea. What the hell am I doing here?"

I freely rolled my eyes. Saylor had been complaining since before we got in. Granted, it wasn't fun bumping together like billiard balls in Katie's trunk, but there wasn't another way.

The car came to a sudden stop, sending me rolling into Saylor and setting off another round of bitching. Cousins or not, we'd never like each other.

Katie popped the trunk, standing over us in killer glitter gold lingerie with a matching glitter eye mask perched on top of her head. "Ugh. I still can't believe she stole my theme. What a vindictive cow. She hasn't forgiven me for calling out her lame reality TV party, so she's one-upping my party."

"She's also ghoulishly reminding everyone of the night she killed Giovanni."

"Yeah. That too." Katie looked around. "No one's looking this way. I'll go in first, then you guys wait five minutes and follow. Forget the sophomore class, it looks like the entire university came out."

We saw for ourselves after Katie left and we climbed out.

The Starling mansion had nothing on the Burkhardt or Wilson mansions, but that wasn't saying much. Three stories of sloped roofs, white brick, and tall windows dominated the view. As for the grounds, it was impossible to tell because every inch of driveway, grass, and flower garden was taken up by cars.

Staying low, Saylor and I quickly shed our jackets and put on our Korean face masks. The masks were my idea. They covered our faces and worked with the sleepover theme. When I told Saylor, she said, "So you're not a complete idiot." Her version of saying great idea.

Together we melded into the crowd of people streaming inside.

Everleigh promised her party would pants Katie's and make it cry on the playground. I hated that she delivered.

Katie had a buffet of sleepover treats. Everleigh had waiters and waitresses in the skimpiest, sexiest sleepwear, strolling through the party carrying cotton candy popcorn balls and s'mores cocktails on a tray. Where Katie built a giant fort in her living room, Everleigh set out dozens of mini-glamping tents decked out in fairy lights around the room. The sleeping bags inside made them perfect for hooking up, and that's exactly what people were doing.

Music pumped from the speakers set up in every room. Dancing, shouting, drinking, kissing, grinding—students were getting wild without a care for how morbid it all was, or a care for basic decency.

A guy knocked into his friend, who fell on a stand and tipped over the vase. He was already walking away with his drink as it crashed to the floor.

"The place is getting trashed," I shouted over the music. "That guy over there is straight writing on the walls."

"Everleigh lets all the guests know that anything goes. Her folks don't even get mad anymore when they come back to a landfill. They know what they've done."

I wasn't going to feel sorry for Everleigh, and I didn't. Lots of people had crappy childhoods and the shitty parents that went with them. But none of those people killed my father and sister.

"Where is she?"

"How the fuck would I know?" Saylor barked. "I've been standing next to you the whole time."

"You are the crankiest person I've ever met, hellbeast."

"Stop calling me that!"

"Will you two get a grip!"

Jerking, I twisted on Katie's angry face. Dean stood over her shoulder, one arm slung around her waist. He winked at me.

I stupidly blushed. *This is dangerous. He does not use his dark powers for good.*

"I heard you both bitching the whole ride over in the trunk. You've got more important things to do tonight than slag each other off."

"Trust me"—Saylor snatched someone's drink and tipped it on my head—"I can do both."

"You—!"

Dean and Katie physically wrestled me back. I slashed the air, trying to get at her retreating back as she flounced off.

"Why is she so evil?!"

"Forget about Saylor," Katie said. "It's almost time."

Breaking free of them, I furiously wiped vodka and chocolate liqueur out of my eyes. "How will I know?"

"You'll know," Dean said before picking a squealing Katie up and carrying her into one of the tents.

I had to avert my eyes quick. I'd never seen anyone get someone out of their panties that fast.

Ducking my head, I weaved through the party—catching a crafty bump or grind as I made for the living room. Well, living room was too small a phrase for the glitzy amphitheater I stepped into. The whole place was turned into a dance floor/viewing area. Projecting on the walls was Everleigh's idea of a sleepover movie: porn.

There were too many people crushed in for me to worry about her noticing one crasher in a face mask. Also, too many for me to find her.

Don't worry, guys. I pressed my fist over my heart. *I'm going to make it right. I'll save you no matter what it takes.*

The music cut off with a wave of screeching feedback.

"Hey!"

"What's going on?"

"Iris?" I'd know that voice anywhere. "What are you doing?"

"Relash, relash," went through all the speakers, quieting people in the other rooms. Iris stumbled onto the deejay's stage.

I watched her out of the corner of my eye. The other eye searched the crowd, trying to find out where Everleigh's voice came from.

"Everyone, let's give it up for the party of the year!"

"Yeah! Whooo!"

Iris yukked it up. "It's about t-time we moved on from all that dark—scary shit and partied Royal-style."

Another wave of hoots and cheers kicked off.

"But if this is a sleepover," Iris continued, "we've got to do it right. A little Never Have I Ever... strip edition."

The roars blew out my eardrums. It was ridiculous how pumped they were for this game. Every Royal party I went to, half the party was out of their clothes by midnight. It amazed me they still got excited over seeing each other naked.

"All right, bitches. Let's start you off with— with— with—" She was skipping like a scratched record. "With an easy one. Never have I ever... had sex!"

Satin tops and silk boxers rained on a laughing Iris. They were all barely wearing anything to begin with. This would be a short game.

Iris stumbled off, down a pajama bottom. Someone else tripped up there to take her place as I approached the stage.

"Never have I ever... slept with a professor."

A surprising number of clothes came off. If I was playing, I'd be down to my thong. Did administration know their staff was regularly partaking in the student honeypot?

A girl with pierced nipples made for the stage steps. I quickly sidestepped and got in front of her, running up past the deejay. He handed me a mic without question. Nobody was going to stop this game.

I cleared my throat, looking out over the crowd that was growing bigger as people came in from other rooms to see. I couldn't spot Everleigh, but I knew she was there.

Watch this, bitch.

"Never have I ever... used the T.O.D. Club to take revenge on someone."

The laughing and jeers hiccupped. A weird pause as people froze with their hands on their hems.

"Huh?"

"What'd she say?"

"What's that?"

"Skip the fake confusion," I said. "A good chunk of the people in this room should be butt-ass naked right now."

"Who is that?" Everleigh's sharp voice sliced through the mumbling. "Who are you!"

I ripped off the mask. Why not? I wasn't here to hide from Everleigh.

"How did—? Security? Call security!"

"Don't bother," I said. "I'll make this quick. For six years, certain people have been using the T.O.D. Club as a means to torment, bully, and terrorize their enemies without ever having to lift a finger. They've let the club members take care of that for them."

"Get her off the stage!"

"A lot of you in this room have been victims of random violence and bullying, and you didn't know why. Exhibit *A*."

The porno cut out. I didn't know which Rogue was on the projectors, but they delivered big-time. Broadcasted on all four walls, my screenshots of the bare, non-anonymous T.O.D. page went up for everyone to see.

"What's that?"

"What's it say?"

"Who did that?" Everleigh screeched.

I flicked across the room and there she was, clambering out of the tent with her panties around her ankles and her top nowhere to be seen. She tripped over her feet, trying to dress herself.

"Turn those off!"

"What you're looking at is Nathan Westchester daring Xero Lantham to rape his ex-girlfriend in revenge. You're looking at Kimber Waverly daring Marcus Brown to cut her supposed best friend's brakes."

"What?!"

"Turn it off!" Everleigh gave up on finding her shirt and shoved through the crowd, beelining for me.

"None of you have to worry about reading off the walls," I said, picking up speed. "Someone made sure that I can't get into your inboxes, but they can't stop you from hitting up mine. If you want to know everything T.O.D.'s done, it's all live and free on this website."

The projectors winked out and the shots were replaced with a single web address repeated dozens of times on the walls.

www.truthordareclubexposed.com

"On that site is a link that you're all really going to be interested in because it takes you right to the place where you can employ my services and the services of the Rogues." I smirked. "Not the four hot sexy Rogues you've known, but the true Rogues that you're afraid to name. Surprise, surprise. They've got new management... and it's me."

"Liar!" Everleigh got stuck behind two half-naked rugby players. "She's a liar! That website is a fake. Someone get her off the stage!"

"I'm not a liar, but I'm not standing up here to prove it to you. It'd be in the best interest of some of you if I never do," I said. "Let me say this flat out, the Rogues are in a new racket: revenge.

"This is to anyone and everyone who's been made a victim of this disgusting club. They farmed out and anonymized their attacks, and now you can do the same. Farm out their retribution. Put in a request through the site, and Rogues will make everyone who hurt you and paid for it, regret what they've done.

"You just tell us how you want it. Castrate the rapists? Expose the blackmailer's secrets? Arrange an accident for the murderers? Whatever you want," I said into a rapidly quieting room. "Anything goes.

"T.O.D.ers, you know who you are. Get ready to spend every single day of the rest of your short life looking over your shoulder. Wondering if the guy looking too closely at you is a Rogue distracting you while the other stabs the knife in your back.

"And if you're thinking you don't have to worry because your victim can't afford us, I wouldn't be so sure of that." I smirked. "Our five-dollar fee is more than affordable."

"What are you saying?"

"You can't threaten people like this," someone screamed. The panic was clear in her voice. "This is criminal. I'm recording everything you say. You'll be arrested."

I shrugged. "Maybe, but I've got friends that'll spring me from prison. Do you have friends that'll save you? I can tell you right now you won't after everyone sees the real T.O.D. Club. But what will save you"—I raised my voice, one eye on the rapidly approaching Everleigh—"is if you confess!

"Confess what you did and what you dared someone to do to the police, and the Rogues will take you off the hit list. Refuse, and we will happily carry out your punishment."

"She's a liar! You're not leading the Rogues, you nobody, Dreg."

"Take your chances that I'm lying. Sooner than later, someone is going to get curious. They'll put in a request through the site just to see what happens, and then some shit is going to happen to you."

Everleigh burst onto the stage. "Give that to me!"

"Five dollars, people. Make the bastards that destroyed your life with some game pay." I dropped the mic and jumped off the stage, shoving past grasping hands for the door on my right.

I escaped into a hallway, Everleigh hot on my heels. I did hear something behind me.

"Hey, bitches," Saylor belted through the speakers all over the house. "You're gonna want to go with the confess option because I'll tell you right now, I'll be using Sinclair's services to make each and every one of you ungrateful bastards pay for turning your backs on me. Did you really think you could be free of the Burkhardts? What kind of dumbasses are you?"

I tuned Saylor out. She was gearing up for a long rant.

I didn't know where I was going. Saylor gave me a rough layout of the mansion, but all that went out the window when surrounded by more rooms, floors, and living areas than a family of three needed.

"Don't run away, Sinclair! I want to hear all about how you bawled and snotted your heart out when Daddy died in your lap!"

I zipped around a corner, taking a staircase up two steps at a time.

"I heard bachtraxin poison shreds your lungs, squeezing the air and life out of you. Did he beg!"

A hurricane of wild eyes, messy hair, and wicked delight haunted my heels. She was gaining on me—fast.

"Did his eyes bulge as he desperately clawed his throat, begging for you to save him?"

"You're insane! You evil, soulless monster!"

"I'm soulless?" She swiped at my back, claws snagging my pajama bottoms. "You just advertised your murder-for-hire club to the whole town."

Ripping free, I lit on an open door at the end of the hall.

"What... were you playing... at?" she huffed. A lifetime of rich-girl pampering didn't prepare her for this hundred-yard dash, though she was keeping up scarily fine. "I've got Wolfgang in my pocket... idiot. I'll have that website shut down... in an hour!"

"I have a better idea!"

I darted inside and found myself standing in a guest bedroom if the lack of personal touches was anything to go by. A modest queen-size bed took up the middle of the room, the end side facing the balcony. I darted around it, putting that flimsy excuse for a barrier behind us.

"I've got an offer for you, Everleigh, and it's the same one I've got for everyone else. Confess."

Everleigh lunged over the headboard. Whipping around, I snatched a lamp off the nightstand and lobbed it at her head.

"Ahh!" It shattered on her skull, dropping her like the flat-back evil skank she was.

Everleigh moaned and rolled on the bed, clutching her forehead.

"As... I was saying," I huffed. "You and I both know it doesn't matter if Wolf shuts down the site. A hundred more will go up in their place. It also doesn't matter if you kill me. I've got my father's laptop. I know every Rogue in the world, and I told them all what you've done."

Rage bled into her eyes as fierce as the blood dripping through her fingers.

"They'll all come after you one after the other until you're sleeping under spotlights because you're terrified of your shadow." I stepped back, climbing a raised platform that housed the sitting area. "Or you can confess what you've done. And I mean all of it. Tell the police that you framed my guys. Force Wolf to give up Victor.

"Do all of that, and we close the chapter on the sad, sorry period where we ever knew each other. You go your way and I'll go mine. Neither of us will chase revenge."

She laughed. "What bullshit are you spouting, Sinclair? I'm not confessing anything to anyone. Maybe those brainless morons downstairs believe an eighteen-year-old girl took over the largest criminal organization in the world, but I'm not that stupid. The second you open your mouth and tell people like Leon Dumont that they have to bow to you, they'll stick a gun in it.

"Besides, even if it is true," she said, grinning. "I can afford bodyguards. I'll be just fine."

If she thought that'd upset me, she was wrong. I smiled back.

"Is that your final answer?" I said softly. "Before you reply, I'd like to give you one last chance to do the right thing—confess your sins. Because if you don't, Everleigh... I'll break you.

"I'll take apart everything you know. Destroy all that you love. Reduce you to the weakest, most pathetic simpering version of yourself."

Her grin dimmed.

"You'll look back at this moment for the rest of your life and remember that you had a choice. And you chose so wrong.

"Last chance. Are you going to confess, or am I going to rip what's left of your desiccated heart out of your chest?"

She laughed. "What are you going on about? You don't scare me, Sinclair. You're just a daddy-less, boyfriend-less, fiancé-less waste of space."

"And you're just a dumb bitch who went on a decade-long crusade to avenge a man who's not dead."

Her face twisted, gleeful mask cracking for a fraction of a second.

"That's right, Everleigh. Your father didn't die that day. All this time, you've had it so wrong."

She glared at me, her bewilderment over what new game I was playing written all over her face. "My dad isn't dead? That's the best you can do? This is you *breaking me*? Fucking hell, you're pathetic."

I blinked lazily. "On that day in June, Everton and my father met for their final showdown. It was an ugly, nasty fight that ended up with Everton in a pool of his own blood. Yes, my father thought he killed him. Two shots to the chest would put down anyone, but on that day, it didn't. After Alistair left, Everton was found, saved, and given a chance to run without anyone looking for him—the feds, the Rogues, my dad. He took it."

Everleigh sat up, dropping her hand. I hissed at the angry, weeping gash on her forehead. "Whatever you're trying to do, stop. This delusion you're spinning is embarrassing."

"Embarrassing?" I laughed. "That's the right word. It is embarrassing that you spent all this time, money, and hatred on avenging a man but zero cents on a private investigator to turn up if he was really dead."

"He is dead! After your piece-of-shit father shot him, he set fire to his body! We had to bury ashes."

"Someone was burned and buried, but it wasn't Everton," I said clearly. "My grandmother told me everything. I admit, I didn't give a shit. Who cares if you're a clueless idiot and Everton is still alive? That knowledge came too late to save my father and sister." My throat choked. "W-what did it matter?"

It took me a beat to collect myself. "But eventually, I accepted that I was wrong. It did matter because telling you would do the most important thing of all. *Hurt you.*"

Everleigh's lips peeled back from her teeth. "Keep spinning your fairy tales, Sinclair. It'll add more weight when I tell the captain that you lost your mind and attacked me. I had no choice but to kill the insane Dreg that came at me."

I carried on like she hadn't spoken. "There was another reason I didn't want to share this story. Because as much as I wanted to hurt you, that's how much I wanted to save my guys from pain."

"Blah, blah, blah." Everleigh picked up a shard of the lamp. She leveled the jagged edge between my eyes. "I've heard enough from you."

"Everton is alive," I snapped. "At first, he wanted to make my father pay by taking everything he loved from him. But after nine years on the run, he wanted someone else. Everton met someone, fell in love, and they decided to fake their deaths and start over."

"No."

"Everton goaded my father into that last meeting. He let slip where he was, and Dad turned up believing they were ending it once and for all. Everton planned that too. He showed up wearing a bulletproof vest. One missed and caught him, but all the blood just sold the lie."

"Nope," she sang. "You're a liar, and I'm not falling for it."

"After Everton successfully fooled everyone." I cringed as it came out of my mouth. "It was Sasha Dumont's turn."

The shard lowered a centimeter. "What?"

"Cato and Rafael's mother," I rasped. "Everton and Sasha fell in love. I don't know anything about her side of the story except this... she blew up her own children to get away."

"You're not even trying to be believable anymore. Sasha Dumont? My dad didn't know her and he didn't want to know her. They had nothing to do with each other, and they sure as fuck didn't run away together."

"They called Astoria five years after they took off. Turns out, you can't get by on just love. When the trust funds run out and you can't access your bank accounts because you're dead, you resort to blackmailing an old woman and threatening to tear down her shining reputation by telling the world her son is the leader of a criminal organization.

"Naturally, she told him to go to hell." Everleigh's brow twitched. "But she did hire someone to track him down, so she'd know where he was if he ever made such a stupid mistake again and came after her."

"Give it up! I don't—"

"That's how she was able to give me his number." I held up my phone, numbers already typed in. "I knew you wouldn't believe me, so I'll let you talk to Everton himself. I'm sure you still remember his voice?"

Everleigh's jaw worked. A thousand emotions flittered across her face until she settled on one—seething rage.

I tapped *call* and put it on speaker before she let loose.

Ring.

Ring.

Ring.

"Hello?"

Jaw slackening, the shard slipped from Everleigh's grip.

"Hello, who is this?"

"Hello," I said, triumph clear and malicious in my voice. "This is Luna Sinclair-Burkhardt, daughter of your old pal, Alistair. I've got someone here who'd like to talk to you."

"Luna Sin— It can't be," he said. "How did you get this number?"

"That's not important. What is important is—"

"Daddy?" Everleigh snatched the phone. "Daddy, is that you?"

"Everleigh?"

"Oh my gosh," she breathed. "Oh my gosh. How—? No, wait. Tell me something only my dad would know."

"Uhh... Listen—"

"My sixth birthday," she blurted. "Where did you take me on my sixth birthday?"

"I don't—"

"Where did we go?"

He sighed. "I chartered a boat and we sailed to Valeria. We learned to make grass skirts and drank out of coconuts on the beach."

Everleigh collapsed, falling flat on her butt and dropping against the bed frame. "It is you," she whispered. "I can't believe it... How? Where have you been?"

"You know where, or you couldn't have made this call." A hard edge steeled his voice.

"Milford, Maryland," I helpfully supplied. "He and Sasha own a popular local restaurant."

Everleigh looked through me. "Maryland? So close? But I don't understand. You've been alive all this time? Why didn't you tell me? Why didn't you come for me?"

"Have you forgotten the situation I was in? A fugitive. Bank accounts frozen. Hated by everyone I knew and everyone I didn't. Living like a castoff out in the woods. It wasn't a life, Everleigh. I had no choice but to fake my death. It was the only way to start over."

"But why didn't you take me with you?"

"I couldn't," he replied. "I would've had to fake your death too. Rip you away from your family, friends, and your parents. It wouldn't have been fair to you."

"What are you talking about? My friends are a bunch of vapid, social-climbing bitches and always have been. Mom and Stepdad treat me like garbage— No, they treat me *worse* than garbage. They act like I don't even exist. You're the only parent I ever had."

"You're exaggerating."

"But you know I'm not," she cried. "You remember what it was like back then. It was always just you and me."

"It wasn't so bad that your mother deserved to think her only child was dead. Come now," he barked. "Be reasonable."

Her lips trembled, eyes wide in confusion. "But... even if you didn't want to do that to Mother, why didn't you let me know that you were alive?"

"No one could know, or it would've all been for nothing."

"I could've known! I didn't tell anyone where you were when you were on the run."

I resisted putting in that she did blab to her friends, writing all about it in their shared diary.

"It was too risky," he said firmly. "This was for your own good as well as mine."

"But I don't understand why—"

"Fucking hell," I burst out. "Are you really this dense, Starling? He didn't want you to know! He didn't want you tracking him down or begging him to let you live with him. Everton faked his death. Sasha blew up her home with her children inside to fake hers. They clearly didn't want a couple of brats getting in the way of their shiny new life.

"Do you understand now? He. Did. Not. Want. You."

"Shut up! You don't know anything, you—"

"I don't know anything?" I laughed harshly. "If I'm wrong... why isn't he correcting me?"

"You are wrong! Tell her, Dad."

Silence.

"Daddy?" She half turned away, flinching from my knowing smirk. "Dad!"

"Okay, just—" He blew out a breath. "I wasn't meant for fatherhood. Your mother used me to get back at my brother. She lied about being on the pill and threw my whole life off track. I couldn't stick around and play daddy. I didn't want to hurt you, Everleigh. I certainly wouldn't have gone as far as Sasha did, but it was better that I made a clean break from your life."

"But I don't understand. I don't understand."

She was a broken record, repeating the same phrase over and over as tears clogged her throat.

"It was for the best. You were better off with your parents."

"Stop saying that," Everleigh shrieked. "I was not better off with those cold, unfeeling monsters! I missed you. I missed you every minute of every day, and I hated the man who took you from me.

"Do you have any idea what I've done for you? I killed Alistair Burkhardt! I—"

"You did what? Did— Did you just say you killed Alistair?"

"Yes, I had to," she sobbed. "I thought he killed you."

"Are you insane!"

The shout blew us both back.

"You stupid, stupid girl! Do you have any idea what you've done! The only reason Astoria spared me is because I swore I'd have nothing to do with her family, and now you've killed her son! She'll never believe this had nothing to do with me.

"Does she know it was you? Tell me she doesn't know."

"She knows," I sliced in. "I told her all about how Everleigh murdered her son and drove her granddaughter to suicide, all in your name."

"Oh no."

I couldn't mistake it. *Fear*. Everton was terrified of a soft-voiced woman in cream pantsuits. He'd seen that side of her. The side that didn't mask her rage.

"How could you do this? What were you thinking!"

Everleigh was full-blown bawling now. I could barely make her out through the snot and tears.

"I d-did it for you. To make them pay f-for what they did to you. I'm sorry, Dad—"

"I'm not your fucking dad! I never should've let you get so attached to me. Now because of you, we have to leave here. Fuck!"

Everleigh flinched, shrinking in on herself.

"You tell her this had nothing to do with me, you hear me? This was all you. I didn't want this, nor did I have a part in it."

"But, Daddy—"

"Stay away from us. Don't ever contact me again."

Click.

"Dad? Daddy?"

Everleigh called back once. Twice. Half a dozen times.

The phone rang and rang while she wailed and cried, pouring desperate pleas and explanations to a man who wouldn't answer.

I looked on in stoic satisfaction. Any other person on any other day, and my heart would swell with pity. I'd hug her and say what a bastard that man was for abandoning the daughter who loved him. I'd say he deserved everything he had coming to him.

But this bitch killed my father and sister. She'd get no pity from me.

"Tsk, tsk, tsk."

Everleigh raised watery, swollen eyes to me.

"Forgive me, but I did give you a choice," I said lightly. "I told you either you confessed and took the easy option, or I'd be forced to rip your heart out."

"This can't b-be true. That wasn't him. My father wouldn't—"

"That was him. You made sure of it yourself, so don't go spinning any fairy tales now. Not a single lie you tell yourself will make up for the fact that you lied, blackmailed, and *killed* all for a man who wasn't dead!" Everleigh flinched. "Ten years, and he's been two hours away from you the whole time.

"For that deadbeat pig, you killed my father. You had my sister tortured and raped—"

"I didn't know he'd rape her!"

"You didn't want to know," I screamed, hauling Everleigh to her feet and shaking her. "You threw money and status at them, then sat back to watch the show. You didn't care what they did as long as they got the job done.

"It was you, Everleigh. *You* destroying innocent lives. *You* betraying your best friends. *You* bringing misery to everyone who has the misfortune of knowing you. And for what? For nothing!"

Racking sobs heaved her chest, rattling her in my grip. "I'm sorry. Oh God, I'm so sorry. I didn't know. I swear, I wouldn't have done it if I'd known."

"You think I give a fuck about your sorry?" Pain laced my words. "Sorry doesn't bring Winter and Alistair back. Your sorry is worthless, but your confession isn't. Admit what you've done— Shut up," I snapped, finally silencing her wailing. "Admit what you've done. Admit you burned down the Gallery and get that poor guy out of jail. Tell the captain all the evidence against my guys is fabricated. Confess your part in making the T.O.D. Club what it is."

"But I can't."

"Yes, you can, Everleigh. You've done so much wrong for so long. Now is your chance to do the right thing. To give the people you've hurt a chance to heal. In the end, your father's true nature as a self-serving bastard won out, but you don't have to be like him. Please," I said, the first trace of gentleness entering my tone. "If you're truly sorry, then this is your chance to make it right. You don't have to be the person you've been anymore."

"Okay," she gasped. "Okay. Get your phone. I'll... record everything. Everything I've done. It's time I make it right."

I released her and went to get my phone from where it had dropped beside the bed.

A blast of cold air hit my neck, turning my head around. "What—?"

Everleigh stepped out onto the balcony.

"Everleigh? Everleigh, no!"

Climbing onto the rail, she jumped off.

Chapter Eleven

"There was nothing I could do."

Adonis and I swayed on the porch swing under a mountain of blankets. My love kept piling them on with every tear.

"It happened so fast. One second she was talking to me, and the next, she jumped over the railing. She said she was going to make it right, Adonis." I smacked the chair arm. "I pushed her too far! I never should've let that heartless bastard talk to her."

"This isn't your fault, Luna." He found my hand under the blankets. "You can convince yourself you're justified in almost anything when you believe you're fighting the worthy cause for someone you love. When all that was ripped away from her, and she saw what a monster she'd become for, in the end, was no reason at all... Well, she couldn't face that truth."

"What do we do now? Rafael, Cato, Lucien, and Wilder are still locked up. Victor is in Wolfgang's clutches. I know what he's going to do next." I sniffed. "He's going to demand I give him everything my father was supposed to give him in exchange for Victor."

"Will you?" he asked softly.

"Of course I will. He can have the fucking laptop. He can have the Rogues. He can have all the money he needs to pay for therapy he desperately needs! I'd give him anything if he'd just tell me what he wants."

"You already gave him what he wants, but it's sweet to know you'd give him everything else for me."

I jerked up and tipped over.

"Luna!"

Shrieking, I crashed to the porch in a pile of limbs and blankets. Victor raced up the steps to me.

"Luna, are you okay?"

"Am I okay?" I stroked his cheek. It was real. He was real. "I don't understand. How are you here?"

"Wolfgang let me go," he said, helping me up. "It's over now. Everleigh's gone, so there was no reason for him to keep playing pretend kidnapper."

"Pretend? He drowned you, Victor, then stole you away. We've been going out of our minds wondering if you're safe. There was nothing pretend about that."

Helping me to my feet, Victor gazed past his shoulder. "I'll let him explain it to you."

Wolf rounded the corner, stepping onto the porch.

"Get out."

He raised his hand in surrender. "Luna, please. I didn't have a choice."

"Don't you dare say that to me, and don't you dare whip out some sob story! You framed your own brother and nearly killed my fiancé. I don't care what you have to say. Turn around and leave."

"It's not a sob story and it's not an excuse. Everleigh discovered something about me that my enemies can never know. She gave me a choice between following her every order or finding out the true meaning of something staying on the internet forever."

I turned away, walking off.

Wolf rushed to speak. "I did what she said, but I tried to help when I could!"

"Help me?" I cried, pulling up short. "What the hell are you talking about?"

"I told you Everleigh's plan that day in the dean's office so you could fight back. I warned you the police were here, waiting for them that day."

I paused, mouth open, but nothing came out.

"I gave Victor CPR when she wanted to leave him for dead," he said. "I kept him safe at my place so that she wouldn't try to kill him again. I did everything I could to help. I'm sorry that it wasn't enough."

I flicked off him to Victor. "Is it true?" I whispered.

"It's true. He locked me up in the apartment to stop me running back to you, but he didn't hurt me. He also told me everything so I'd understand why. Everleigh was out of control."

"Oh, Victor." I jumped in his arms, squeezing the life out of him.

Victor grasped my head and kissed me hard—exploding heat, light, and love inside my body. He was here. He was safe. And everything was still so horribly wrong.

"But it doesn't have to be." I untangled from Victor but kept him close. "You can undo what you've done. Tell the police everything they've got on the guys is fake. You made it up."

"I can make the fake evidence disappear as easily as I made it appear, but I can't delete the cops' memories. They found those weapons in the ashes of the Gallery. They've got more than enough from that to lock them up."

I deflated. He was right. The Rogues were in trouble long before Wolf made it worse. They wouldn't be terrorists. Instead, they'd go down for hoarding illegal weapons and chemicals.

"I knew that. I guess I hoped with Everleigh confessing that she had the guys framed, killed my father, used the T.O.D. as a hit squad, and a million other terrible things, the police see that she'd done so much evil, it wasn't a stretch to believe she planted all those weapons too.

"But I've got nothing. No Everleigh. No confession. No nothing." I buried my face in Victor's shoulder. "What do we do? It can't end this way. We've only been together a short time. I wanted forever with you guys."

"You'll have it, baby." Victor's fingers were soothing on my scalp. "We'll figure this out. I promise."

"Hold on." Wolf stepped forward. "Did you just say you needed a confession?"

"Yes, but it's too late," I replied. "Everleigh's gone. At this point, I'm going to break them out of jail. They'll be fugitives, but at least we'll be together."

"I'm mildly interested in how you'd pull that off," Wolf supplied, "but I've got a better idea."

Taking out his phone, he tapped the screen, then held it up.

Everleigh's voice flowed out of the speakers.

My eyes widened the longer I listened.

"I told you," Wolf said, smirking that smirk I was quickly becoming fond of. "The first time she called, I recorded everything she said to take to the police. You've got your confession."

Epilogue
One Year Later

I dug my toes in the sand, relaxing as the warmth spread up my feet.

True paradise. We'd found it.

"Sinclair." Wilder dropped down and handed me a piña colada from the beach bar. His six-year-old companion giggled from around his shoulders.

"Uncle Wild," Liam said. "I want to swim."

"You don't know how to swim."

"That's not true!"

No one on earth had ever been more outraged at the blatant truth.

I laughed, tickling the little boy under the arm. Shrieking, he squirmed and nearly kicked his uncle in the face.

A year ago, after I sprung my boyfriends from prison, Wolfgang introduced us to the person who changed his life—the one Everleigh used to blackmail him.

Wolfgang had enough enemies gunning for him. The one thing they could never know is he had the biggest weakness of all—a son. Wolf wanted him to have the normal life his mother denied him and Wilder, and it was that realization that woke him up to how awful their childhood was and how badly he'd treated Wilder.

"I rationalized and explained everything I did until I asked myself what I'd do to the person who treated my son like that. The torture I'd put them through hasn't been invented yet," Wolf told Wilder that day. *"I was wrong, brother. I don't expect your forgiveness, but I give my apology."*

"Is it weird that we brought this little ankle biter on the honeymoon?"

I smooched Liam's cheek. "Not weird at all, especially because it's not a honeymoon. You need a wedding for that."

"Made sense to cancel." Victor plopped down on my other side, his drink in hand. "We're young. Dad finally retired. We've got plenty of time to get married. So we ditched the wedding but still went on the trip."

"It's summer vacation," I said. "Now is the time to sun it up, plan for the future, take care of business."

"Speaking of business, we've got another job." Wilder handed me his phone.

Months and months later, the new Rogues handled all the revenge commissions based on the now-dead T.O.D. Club. At first, a wave of them came in because no one confessed. They all stupidly thought I was bluffing.

When the twelfth trust-fund baby wound up in a ditch, the Royals got the hint. A mess of them moved out of Regalia, thinking they'd escape punishment, but all it did was take the franchise global. Rafael, Cato, Lucien, and Wilder dropped out of school to handle the out-of-state and overseas business.

As for the rest of the Royals, Saylor and I brought part *b* of the plan to her father and grandfather, who took to it easier than we expected. Any Royal who didn't leave on their own was evicted.

Regalia, home of the über-rich and connected, was no more. The Burkhardts sent all their renters packing, then Dario donated the land and homes. Regalia was now a collection of fancy orphanages, women's shelters, refugee housing, and housing for homeless or low-income individuals.

The stack of applications wrapped around the world when Uncle Dario announced he was donating all those mansions for practically nothing. He didn't profit from the gesture, but he did win the presidential election by a landslide.

With the Royals scattered all over the world, making new business and social connections separate from the Royal line, that was the end of the system. Saylor didn't protest this loudly or at all. Thanks to the text messages, she would've inherited a Royal line that hated her and tried to sabotage her at every turn. She accepted that it wasn't worth the headache, and she'd keep the billions coming through her inheritance instead. Not a bad trade-off.

Saylor looked up from her lounge. "What's the job? Anything that'd interest me?"

Well, she thought that for less than a month. Turned out, she didn't take to having nothing to do and no one to dangle at the end of her puppet strings. She came over to the Rogue side, and I was only too happy to accept her. I'd seen firsthand how good she was at making people suffer. Why not use her dark gifts for good?

"Stepfather married her rich mother, they went on vacation, Mom suffered a freak *accident*, and then a new will appeared that gave him everything and cut the kids out," Wilder explained. "They know he killed her and forged the will, but there's no proof. They want to hire us to get the money back... and make sure he has a freak accident too."

"That does interest me. Give it here," Saylor said, requesting the phone. "And get me a piña colada too. Extra pineapple with a straw. Don't doddle."

I rolled my eyes. "Saylor, it's both irritating and admirable how steadfastly *you,* you are."

She shrugged, returning to her sunbathing.

Twisting around, I landed on Rafael, Cato, and Lucien chatting at the beach bar.

"I'm glad they took time away from the search and joined us," Victor said softly. "Their mom is good. Not even we can find her."

I nodded. It crushed my heart when I had to tell Rafael and Cato that their search for their mother's killer was over. She wasn't actually dead.

To say they didn't handle the news well was an understatement. Cato went on an arson spree, burning down every place connected to their mother, and Rafael straight denied it. He said he wouldn't believe their own mother blew them up to cover her fake death until he heard it from her.

Unfortunately, after that fateful night with Everleigh, Everton and Sasha left their small town and went deeper into hiding. We still hadn't found them.

"They needed this," I said. "Good food, the beach, and surrounded by everyone who loves them. Finding out your own mother carelessly tossed away your life would put anyone in a dark place."

Rafael saw me looking and smiled. The three of them came over.

"You gonna keep eyeballing me, gorgeous, then I'll have to invite you for a walk down the beach."

I giggled. "Fine by me."

Victor and Wilder stood up too, to join us. Wilder plopped Liam on Saylor.

"Wolfgang and Adonis will be back soon," Wilder said. "They went to grab food."

Liam bounced on her lap. "Auntie Saylor, Auntie Saylor, swim with me."

"I'm not your aunt, kid," she said, even while dropping everything and carrying him to the water, peppering his face with kisses the whole way. Liam loved Saylor even more than he loved me, and she loved him back.

The six of us set off down the beach.

"Can you believe how far we've come?" I mused. "Everything's changed so quickly. I barely remember that girl you guys kidnapped from the ABC party."

Rafael chuckled. "Everything has changed. The Rogues disbanded. Us running the new Rogues. Regalia as we knew it, gone. You went from engaged to the most eligible bachelor in the country to dating a bunch of college dropouts."

I laughed. "I'm very happy with all of that. The only reason I stayed in Regalia U is that it's still my dream to become a therapist and help at-risk young people. The Rogues help a lot of people, but there's more I can do. For Winter."

Victor laced his fingers through mine. He hadn't dropped out either, of course. Adonis was teaching and writing novels. That left him to take over the family business.

Together we strolled down the sand, wandering away from crowds and families to the private stretches of beach claimed by the owners of the nicer and grander homes we passed.

"I wish Alistair and Winter could've seen all of this," I said. "I wish we had a chance to be a family."

I looked at my guys, overflowing with love for all of them. "Thank you for being my family. For being there for me when no one else was. I love you so much my heart physically aches all the time."

"We love you, Cloud Girl," Rafael said, spinning me off my feet. "It was always you."

"It was not always you," Victor put in, "until it was."

"Mine," Cato said simply.

Laughing, I ran around them, kissing them all in turn.

Wilder snagged me and lifted me onto his back. "This is it," he said, turning up a stone path.

A gorgeous peach-painted beach house glittered under the sun. It was a lovely, two-story masterpiece with a wooden balcony and thatched roof.

"I like it," I said. "Let's take it."

"Whatever you want," Lucien replied, "is yours. I bet we get it for a good price."

"We should vacation here every summer. The Maldives is as close to paradise as it gets."

I skipped up to the front door and knocked. After a minute, I heard movement on the other side.

He threw open the door. One look and the smile melted off his face.

"Hello, Levi," I sang. "I know your ass didn't think you'd get away from me that easily."

Wilder shoved him inside.

I inhaled a deep lungful of fresh, island air as the screaming started. "I miss you, Dad, Big Sis," I whispered. "My life can't be perfect without you, but this is pretty close."

***

Keep In Touch

Join Ruby's mailing list for news, teasers, and more: https://www.sub-
scribepage.com/rubyvincentpage
Join Ruby's Facebook Reader Group:
https://bit.ly/3bNuCOq

ABOUT THE AUTHOR

Ruby Vincent is a published author with many novels under her belt, but after taking a fun foray into contemporary romance, she found her love of saucy heroines, bold alpha males, and weaving a tale where both get their happy ever after.